VICTORY FOR THE FOYLES BOOKSHOP GIRLS

ELAINE ROBERTS

B

Boldwood

First published in Great Britain in 2025 by Boldwood Books Ltd.

Copyright © Elaine Roberts, 2025

Cover Design by Colin Thomas

Cover Images: Colin Thomas

The moral right of Elaine Roberts to be identified as the author of this work has been asserted in accordance with the Copyright, Designs and Patents Act 1988.

Every effort has been made to obtain the necessary permissions with reference to copyright material, both illustrative and quoted. We apologise for any omissions in this respect and will be pleased to make the appropriate acknowledgements in any future edition.

A CIP catalogue record for this book is available from the British Library.

Paperback ISBN 978-1-80549-722-6

Large Print ISBN 978-1-80549-721-9

Hardback ISBN 978-1-80549-720-2

Ebook ISBN 978-1-80549-724-0

Kindle ISBN 978-1-80549-723-3

Audio CD ISBN 978-1-80549-715-8

MP3 CD ISBN 978-1-80549-716-5

Digital audio download ISBN 978-1-80549-718-9

This book is printed on certified sustainable paper. Boldwood Books is dedicated to putting sustainability at the heart of our business. For more information please visit https://www.boldwoodbooks.com/about-us/sustainability/

Boldwood Books Ltd, 23 Bowerdean Street, London, SW6 3TN

www.boldwoodbooks.com

To my cruise friends who have helped me through a difficult time and gave me lots of valuable advice and lots of laughs, thank you x

1

Alice stifled a yawn as she stood huddled with her friends Victoria and Molly near the counter in Foyles Bookshop, their voices low as they snatched a moment between customers to catch up.

Molly eyed Alice. 'You're looking tired – maybe you're trying to do too much? I mean you work here, drive an ambulance and that's without the family time, which I'm sure keeps you busy on its own. Are the boys keeping you awake at night? They must get frightened when the bombs drop, let alone the ground shaking and all the shouting that goes on as people rush for cover.'

Alice stared down at her hands, the knuckles white as one hand gripped the other. 'They don't know what it's like to live in peacetime. This so-called Great War has gone on for so long they don't very often stir. Thankfully, living with my parents, along with my brother and sister, and Mrs Headley, who all love to look after the children as much as they can, frees up a lot of my time. Of course, like others, I now sleep in the basement with them so we don't have to wake the boys to take them down there in the middle of the night when the bombs are dropping.' Her gaze travelled between her friends. 'Freddie has had difficulty sleeping at night for some time, but his nightmares seem to be getting worse, or at least more frequent. It seemed sensible for me to stay in the basement with the boys, with them both being under four, and he stays upstairs. At least there they can't hear him and don't get frightened when their father shouts out in his sleep.'

Victoria reached out and squeezed Alice's arm. 'You never said. You know we're here for you.'

Alice nodded. 'Thank you, it means a lot to me. I don't know where I'd be without our friendship. But I'm not the only one going through this; we all are. We must just try and survive it the best we can and be there for each other like we always are.' Glancing at Molly she smiled. 'What is it you always call us? The three musketeers, "all for one and one for all".'

Molly giggled. 'That's right, and it's got us through this never-ending war.'

Smiling, Alice shifted her gaze around her. 'Of course, there's the other half of that quote, "united we stand, divided we fall", which also describes our friendship.'

Victoria laughed. 'So, we really are the three musketeers.'

The warm June sun filtered through the large windows of London's Foyles Bookshop, casting a glow on the rows of second-hand books lining the shelves.

Alice shook her head. 'The trouble with this time of year is the sunshine shows up all the dust.' She glanced around. 'It's been fairly quiet today.'

'I expect everyone is at the park enjoying the sunshine.' Molly peered over her shoulder at the shelves. 'Trust you to notice the dust. Let's hope Mr Leadbetter hasn't – otherwise we'll all be on dusting duties again.' She rolled her eyes. 'I swear, if I have to shelve one more book on the shelf, I'll scream. Whatever happened to losing yourself in another world away from this one?' She brushed a stray strand of blonde hair from her face.

Victoria laughed, her engagement ring catching the light as she gestured. 'Well, at least you're normally in the children's section, which has lots of different worlds to escape to. Although I know what you mean. I've been trying to push some of the new poetry collections. I even put some in the window display, but I don't think it has made any difference. I thought a bit of beauty to balance out all the... well, you know.'

Alice nodded, her eyes darting to the door as the bell chimed, signalling a new customer.

Victoria frowned. 'I'm concerned you've never mentioned Freddie's nightmares before. Has he always had them? I mean, since he came back from the front?'

Alice nodded. 'Not so much at first, but I know from listening to the soldiers at Victoria train station and at the hospital that it's quite normal. When Freddie came home, the war didn't appear to have affected him as much as others; he was just glad to be home, and I was pleased to have him back.' She sighed. 'But I think his nightmares are getting worse and I don't know how to help him, especially as he won't talk about it. He just pretends it isn't happening.'

Molly raised her eyebrows. 'How did he manage to hide them when he came home? I mean, Andrew has the nightmares but when he's not at the bank, he's throwing himself, day and night, into helping other veterans – you know, trying to find them work and somewhere to live. Most of the time he looks worn out, but he won't talk about it either.'

Alice lowered her eyes. 'I don't think he hid them in the way you mean; he just didn't want to worry, or frighten, me and the children. It soon became apparent he was sleeping less and less each night for fear of waking us up with a start. I think he has a sleep at the police station before he starts work and at lunchtime, as well as before he comes home, although he says he doesn't.'

Victoria shook her head. 'It's difficult for you, Alice. I mean it's difficult for Molly too, but because you live with your family and you have the boys, you obviously don't want to get into an argument over it, whereas Ted and I can have proper frank discussions because Daisy is often working at the police station.' Daisy was Victoria's younger sister.

'Have you talked to him about seeing someone?' Molly asked, reaching out to squeeze Alice's hand.

Alice shook her head. 'You know Freddie. He insists he's fine, that he just needs time. But it's been a couple of years now, and with the boys…'

Their conversation was interrupted by Mr Leadbetter's voice calling from the back room. 'Ladies, I know it's quiet in the shop today, and it won't be long before we're shutting up for the night, but Albert is swamped in the basement so maybe we could find someone to help him check the books.' He pulled at the bottom of his black waistcoat as he walked into the shop before glancing at Victoria. 'Miss Appleton, I know you three are good friends, but can I please remind you that you're paid to make sure everything runs smoothly and not to stand around chatting.' He gave a faint smile. 'Mrs Greenwood, should you not be upstairs in the children's section?'

Molly nodded. 'Yes, sir.' She stepped away from her friends.

Mr Leadbetter raised his eyebrows. 'If it's also quiet upstairs, everyone can start dusting the shelves and the books that sit on them. I'm surprised you ladies hadn't noticed the dust in this sunshine.'

Alice leaned over the counter and picked up a rag. 'I'll start near my counter because I can then keep an eye out for customers as well.'

'Thank you, Mrs Leybourne, we've always taken pride in what we sell here so let's keep it that way.' Mr Leadbetter turned away and noticed a soldier down one of the aisles browsing the books. He wondered if he was there for the solitude and the peace that came with books. The man looked up and Mr Leadbetter nodded before going back to his office.

With sighs and knowing smiles, the three friends dispersed, each lost in thought about the challenges that awaited them beyond the sanctuary of the bookshop. As they worked, surrounded by the comforting smell of paper and ink, each woman silently drew strength from the bond they shared, a friendship forged in peacetime but tempered by war. They knew all too well the toll the war had taken on those who'd returned.

* * *

Alice picked up the clean tea towel to start drying the soapy dinner plates Mrs Headley, the housekeeper, had been washing up in the sink.

Mrs Headley smiled. 'You shouldn't be doing that; you'll get me the sack. You should be upstairs playing with them boys.'

The house on Bloomsbury Street echoed with the sound of children's laughter and the clatter of dishes. Alice stood near the draining board, a small smile playing on her lips as she strained to hear Freddie's deep voice regaling their sons with a bedtime story.

'And then the brave knight raised his sword high...' Freddie's voice grew louder and drifted downstairs from the boys' bedroom, followed by excited gasps from three-year-old Arthur and a giggle from seven-month-old David.

Mrs Headley chuckled. 'You know I remember you having Arthur like it was yesterday.' She shook her head. 'I don't think there's a sound in this world that beats a child's laughter. Mr Leybourne is clearly tickling young David while telling Arthur his story. He's a good man.'

Alice's smile slowly faded. She remembered a time when Freddie's stories might have been filled with dragons and magic, not knights and battles. The war had changed him in ways she was still trying to understand. 'Yes, he is, Mrs Headley, but don't forget it's thanks to you that Arthur was born safely. If you remember I didn't even realise I was in labour until my waters broke. You saved the day. I hope you realise you are much more than a housekeeper to us; I can't remember a time when you weren't part of this family, but now it's much more than that because you delivered my precious Arthur safely, and here in my parents' home.'

Mrs Headley glanced up from the suds in the sink. Her voice cracked when she spoke. 'That's a very kind thing to say but it's important to remember my position, if only because I love working here.'

Sarah Taylor's heels clipped the tiles as she walked into the kitchen. 'Ahh, there you are, Alice. I thought you were upstairs with the boys.'

Alice shook her head. 'No, Ma, I thought I'd help Mrs Headley with the washing-up. It's a lot for one person to do.'

Stepping nearer, Sarah grinned. 'Of course. I'll take over while you go up and help carry them into the basement and settle them down – otherwise Freddie will be playing with them all night.'

Alice frowned. 'He enjoys making them laugh. I think it takes his mind off the war and being a police officer.'

Sarah nodded. 'That I do understand. Every day I pray we'll see an end to this terrible war.' She reached out to take the tea towel. 'Now go on and give them boys a kiss from me, and from Mrs Headley.'

Laughing, Alice dried her hands on her apron. 'I will, thank you.' She tried to climb the stairs quietly, but every other step seemed to creak under foot. She made her way to the bedroom door, leaning against the frame to watch her family.

Freddie sat on the edge of Arthur's bed, his police uniform still crisp despite the late hour. His face, once boyish and carefree, now carried lines of worry and fatigue. But as he looked up and caught Alice's eye, a warmth spread through his features that made her heart skip.

'All right, lads,' Freddie said, ruffling Arthur's hair. 'Time to go to the basement so you can get some sleep. You've got your brave knight to protect you from any monsters under the bed.' He lifted Arthur up and held him tight.

Alice strolled into the bedroom and kissed each boy in turn three times, then scooped David up into her arms. 'That was a kiss from Grandma, Mrs Headley and me.'

Arthur yawned. He counted each person on his fingers. 'Grandma, Mrs Headley and you, Ma – that's three kisses.'

Alice leaned in and hugged him tight. 'You're so clever. David is very lucky to have a big brother like you.'

Freddie and Alice trundled down the stairs into the basement, ignoring the creaking floorboards as they went. Freddie opened the door and wrinkled his nose as the smell of dampness engulfed him. 'I'll be glad when the children won't have to keep sleeping down here.'

Rays of daylight were still streaming into the basement as they laid the boys in their beds. David wriggled in his cot as Alice pulled a blanket over him. She turned and watched Freddie do the same with Arthur in his small bed.

Alice yawned. 'Now close those eyes and I'll see you both in the morning.' She stepped quietly towards the stairs with one last glance over her shoulder. 'Goodnight, and pleasant dreams.'

As the boys settled down, Freddie joined Alice, wrapping an arm around her waist. 'How was work today?' he asked, his voice low.

Alice leaned into him, savouring the moment of closeness. 'Oh, you know the usual, books to sell and customers to please. Molly and Victoria send their love.' She paused, then added carefully, 'Freddie, I was thinking... maybe we could talk to Dr Harrison about your nightmares. I mean, you look so tired – I'm assuming they are happening more often or getting worse. Apparently, the doctor has been helping some of the other returned soldiers, and—'

'Alice, we've been through this.' Freddie's body stiffened, and he pulled away slightly. 'I'm fine. It's just... it takes time, that's all. I don't need to talk to anyone.'

Alice bit her lip, not wanting to push but worried all the same. 'I know, love. I just... we're here for you – you know that, right? Me, the boys and the family, for whatever you need.'

Freddie's expression softened, and he pulled her close again, pressing a kiss on her forehead. 'I know, Alice. I know. Come on, let's have a cup of tea before bed. You can tell me all about the latest scandals at Foyles.'

As they made their way to the kitchen, Alice couldn't shake the feeling that there was more going on with Freddie than he was letting on. But for now, she would take this moment of peace, this slice of normality, and hold on to it with both hands.

* * *

Victoria sat at her dressing table, her notebook open in front of her, every page filled with lists and sketches, each one a testament to everyone's determination to make her wedding to Ted perfect. But she knew it would never be that, because her mother and father were not there. There weren't going to be any words of wisdom from her mother, or her father proudly walking her down the aisle. She thought back to that day eight years ago when a policeman had knocked on the front door to tell her their parents had died in a train derailment in Brighton. At the time she had never understood why her parents had gone to Brighton, but that day changed her life along with the lives of her younger brother and sister: Stephen and Daisy. It had turned their world upside down. At sixteen years old, Victoria had instantly taken on a mother's role to them. It was only a few years later when Alice and Molly persuaded her to unlock her parents' bedroom door that she started to get the answers she had been looking for. When she thought back to that troubled time, she realised they had all come a long way.

Looking up, Victoria caught sight of her reflection in the mirror, and the worry lines creasing her forehead.

A soft knock at the door pulled her from her thoughts. 'Come in,' she called, hastily arranging her face into a smile.

The door handle turned, grating as it did. Ted pushed open the door and strolled in, his tall frame filling the doorway. He looked handsome in his civilian clothes, but Victoria couldn't help noticing the slight tremor in his hands, the way his eyes darted around the room as if searching for something.

'Hello, darling,' Victoria said, rising to greet him with a kiss. 'I didn't expect you back until later. Is everything all right?'

Ted nodded, but his smile didn't quite reach his eyes. 'Just thought I'd let you know the hospital seem pleased with my eyesight. Apparently it's improved a little, but I don't think they are expecting it to get any better than it is now.' He gestured to the array on the dressing table. 'So, how's the planning going? Looks like you've been busy.'

Victoria led him to sit on the edge of the bed, taking his hands in hers. They felt cold despite the warm June weather. 'It's coming along.' She glanced back at the dressing table. 'You know I never wanted all this fuss; it feels like I've been swept along by everyone else.'

For a moment, Ted's eyes seemed to focus, and he squeezed her hands. 'You should have the day you want and, don't forget, you'll look beautiful no matter what.'

Victoria squeezed Ted's hand. 'I don't want to let everyone down. There have been lots of offers of help, and with my grandfather in Brighton wanting to pay for the day it seems churlish not to have a big day with all the works.'

Ted peered down at their entwined hands for a moment before looking up at her. 'This wedding should have happened years ago, and if I hadn't been a coward and run away when your parents died it would have done. All I care about is us being together and your happiness. I can't get back the years we lost but I love you with all my heart, so as long as we get married that's all that matters to me.'

Victoria's heart raced, her eyes bleary from unshed tears. 'That's all I want too, but how do I tell everyone—' She broke off as a car backfired in the street outside. Ted flinched violently, his body going rigid, eyes wide with fear. In an instant, he was no longer in the cosy bedroom but back in the trenches, surrounded by the sounds of war. 'Ted? Ted, it's all right. You're safe. It was just a car,' Victoria said softly, her heart breaking as she watched him struggle to come back to the present.

Slowly, awareness returned to Ted's eyes. He looked at Victoria, shame and frustration evident in his expression. 'I'm sorry,' he muttered. 'I don't know why I can't... why I can't just forget it all.'

Victoria cupped his face in her hands, forcing him to meet her gaze. 'You have nothing to be sorry for. We'll get through this together – I promise. Maybe... maybe we could talk to someone? I've heard there are doctors who specialise in helping injured soldiers live with the things they've seen and heard.'

'No, someone told me they use electric shock therapy, and I'm not putting myself forward for that. Who knows how that could end up.' Ted pulled away, shaking his head. 'I just need time. I'll be fine, Victoria. Just plan our perfect day and not everyone else's.' He stood up. 'I'll make us a cuppa. Don't worry, everything is going to be all right.'

Victoria jumped up to follow him, but a knot of anxiety tightening in her stomach held her where she was. She loved Ted with all her heart, but she couldn't shake the fear that their 'perfect day' might be overshadowed by the war that felt like it would never end, and for Ted perhaps it never would.

After Ted left, Victoria sank back onto the bed, her eyes falling on the wedding plans scattered across her dressing table. The joy she had felt in planning their future together now seemed tainted by the harsh realities. She thought about the other war brides she knew: women who had married in haste before their sweethearts shipped out, or those who, like her, were trying to build a life with men forever changed by their experiences. And then, of course, there were those men who would never be coming home to their wives and sweethearts. None of their lives would ever be the same again.

She reached for a framed photograph on her bedside table, a picture of her and Ted her father had taken just days before her parents died. Their smiles were carefree, their eyes full of hope and innocence. Victoria traced Ted's face in the photograph, remembering the boy he had been, loving the man he had become, scars and all.

With a deep breath, she stood and returned to her dressing table. She may not be able to erase Ted's traumatic memories or heal his invisible wounds overnight, but she could create a day filled with love, support, and new, joyful memories to stand alongside the painful ones. Victoria picked up her pen and began to write, not wedding plans this time, but a letter to Ted, pouring out her love, her fears, and her unwavering commitment to their future together.

As she wrote, a new determination filled her. Their wedding might not be the fairy tale she had once imagined, but it would be real, honest, and a testament to the strength of their love. Whatever challenges lay ahead, they would face them together, starting with this first step into their new life.

2

Molly stood in the large bedroom of the red-brick, four-storey house she shared with her husband, Andrew, in Bury Street. It had been his family home, very different to the small, terraced house she had grown up in. Her mother and father had worked hard for the Gettin family, Alice's wealthy grandfather, which was how Molly and Alice became childhood friends. But Molly had always felt she was caught between the two worlds and never understood where she fitted in, despite being good friends with Alice and Victoria.

Staring blankly at the small blue floral bowl with its matching jug, she felt so sick again. She'd been feeling like this for at least a week now and was almost too scared to leave the room in case she vomited again. She took a deep breath. Her mother and father had been so proud when she married Andrew and moved into his big house. Molly sighed remembering it took her father being taken into hospital to realise how important and loved they were. As an only child she sometimes felt the burden of responsibility to produce grandchildren, but she never spoke about it, not even to her friends.

Her stomach lurched up into her chest. Grabbing the bowl, she sat down on the edge of the bed and held it on her lap with her trembling hands. Was she pregnant? Was this the morning sickness she'd heard women talk about? If she was it would be life-changing. Frowning, she wondered how Andrew would feel about becoming a father, especially as all his spare time was taken up with looking after soldiers returning from the front. Her mind whirled with a mixture of emotions: joy, fear, excitement, and overwhelming uncertainty. There was a light knock on the door, jolting Molly out of her troubled thoughts.

'Molly? Are you all right in there?' Andrew's soft voice came through the door, tinged with concern.

She looked up as the door opened and Andrew walked through the doorway. 'Yes, I'm fine... I'm just feeling a little queasy. It must be something I've eaten,' she answered, her voice higher than usual.

Taking a deep breath, Molly picked up the jug and poured some water into the bowl she was holding. Placing it on the chest of drawers she quickly splashed some water on her face and looked at herself in the mirror. Did she look different already? Could Andrew tell? She wasn't ready to share the possibility yet – not until she'd had time to process it herself and know that it was true.

Andrew's brows furrowed. He stepped forward and gently rubbed his hand up and down her back. 'You've been in here a while, and I was getting concerned.'

Molly forced a smile. 'I've got a bit of a headache coming on. What with that and feeling a little sick...' She sighed. 'I'm sure it's nothing and will soon pass.'

Andrew nodded, but she could see he wasn't entirely convinced. 'Would you like to have a lie-down? I can leave you in peace.' He studied her. 'You do look a little pale.'

Molly forced a smile. 'Don't you go worrying about me. It will soon go.'

Andrew's eyes didn't leave her. 'If you're sure, we can always get a doctor.'

Molly's eyes widened. 'No, no honestly I'll be all right.'

Andrew shrugged and turned to head back to the living room.

Following Andrew, Molly watched as he settled back into his armchair, surrounded by papers and pamphlets. The Silvertown munitions factory explosion, and all the devastation it caused had changed everything. She remembered continually screaming out his name when she hadn't been able to find him amongst all the rubble, ignoring her own injuries. That was where Alice and Victoria had found her. She had been distraught at the thought of losing him. They had taken control and got Molly's wounds looked at and found out he could have been taken to hospital. They were up all night searching for him and did eventually find him unconscious but safe.

When Andrew recovered, he eventually accepted his old job back at the bank. He had worked there before the war started, but he struggled with going back. He talked about how he was no longer contributing to the war effort – at least at the factory he had been helping to get the munitions built and out to the front line. That was until he chatted to a veteran begging in the street, and that had made him realise he could be of use to those who had returned and had nothing, so when he wasn't working at the bank he had thrown himself into veteran support work with a fervour that sometimes frightened her.

'More letters to write?' Molly asked, perching on the arm of his chair.

Andrew nodded, his eyes scanning a list of names. 'So many of the lads are struggling to adjust, let alone find work. Some were promised that their jobs would still be here when they returned from the front, but that wasn't always true. Someone's got to help them, you know, stand next to them, prop them up and help fight their corner.'

Molly thought about her friends at Foyles – Alice with her quiet strength, Victoria with her unwavering optimism. They had all changed so much since the war began, grown in ways they never could have anticipated. Perhaps, if she is pregnant, this baby was her next step in that journey of growth and change.

She ran her fingers through Andrew's hair, her heart swelling with love and pride, even as her own anxiety gnawed at her. How would he react to the news of the baby? Would he see it as a joy or another burden in a world already weighing heavily on his shoulders? She caught sight of the newspaper on the side table. The headlines screamed about the war, about the mounting casualties and the strain on the home front. Her hand instinctively went to her still-flat stomach. What kind of world would she be bringing a child into?

'Andrew,' she said softly, her heart pounding. He looked up, his eyes tired but attentive. Molly opened her mouth, the words on the tip of her tongue. But at the last moment, she faltered. 'I… I love you,' she said instead, leaning down to kiss him gently.

Andrew smiled, some of the tension leaving his face. 'I love you too, Molly, more than ever.'

As Andrew leaned into her touch, Molly decided to stick with her original resolution. She would wait to tell him, just for a little while. Give herself time to come to terms with this possible new reality, to figure out how to share the news in a way that would bring light to Andrew's often-shadowed eyes. For now, she would carry the secret close to her heart, a tiny spark of hope in uncertain times.

* * *

Victoria hummed softly as she arranged flowers in a vase, the late afternoon sun streaming through the front room window. She'd spent the morning at Foyles, but Mr Leadbetter had insisted she take the afternoon off to finalise her wedding plans. She stood back and admired the flowers before leaning in to sniff their fragrance. She shook her head and thought about Mr Leadbetter's kind gesture. The initial excitement of her engagement had worn off. In fact, sometimes she wasn't even convinced there would be a wedding. Since they had announced they were going to marry, Ted appeared to be more anxious and less able to relax. She had said the wedding could wait but he said he wanted to marry her. Victoria sighed. They had booked the church, but she hadn't thought about her dress or the bridesmaids. The more she thought about it the more she thought now was not the right time for Ted. She sniffed as tears rolled down her cheeks – maybe it was never going to be the right time.

Victoria knew she had to talk to Alice and Molly and be honest about everything she was thinking. Maybe she should walk to Alice's house to try and straighten out her mind before her confusion truly took hold. Walking into the hall she glanced at herself in the mirror. Her lips tightened as she took in her ashen features and the darkness around her eyes. Grabbing her jacket off the coat hook, and pulling open the front door, Victoria stood rooted to the spot as she stared at Alice with her hand up ready to knock on the door.

Alice's eyes widened. 'You made me jump. I thought I'd come and see you. I hope that's all right?'

Victoria blinked rapidly. 'Of course... I was just going to walk round to see you.'

'I went to Foyles but Molly said Mr Leadbetter had sent you home to finish off your wedding plans.' Alice paused. 'And the thing is we haven't been shopping for your dress yet, so here I am.'

Victoria stepped back into the hall. 'Come in, I'll make some tea.'

Alice stepped inside and shut the door behind her. 'Don't worry about the tea. I'm here because I want to either take you wedding dress shopping or find out what's going on.'

Victoria forced a smile. 'There's nothing going on.' She turned away and walked into her front room.

Alice eyed her friend before following her. 'I don't think that's true, but you were coming to see me, so you obviously wanted to talk to me about something, so we'll talk about that first.'

Victoria took a deep breath before dropping her jacket on the back of the armchair. She turned to face Alice. 'I'm worried about Ted. He's not in a good way, so I'm not even sure we should be getting married.'

'Do you still love him? I mean, do you want to marry him?'

Victoria nodded.

'Does he want to marry you?'

Again, Victoria nodded, trying to blink away the tears that were threatening to spill over her lashes.

Alice shrugged. 'Isn't that all that matters? You have waited a long time to be Ted's wife. We both thought it was never going to happen and yet here we are.'

Victoria flopped down onto the armchair. 'I don't know, I can't help thinking he's got worse since we set the wedding date, so he's either changed his mind or something else is going on that he won't talk about.'

Alice knelt at Victoria's feet and clasped her hands in hers. 'It's probably to do with the war. I get the impression most men won't talk about it. Freddie's the same. It's like they are trying to protect us from it all.'

'I understand, but don't they know they're worrying us more by not talking about it?' Victoria took a breath. 'Last week I finally managed to persuade Ted to see Dr Harrison, and despite his good reputation Ted won't let me go with him. He has always said no to talking to anybody about it, but I think that's more out of fear he will be offered electric shock treatment, which none of us want him to have. But he's getting worse and shutting out any help that's available isn't going to solve the problem.'

Alice looked solemn as she jumped up. 'You know we can't help them if they don't want our help, and worrying won't change anything.' She forced herself to smile. 'I say we go out, take our mind off things, and buy your wedding dress. It's not long now and we've all been so wrapped up in other things, we've let the excitement of your wedding drift away and that's not right.'

Victoria forced a smile. 'Thank you, but I don't think I'm going to have the wedding that everyone expects.' She took a deep breath. 'Don't be cross with me, but I'm not convinced it's even going to happen, so I don't want to waste my money on it.'

Sadness washed across Alice's face. 'But you've wanted to be married to Ted for such a long time.' Looking thoughtful, she sat down in the nearby armchair. 'Right, well, you sound determined not to buy a wedding dress but we could still go to the shops and look around to see what the options are.'

Victoria's throat tightened as she held her tears in check. 'That's very kind of you but, if it ends up happening, I'll wear something I have in the wardrobe. I just can't seem to think about it without being gripped with anxiety that something awful will happen.'

Alice nodded. 'I understand the worry but please don't let it spoil your day.'

Victoria tried to focus on the happiness at marrying Ted, who she knew she couldn't love any more than she did. The sound of the front door opening made her smile. 'Ted?' she called out. 'We're in the front room. How did it go with Dr Harrison?'

There was no response, just the sound of heavy footsteps in the hallway. Victoria's smile began to fade. 'Ted? Is everything all right?' She glanced at Alice before moving towards the door, but before she could reach it, Ted appeared in the doorway. The sight of him made her gasp. His face was ashen, his eyes wild and unfocused. His usually steady hands were shaking violently.

'Ted, darling, what's wrong?' Victoria asked, reaching out to him.

But as her hand touched his arm, Ted recoiled, his body going rigid. 'No,' he shouted, his voice raw with fear. 'Stay back – it's not safe.'

Victoria froze, her heart pounding. She'd seen Ted have difficult moments before, but nothing like this. 'Ted, it's me. It's Victoria. You're home. You're safe.'

But Ted didn't seem to hear her. His eyes darted around the room, seeing not their cosy front room but some unseen horror. 'Gas,' he cried out. 'Everyone, get your masks on. Be quick about it.'

He stumbled backwards, knocking over a small table. The vase Victoria had just arranged crashed to the floor, water and flowers scattering across the rug.

The sound seemed to jolt Ted. He blinked rapidly, confusion replacing the terror in his eyes. 'Vic... Victoria?' he mumbled.

'I'm here. You're home and safe,' she repeated, her voice calm despite the fear coursing through her.

Slowly, recognition dawned on Ted's face. He looked around the room, taking in the overturned table, the scattered flowers and Alice trying to hide her sadness. 'Oh God,' he whispered, his face crumpling. 'I... I'm sorry. I don't know what happened. At the doctor's, there was a smell... something chemical... It was so strong... and then...'

Victoria rushed to him, enveloping him in her arms. 'Shh, it's all right.' As she held him, feeling his body shake with silent sobs, Victoria's mind raced. How could she help him? How could they build a life together with the war still raging in Ted's mind? But as she stroked his hair, murmuring words of comfort, she knew one thing for certain: she wouldn't give up on him. No matter what it took.

* * *

The Sunday roast was a tradition in the Taylor household, a time for the growing family to come together and forget, if only for a few hours, about the troubles of the world outside. Alice sat at the crowded table, wedged between her younger brother, Charles, and her younger sister, Lily, the familiar chatter and clinking of cutlery a comforting backdrop. Arthur's laughter rang out from upstairs. Freddie peered across at Alice and matched her smile at their son's giggles. Their three-year-old was obviously having fun with Mrs Headley.

The only thing that was missing was the roast meat. Alice could remember her father at the head of the table carving the meat with practised precision. But all of that was before the food shortages. Alice watched him as her mother ladled the stew on to plates before passing them around the table. The war had changed her father and he was no longer its champion. Losing Alice's older brother Robert and seeing the men suffering on their return had affected him badly. He had sat as a volunteer with men as they lay dying in hospital, holding their hands until they had taken their last breath. Alice tried to reconcile the man before her, his silver hair neatly combed, his Sunday best impeccable, with the suspicions that had been gnawing at her for months, no matter how she tried to ignore it.

She shook her head. The war had changed everyone. Thoughts of Ted jumped into her head. What if what she had seen at Victoria's was a regular occurrence? She'd talk to Molly to see whether they could help Victoria in some way. Ted appeared to be suffering more than Freddie. She sighed. There must be something they could do to help them both.

'Pass the potatoes, would you, Alice?' Lily's voice broke through her reverie.

As Alice handed over the dish, Lily leaned in close, her voice low. 'Have you noticed anything... odd about Father lately?'

Alice frowned, glancing quickly at their parents to ensure they couldn't hear Lily. 'Odd how?'

Lily's eyes darted to their father before meeting Alice's gaze again. 'Those business trips to Norfolk. Don't you think they've been more frequent? And longer?'

A chill ran down Alice's spine. She had noticed, of course, but had pushed the thought aside, not wanting to give voice to her suspicions. She forced a smile. 'I think since you've been a policewoman, you're always looking for dubious behaviour, even where there isn't any. He's always had business in Norfolk. If I remember rightly, he used to go there a lot before the war started,' she whispered back. 'So, what are you getting at, Lily?'

Her sister's expression was a mix of worry and determination. 'I went into his office to get some paper and it felt like I had interrupted something. He clearly wasn't pleased to see me and immediately covered the letter he was writing and, to my mind, he looked guilty of something. So, it makes me wonder what he could be guilty about. I mean, do you think he's having an affair or something? None of it feels like business to me.'

Alice wondered for a moment what Freddie would make of this conversation. She opened her mouth to respond to defend their father or demand more information, she wasn't sure which, when her brother's low tones cut through their conversation.

Charles leaned in towards them. 'What are you two whispering about?'

Alice nudged his arm. 'Nothing, Lily's just messing about. You know, girls' stuff.'

Their mother, Sarah, glanced across at them. 'Girls, is everything all right? You're being awfully secretive, so I'm intrigued.'

Both sisters straightened up, plastering on smiles. 'Just girl talk, Mother,' Lily said smoothly. 'Alice was telling me about a particularly demanding customer at Foyles.'

As the conversation around the table turned to other topics – the latest news from the front, the upcoming church fete – Alice found herself studying her father more closely. Was there a hint of guilt in his eyes when he glanced at their mother? A slight hesitation in his usually confident manner?

Or was she simply seeing what Lily's suspicions had primed her to look for?

As the meal wound down and the family moved to the sitting room for tea, Alice felt a weight settle in her stomach. He had always been a stickler about the girls not working and how it would make him look bad if they got jobs, but when they took up war work he was proud and told anyone who would listen. She loved her father, had always seen him as a pillar of strength and integrity, even if some of his ideas were old-fashioned. The thought that he might be leading a double life, that there might be another family in Norfolk... it was almost too painful to contemplate.

But as she caught Lily's meaningful glances, Alice knew she couldn't simply ignore the possibility. For her mother's sake, for the sake of the family she loved, she would have to dig deeper. The truth, whatever it might be, was out there. And Alice was determined to find it. Perhaps she'll talk to Freddie about it all, he was always logical in his thinking, except when it came to looking after himself.

3

Alice's hands trembled as she held the yellowed envelope, her father's familiar handwriting addressing it to an unfamiliar name in Norwich. It felt like she was meant to see the letter, especially as it was only a few days after having that conversation with Lily at the dinner table. She studied the unposted envelope hard. Had someone been waiting to hear from him? Sadness overwhelmed her. She had stumbled upon it quite by accident, tucked away in an old book while helping her mother clear out the attic only two days ago. Now, sitting cross-legged on her bedroom floor, surrounded by dust particles dancing in the late afternoon sunlight, she felt as though she was standing on the edge of a precipice.

She knew she shouldn't read it – she had been telling herself that since she found it. It was private, not meant for her eyes. But the niggling doubts that had been plaguing her, the whispered conversations between her parents that stopped abruptly when she entered a room, the frequent business trips to Norfolk that never quite added up, Lily's suspicions, it all seemed to converge on this moment, this letter.

With a deep breath, Alice carefully extracted the letter from its envelope, unfolding it with reverent care. As she began to read, her eyes widened, her breath catching in her throat.

'My dearest Margaret,' the letter began, 'I cannot express how much joy your news has brought me. A son, I can scarcely believe it. I find myself daydreaming about him, wondering whose eyes he has, whose smile...'

Alice felt as though the floor had dropped out from beneath her. A son? Her father had another child. The implications whirled through her mind, each more distressing than the last. How long had this been going on? Did her mother know? And this child, their half-brother, did he know about them?

She read on, her hands shaking so badly she could hardly make out the words. Her father wrote of his torn feelings, his love for this Margaret and their child warring with his duty to his family in London. He spoke of the impossibility of their situation, of the pain of living a double life.

As she reached the end of the letter, Alice felt tears streaming down her face. Her watery gaze jumped to the top of the page, she gasped at the date, 30th March 1903. Alice wiped her fingers across her wet cheeks. The father she thought she knew – steadfast, honourable, devoted to her mother – suddenly seemed like a stranger. The foundations of her world, already shaken by the war, now felt as though they were crumbling beneath her feet.

A soft knock at her door made Alice jump. She hastily folded the letter and shoved it under her pillow. 'Come in,' she called, trying to keep her voice steady.

Her mother entered, a concerned look on her face. 'Alice, dear, are you all right? You've been up here for hours.'

Alice nodded, not trusting herself to speak. Her mother's presence, usually a comfort, now felt like an accusation. How could she look at her mother, knowing what she knew? How could she keep this secret?

As her mother chatted about the progress they'd made in the attic, Alice's mind raced. Should she confront her father? Tell her mother? Pretend she'd never found the letter? The weight of this knowledge pressed down on her, making it hard to breathe.

'Alice?' Her mother's voice cut through her thoughts. 'You look pale, darling. Are you sure you're feeling well?'

Alice managed a weak smile. 'Just tired, I think. It's been a long day and I'm worried about Victoria.' She sighed. 'Ted isn't in a good place and she's refusing to buy herself a wedding dress. It's not fair; she's wanted to marry Ted for so long and I think she believes it isn't going to happen.'

Her mother nodded sympathetically. 'I don't know what to say; maybe it's all too much for her and they need to postpone it for a while, or you could always suggest to Victoria that she wears your dress, if it will fit her?' Sarah paused. 'The trouble is everyone is war-weary. It's gone on for nearly four years now and the men that are coming back are troubled, admittedly some more than others, but we can only be there for the people who need us.' Stepping towards the door, she frowned. 'Your father's trips to Norfolk are becoming more frequent,' she said, an odd note in her voice. 'I do hope his business there wraps up soon. I worry about him travelling; after all, you never know where or when the bombs are going to fall.'

As the door closed behind her mother, Alice felt a chill run down her spine. Did her mother suspect something? Or was Alice simply reading too much into an innocent comment?

The bedroom door swung open again. 'Oh Freddie, you made me jump.'

Freddie studied her for a moment. 'Are you all right? As your mother would say "you look a little peaky".' The door clicked as he shut it behind him.

Alice took a deep breath. 'I'm glad you're here, I've been wanting to talk to you about father.'

Freddie frowned. 'What about him?'

Alice tightened her mouth for a moment.

Freddie took the couple of steps to sit on the bed next to his wife. He rested his hand on hers. 'What is it?'

She closed her eyes. 'I don't know how to say it, but to put it bluntly, Lily and I were wondering if father had another life in Norfolk.' She blurted it out, her words tumbled over each other. 'After all he's always going there and he's never offered to take us with him, maybe he has a secret life we know nothing about.'

Freddie chuckled. 'I've never heard anything so ridiculous. This is Lily's doing, isn't it? Your father has always been a man of moral standing, remember when I asked for your hand in marriage and the interrogation that followed that.' He leaned in and gave his wife a hug. 'Don't let Lily lead you astray, she's never had much time for your father.' Freddie stood up and walked over to his side of the bed. 'I've got to go back to work, I only popped home for some papers I had forgotten.' He picked up a stack of pages, they rustled as he straightened them before walking towards the door. 'Are you all right Alice? I don't want to leave you if you're upset.'

Alice forced a smile. 'Don't worry, get back to work, I don't want you getting into trouble.'

Freddie smiled. 'I'm a sergeant so there's no fears of that happening.' He quickly stepped back towards her and gave a light kiss on top of her head. 'I'll be back soon.' He rushed out of the bedroom leaving behind him the sound of the creaking stairs as he ran down them.

Alice retrieved the letter from under her pillow. Perhaps she should have shown it to Freddie, but his reaction to just the thought of it all told her now wasn't the time. She stared down at it as if it might offer some solution. But she knew the answers she sought wouldn't be found in these faded words. She would have to dig deeper, to uncover the truth that had been hidden from her for so long.

As the sun set outside her window, casting long shadows across her room, Alice made a decision. She would go to Norfolk herself, find this Margaret and the half-brother she'd never known. Whatever the consequences, whatever pain it might cause, she had to know the truth.

With a new sense of purpose, Alice carefully resealed the letter in its envelope. The war had already changed so much in their world. Now, it seemed, it was time for the secrets closer to home to come to light as well. Whatever she discovered in Norfolk, Alice knew her life would never be the same again.

* * *

Victoria stood in front of the military history section, reorganising the books that had become dishevelled. She sighed, not understanding why customers wanted to read anything from this section with a war going on. As she worked, her mind wandered to the conversation she'd had with Mr Leadbetter earlier that morning.

He'd approached her with an unexpected proposition: would she consider taking on a more managerial role at Foyles? With staff shortages and the future uncertain, he needed someone he could rely on to help run the day-to-day operations of the shop, as well as helping when and where required.

The offer had taken Victoria by surprise. She'd always seen her work at Foyles as temporary, a job to tide her over until...

until what? Until the war ended? Until Ted was well enough for her to focus on being a full-time wife, or mother? But now, faced with this opportunity, she realised how much the bookshop had come to mean to her.

As she shelved a volume on another battle in history, Victoria's thoughts turned to Ted. His recovery was slow, the nightmares and anxiety still a daily struggle. How would he feel about her taking on more responsibility at work? Would he see it as a lack of faith in his ability to provide for them?

But then again, hadn't this war changed everything? Women all over the country were stepping into roles they never would have considered before. Why should she be any different?

'Victoria?' Alice's voice broke through her reverie. 'Are you all right? You've been staring at that book for ages.'

Victoria turned to her friend, a small smile on her face. 'I'm fine. Just... just thinking. Alice, can I ask you something? Do you think it's selfish of me to want more than just being a wife? To want to have proper work, to make a difference in my own right?'

Alice's eyes widened in surprise, then softened with understanding. 'Oh, Victoria, of course it's not selfish. We've all changed so much during this war. Why shouldn't our dreams change too?'

Victoria nodded, feeling a weight lift from her shoulders. She hadn't realised how much she'd needed to hear those words.

'Mr Leadbetter offered me a promotion,' she said softly. 'A managerial position. I'm... I'm thinking of accepting it.'

Alice's face lit up. 'Victoria, that's wonderful! You'd be perfect for it. But... what about Ted? Have you talked to him about it?'

Victoria shook her head. 'Not yet. I wanted to be sure of my own feelings first. But I think... I think he'll understand. We're partners, after all, in everything.'

As they continued to work, discussing the possibilities this new role could bring, Victoria felt a sense of excitement building within her. The world was changing, and she was changing with it. Whatever challenges lay ahead, she would face them head-on, balancing her love for Ted with her own ambitions and dreams.

The war had taken so much from them all, but perhaps it had also opened doors that might otherwise have remained closed. And Victoria was ready to step through, into whatever future awaited on the other side.

Later that evening, as Victoria walked home, her mind was still whirling with possibilities. The streets of London, once so familiar, seemed different somehow, full of new potential. She found herself noticing details she'd overlooked before: women in uniforms hurrying to important jobs, shops run entirely by female staff, posters encouraging women to do their part for the war effort.

As she approached Percy Street and the small house she shared with Ted, her sister Daisy and younger brother Stephen, Victoria felt a flutter of nerves. It had taken a lot of persuading to get Ted to move into her home after leaving the hospital. She had shocked everyone, including herself, when she asked him to marry her, but she didn't care what other people thought – she wasn't going to lose him a second time. She had been desperate to be there for him, to look after him while his blindness slowly improved with time. Getting him to see Dr Harrison had been no different; she recognised Ted was a proud man. Victoria now wondered what was the best approach to take on the subject of her potential promotion? How would Ted react?

She found him in the sitting room, poring over a newspaper. He looked up as she entered, a smile lighting his face. 'There you are, love. How was your day?'

Victoria took a deep breath. 'It was… interesting. Ted, there's something I need to talk to you about.'

She sat beside him, taking his hand in hers as she explained Mr Leadbetter's offer and her own conflicted feelings about it. As she spoke, she watched Ted's face carefully, trying to gauge his reaction.

To her surprise and relief, Ted's smile grew wider. 'Victoria, that's wonderful news. Of course you should take the position. You'd be brilliant at it.'

Victoria felt tears pricking at her eyes. 'You really think so? You wouldn't mind if I... if I wanted more than just being a wife?'

Ted's expression softened. He reached out, cupping her face gently. 'Victoria, my love, I fell in love with you because of your spirit, your intelligence, your dreams. The war may have changed a lot of things, but it hasn't changed that. I want you to be happy, to fulfil your potential. If this job at Foyles does that, then I'm all for it.'

Victoria felt a wave of love and gratitude wash over her. She leaned in, kissing Ted softly. 'Thank you, for understanding, and for supporting me.'

As they sat there, discussing the possibilities this new role could bring, Victoria felt a renewed sense of hope for their future. Yes, there were still challenges ahead – Ted's ongoing recovery, and the uncertainties of the war. But together, supporting each other's dreams and ambitions, they could face anything.

The wedding plans, which had seemed so all-consuming just days ago, now felt less urgent. Perhaps, Victoria thought, it wouldn't be such a bad thing to postpone the ceremony for a bit longer. She wanted Ted not to feel so threatened by his time at the front, and to give themselves time to grow into these new roles. These new versions of themselves that the war had shaped.

As night fell over London, Victoria and Ted talked long into the evening, dreaming and planning for a future neither of them could have imagined.

* * *

Molly's morning sickness had been manageable at first, just a bit of queasiness that she could easily hide. But as she stood in the cramped toilet at Foyles, splashing cold water on her face for the third time that day, she knew she couldn't keep this secret much longer.

She stared at her reflection in the small mirror, noting the pallor of her face, the slight shadows under her eyes. How long before the others noticed? Before Mr Leadbetter started asking questions?

Taking a deep breath, Molly straightened her white blouse and black skirt before pinching some colour into her cheeks and stepping back into the shop. She could do this. She just wanted to wait a few more weeks before telling Andrew, and then...

The thought of telling Andrew filled her with a mix of excitement and dread. He'd been so focused on his work, whether it was at the bank or with the veterans, trying not to show he was haunted by his own experiences on the front line. With no children of their own he had found a way to fill his time and she had supported him. But gradually she had come to recognise the signs he had tried so hard to keep hidden.

'Everything all right, Molly?' Alice asked, noticing her hovering nearby. 'You look a bit peaky.'

Molly forced a smile. 'Oh, just a bit tired. Didn't sleep well last night.'

Victoria reached out, squeezing her hand. 'The war's got us all on edge. Make sure you're taking care of yourself, won't you?'

Molly nodded, the lie sitting heavy in her throat. As she turned to help a customer, Molly's hand unconsciously went to her stomach. Soon, she promised herself. Soon she'd share her secret. But for now, she had to focus on getting through each day, one hour at a time, keeping her growing child safe in a world that seemed increasingly dangerous.

The day wore on, each hour a test of Molly's endurance and ability to keep her secret. The nausea came and went in waves, forcing her to develop a series of subtle strategies to cope. She found herself strategically positioned near the exits, always ready for a quick dash to the lady's room if needed. She kept crackers hidden in her pockets, sneaking bites to keep the queasiness at bay when no one was looking.

But it wasn't just the physical symptoms that were becoming harder to hide. Molly found her emotions increasingly difficult to control. Remembering a touching scene in a novel she was placing on a shelf brought unexpected tears to her eyes. A customer's offhand comment about the war made her heart race with anxiety for Andrew and their unborn child.

As closing time approached, Molly found herself in the children's section, straightening a display of picture books. Her hands lingered on a beautifully illustrated copy of *Peter Rabbit*, and she found herself imagining reading it to her own child. The thought filled her with a mixture of joy and terror. How could she bring a baby into this world, with all its dangers and uncertainties?

'Molly?' Mr Leadbetter's voice startled her from her reverie. 'A word in my office, if you please.'

Heart pounding, Molly followed him. Had he noticed something? Was her secret about to be exposed?

'Molly, my dear,' Mr Leadbetter began, his voice gentle, 'I couldn't help but notice you've seemed... out of sorts lately. Is everything all right? You're not coming down with something, are you?'

Molly felt a wave of relief, quickly followed by guilt at the genuine concern in her employer's voice. 'No, sir, I'm not ill. Just... just a bit tired, that's all. With everything that's going on...'

Mr Leadbetter nodded sympathetically. 'These are trying times for us all. But, Molly, if there's anything you need – time off, or a change in duties – you must let me know. We take care of our own here at Foyles.'

Molly felt tears pricking at her eyes, touched by his kindness and frustrated by her inability to be honest. 'Thank you, Mr Leadbetter. I appreciate that more than you know.'

As she left his office, Molly realised she couldn't go on like this for much longer. The strain of hiding her condition, of carrying this joy and fear alone, was becoming too much. Soon, she resolved, she would tell Andrew. Whatever his reaction, whatever challenges lay ahead, they would face them together.

With this decision made, Molly felt a weight lift from her shoulders. As she re-joined Alice and Victoria to close up the shop, she allowed herself, for the first time, to fully embrace the reality of her situation. She was going to be a mother. In the midst of war, a new life was growing. It was terrifying, yes, but also miraculous.

The bell chimed as the last customer left, and Molly looked at her friends, these women who had become like sisters to her. Soon, she thought, she would share her news with them too. Soon, she wouldn't have to face this journey alone.

4

Freddie sat at the kitchen table, surrounded by a sea of papers, his police uniform jacket draped over the back of his chair. The lamp cast a warm glow over the scene, but it did little to soften the hard lines of worry etched on his face.

Alice watched him from the doorway, toying with the idea of talking to him about her father's unposted letter. Frowning, she stared down at the cup of tea cooling in her hands. She'd meant to bring it to him from the front room, but now she hesitated, not wanting to interrupt his concentration. Dinner had long since finished and the boys were fast asleep. The only sound was the murmured voices of her mother and father coming from the front room.

'Freddie?' she said softly. 'It's getting late. Don't you think you should get some rest?'

He looked up, blinking as if surprised to find himself still at the table. 'Oh, Alice, I'm sorry, I didn't realise the time.' He gestured to the papers before him. 'There's just so much to do. So many of the lads are struggling, and...'

Alice set the tea down and moved behind him, placing her

hands on his tense shoulders, realising now was not the time to burden him with her worries. 'I know, love. But you can't help anyone if you run yourself into the ground.'

Freddie sighed, leaning back into her touch. 'I know. It's just... I feel like I owe it to them, you know? The ones who didn't make it back their families are struggling to feed themselves, and the ones who did aren't much better off. I saw Ted today, and he's in a terrible way. He's trying to hide it from Victoria because he wants to protect her but I think that's causing him more problems.'

Alice shook her head. 'Victoria thinks their wedding won't go ahead because Ted is getting worse. I was there when he came home and thought he was still on the front line. It was awful to see the fear play out. Victoria was trying to reassure him he was home and safe, but he seemed unable to hear her.'

Freddie took a deep breath. 'And he's just one of many who are unable to cope because sounds and smells trigger something in their brains. I'm lucky. Yes I have nightmares, but at least it doesn't affect my day-to-day life. Having seen it for yourself you must see why I must try and do something to help, I can't let it all go just because I'm all right.'

Alice's heart ached at the pain in his voice. She knew about the nightmares that still plagued him. They had rarely acknowledged them, until now. She didn't want to force that conversation, hoping he would talk about them when he was ready, but the guilt he carried for surviving when so many others hadn't was getting worse every day. It was all there to see in the way he held himself, at least for anyone who cared to look deeper than the surface smile. 'You are doing something,' she said gently. 'Every day, with your work in the police force, and with these veterans' groups, but you also need to take care of yourself.'

He nodded, then turned to face her, his eyes haunted. 'I saw Private Cooper today. Do you remember him?'

Alice nodded, remembering the cheerful young man who'd visited them before the war.

'He's... he's not well, Alice. I think he's getting a bad cold; it could even be this influenza I keep hearing about people catching, and what with his war injuries... I'm worried he won't make it.'

Alice pulled him close, feeling his body shake with suppressed emotion. 'Oh Freddie, I'm so sorry.'

As she held him, Alice's mind raced. How much more could they all take? Constantly struggling to rebuild their lives... with what little food there was rationed and some folk short of money to buy what was available. It seemed never-ending. But as Freddie's breathing steadied, she made a silent vow. They would get through this, all of them, together. They had to.

* * *

Victoria busied herself vigorously sweeping the kitchen floor. Tears pricked at her eyes, but she blinked them away. Tomorrow was her wedding day, and she should be filled with excitement. The thud of the door knocker stopped her in her tracks. Her mind immediately rushed to Ted – had something happened to him? Her lips tightened as she strode towards the front door. Pulling back her shoulders and taking a deep breath she pulled open the door.

Alice and Molly beamed at her.

Molly reached out to clasp Victoria's arm. 'Is everything all right? Only you look a little pale.'

Alice stepped inside. 'I expected to see you with your hair in braids, you know, getting ready for the morning.'

Victoria forced a smile.

Molly followed Alice inside. 'Victoria, I want to say I'm sorry for not giving your wedding the attention I should have. I'm afraid I've been wrapped up in my own problems, which actually didn't turn out to be problems.'

'Don't worry, Molly, I understand. We've all been thinking about things that have been going on in our own lives.'

Alice nodded. 'Well, better late than never. We're here to change that.' She lifted her hand, which was holding a large carpet bag tight.

Victoria frowned. 'What's that? I mean I can see it's a bag but you both seem quite pleased with it.'

Molly grinned. 'Open it, Alice. Show Victoria what's inside.'

Trying to catch her friend's excitement Victoria forced a smile. 'First, let's go and sit in the front room and then you can let me in on your secret.'

They giggled as they followed Victoria.

'It's nothing to worry about, Victoria.' Molly stopped laughing. 'We know we've let you down and we're just trying to make up for it.'

Victoria glanced over her shoulder. 'There's no need; everything is good. Please take a seat and I'll make us all a cup of tea.'

'The tea can wait, thank you.' Alice placed the bag on the chair and began to open it. 'Now I want you to take this with the good heart with which it is given—'

'Just get on with it.' Molly laughed.

Victoria's gaze moved from one to the other before focusing on the bag. 'Alice, you are clearly worried about it, so just tell me what it is you have in there.'

Alice cleared her throat before pulling out a long white dress. 'You'll probably recognise it as the one I got married in; I'm hoping it will fit you.' She glanced at Victoria's troubled face. 'It seemed like a good idea this morning, but now I'm not so sure.'

'Thank you for thinking of me, Alice, but it really isn't necessary.'

Molly frowned. 'Have you got a wedding dress?'

Victoria shook her head.

'Are you planning to go out today to buy a dress?' Molly persisted.

Again, Victoria shook her head.

Molly stared at Victoria. 'Then can I ask what were you planning to wear? My dress would have been too big for you, otherwise that would also be in the bag to give you a choice, but we're running out of time.'

Victoria's tears spilled over her eyelashes.

Molly quickly stepped forward and wrapped her arms around her. 'I'm sorry, I didn't mean to upset you, but we do want you to have the best day. You've waited so long to marry Ted.'

Victoria wiped her hands over her cheeks, clearing away her tears. 'I... I haven't bought a dress. To be honest I'm not convinced the wedding will go ahead tomorrow.'

Alice's head jerked up. 'Why? Why do you say that?'

Victoria sniffed. 'Ted is very unpredictable. Don't get me wrong – when his head is clear I know he loves me, but a noise or smell can put him straight back at the front and then he doesn't hear me. If that happens tomorrow, then I can't see how the wedding can go ahead.'

Molly lowered her eyelashes. 'And that's why you haven't planned much for your big day.' She peered wide-eyed at Victoria. 'Are your family from Brighton coming?'

Victoria shook her head. 'I told them because of the war I wasn't sure it would go ahead, and if it did then I would only have witnesses there.'

Alice frowned. 'I don't know what to say. I mean, I saw Ted here, so I knew he wasn't in the best state of mind and I knew you were worried that the wedding might not go ahead, but I didn't think things were really that bad because you didn't call the wedding off. Why didn't you say something?'

Victoria shrugged. 'It seems we've become three friends who now keep our fears and problems to ourselves.'

Molly sat down on the nearest armchair. 'I'm definitely guilty of that, but I don't want you to think it's because I don't value our friendship, because I do.'

Alice raised her eyebrows. 'I'm also guilty of keeping my thoughts to myself, and it's not because I don't trust our friendships; besides my children and my husband, you two are up there as two of the most important people in my life.'

Molly eyed her friend. 'So what thoughts are you keeping from us?'

Alice smiled. 'I promise to talk to you both about that after Victoria's wedding. Today is about her trying on the dress and getting butterflies fluttering inside at the thought of being married to the man she has loved since she was sixteen.'

* * *

The morning of Victoria's wedding dawned bright and clear, a rarity in London's usually gloomy weather.

'Daisy will be up shortly. She wants to be the one to help you into your dress,' Alice whispered as she stepped over the threshold, pushing the door to behind her.

Molly stared at the beautiful white taffeta dress, with its layers of trumpet sleeves and lacework on the bodice, ending at the base of the neck. 'I'd forgotten how beautiful the dress was.' She turned to Victoria. 'You're going to look stunning. Ted's a lucky man.'

Victoria gave a small smile. 'It has a lot of history behind it, so

I hope I do it proud.' She turned to Alice. 'I don't want your grandmother turning in her grave because I've ruined the good luck, the happiness that seems to be sewn into every stitch of it.'

Alice laughed. 'Don't be daft. You've waited a long time for this day so just enjoy it and stop worrying.'

Victoria nodded. 'You're right of course, but it does feel my wedding is a bit of a botch job. I'm wearing your wedding dress, you are wearing my bridesmaid dress that I wore to your wedding and Molly's wearing hers, and Daisy's wearing the bridesmaid dress I wore to Molly's wedding.'

Molly looked up from examining her dress. Memories of Alice's and her wedding day came flooding back. 'But these are beautiful, and it would be criminal not to give them all a second wear.' Molly ran her fingers over the soft, dark blue lace that overlaid the pale blue dress. The long sleeves were cuffed with the same detail. She let her fingers rest on the hard surface of the navy sequins, which had been sewn onto the lace appliqué. 'The good news is I know it still fits me – and don't forget we've got matching navy-blue hats.'

Alice chuckled. 'They are wonderful.' She glanced at Victoria. 'Victoria, this isn't a botch job, there's a war going on, so we are making the most of what's available to us.'

Molly laughed. 'That's right. Come on, Victoria, we expect better from you so start enjoying your day.'

The creak of the bedroom door made them all look across and see Daisy walk in. 'Is everything all right? You all look like you've been up to no good. You've got guilt written all over you.'

Molly laughed. 'Watch yourself, girls, there's a policewoman in the house.'

Alice giggled. 'I know all about living with a policewoman. Lily is suspicious of everything these days.'

The next hour passed with them all getting dressed. Daisy

tried on her bridesmaid dress. The white lace and pale pink satin underlay of the column dress swished around Daisy's calf, and the neat white shoes just about fit her, although they were a little tight. Daisy wasn't convinced she could wear them all day, but she would try; after all it was the day Victoria had thought would never come so it was the least she could do.

Victoria had been unsure about Daisy wearing a different style of dress, but the others assured her that it all went well together and as her sister was walking her down the aisle the different dress gave her more status. Victoria decided they could be right.

As Victoria stood before the mirror in her childhood bedroom, adjusting her veil with trembling hands, she had a sense of foreboding and felt anything but sunny.

Molly bustled around the room, fussing with the train of the dress and chattering nervously about last-minute details. But Victoria barely heard her. Her mind was with Ted, wondering how he was faring, praying that today of all days, the shadows of war would leave him in peace.

A soft knock at the door interrupted her thoughts. 'Come in,' she called, half expecting to see her sister, Daisy, or perhaps Alice, who had gone downstairs for a glass of water.

Alice slipped into the room, her face pale with worry. 'Vic,' she said softly, 'I've just had word from Freddie. There's... there's been an incident.'

Victoria felt her heart drop. 'What kind of incident?' she asked, already knowing the answer.

Alice glanced at Molly, who had gone quiet, then back to her friend. 'Ted had a bit of a... moment this morning. The noise of a car backfiring... well, it set him off. They're trying to find him so they can calm him down, but...'

Victoria closed her eyes, fighting back tears. This was what she had feared, what had made her consider postponing the wedding in the first place. But Ted had been so determined, so eager to start their life together, that she had tried to push her doubts aside.

'What should I do?' she whispered, more to herself than to anyone in the room.

Molly stepped forward, placing a comforting hand on her shoulder. 'That's up to you. If you want to postpone, we'll all understand. These are difficult times for everyone.'

But as Victoria looked at herself in the mirror, at the dress she had borrowed from Alice, and the ring sparkling on her finger, she felt a surge of determination. 'No,' she said firmly. 'We're doing this today. Ted needs me, and I need him. We promised to face everything together, and that starts now.'

She turned to Alice. 'Tell Freddie I'm coming to help find him. I want to see Ted.'

As she swept out of the room, her veil trailing behind her, Victoria felt a strange mix of fear and resolve. This wasn't how she had imagined her wedding day, but then again, nothing about their love story had been conventional. Whatever challenges lay ahead, they would face them side by side. She ran down the stairs into the narrow hall and pulled open the front door. She gasped at the frazzled man standing in front of her. 'Ted, are you all right?'

Ted's wild gaze darted around Victoria. 'It's not safe. We need to hide.' He ran inside and slammed the door shut.

Victoria took a breath. 'Ted, it's me – Victoria, remember? It's our wedding day. I was just coming to see you.' She reached out to take his hand. 'Everything is going to be all right.'

Ted was breathing hard, his wedding suit wrinkled from where he'd gripped it too tight. Instead of panicking, she simply sat with him, her own wedding preparations forgotten as she helped him count his breaths, grounding him in the present moment.

Ted stared at her wide-eyed. His wild gaze slowly faded away, as he studied her, as if for the first time. 'You're wearing a wedding dress.'

Victoria tried to add a smile to her voice. 'Do you like it? Today is our wedding day; we will soon be man and wife. Remember that's what we've wanted for so long. I'm going to be Mrs Marsden.'

Dropping to the floor, Ted nodded. 'I'm sorry.' He sobbed. 'I can't seem to control what's going on. I don't think we should get married. It's not fair on you. I can only see misery for you. I'm sorry,' he whispered, shame colouring his voice. 'You deserve better than this.'

Victoria took his face in her hands then, forcing him to meet her eyes. 'I deserve you,' she had said firmly. 'All of you, Ted Marsden. The man you were before the war, the man you are now, and the man you're becoming. I choose all of it.'

Victoria lowered herself to the floor in front of the man she loved, her eyes filling with unshed tears as she peered at him. He was broken; his spirit and fight had left him today and she didn't know how to help him. She reached out and took his hands in hers. 'It's going to be all right. We love each other, don't we?'

Ted gazed down at the floor. 'It's because I love you that I want to make you happy, and I don't think I can. I'm sorry.'

Victoria's tears silently spilled over and rolled down her cheeks. 'Don't we owe it to ourselves to at least try? I have loved you for so long and I can't give up on us without a fight. If I'm prepared to try, isn't that enough?'

Molly stood on the stairs watching the scene in front of her.

There was a rap on the front door, Alice pulled it open, and

Freddie came rushing in. Victoria held up her hand to immediately stop him in his tracks.

Ted glanced around him. 'I've messed up, haven't I?'

Victoria smiled at his troubled features. 'No, you haven't. There is still time.'

Freddie stepped forward. 'Ted, we need to let the girls finish getting ready so you can finally marry the love of your life. I'll be with you, and I promise to look after you.'

Ted stood up. He nodded at Freddie.

Victoria reached out to Ted. 'Before you go to the church, let me give you a hug.'

Ted wrapped his arms around Victoria and squeezed her tight. 'I am sorry.'

'Shh, it's all right. We are going to be all right because we love each other.'

* * *

The July afternoon sunlight filtered through the stained-glass windows of St Michael's Church, casting a kaleidoscope of colours across the worn wooden pews. Victoria stood in the small vestibule, her fingers tracing the delicate lace on Alice's wedding dress, now hers for this special day. She remembered her words earlier to Alice and she did believe the vintage gown held memories of joy within its fabric, and she truly hoped that would be true for her and Ted.

'You look absolutely perfect,' Molly whispered, adjusting the train with gentle hands. Alice, standing beside her fellow bridesmaid, dabbed at her eyes with a tissue.

'I never thought I'd cry seeing someone else wear my dress,' Alice laughed softly, 'but you've made it even more beautiful than when I wore it.'

Through the door, they could hear the murmur of guests finding their seats, the subtle notes of the organ warming up. The small church, which had stood for over a century, seemed to embrace them in its intimate atmosphere.

Victoria took a deep breath, smoothing non-existent wrinkles from the silk. 'I can't believe we're actually here.'

In the adjacent room, Ted fidgeted with his bow tie while Freddie, his best man, swatted his hands away. 'Stop that.' Freddie chuckled. 'You'll undo all my hard work. Though I have to say, you're much calmer than I was before my wedding.'

'That's because you were marrying into the Gettin family, which I know strictly speaking isn't true – it was the Taylor family – but let's face it Alice's grandfather is much more powerful than her father is. From what I've heard her great-grandfather and his son were a force to be reckoned with. They had a reputation for doing dodgy accounts for some of their clients, but I don't think her grandfather was a part of that. Although, I believe, that's how Alice's parents met,' Ted replied with a grin. 'And if what I heard is true he had to threaten you with bodily harm if you ran.'

Freddie laughed. 'That's not true at all. I've always loved Alice. Now you're just making things up.'

Ted smiled. 'Yes, but it helps to ease my nerves. I know I don't deserve Victoria; I've led her a merry dance over the years.'

Freddie frowned. 'We've all made mistakes, but what's important is she forgives and loves you and of that there is definitely no doubt.'

The old wooden doors creaked open, and the organ music shifted, signalling the beginning of the ceremony. The priest stepped forward and the chords of the pipe organ filled the air. The congregation stood up as one, as Molly and Alice slipped out first. With Alice leading the way, the two bridesmaids slowly walked down the aisle, in single file, towards the waiting priest, in step with each other and Mendelssohn's 'Wedding March'. Their blue dresses caught the light as they took their places at the altar.

Victoria, radiant in the borrowed dress that carried so much love in its history, stood next to Daisy, their arms interlinked.

Daisy leaned in and whispered, 'I love you, Victoria. Thank you for being my mother and my sister.'

Victoria could feel her tears threatening to overflow. 'I love you too, Daisy. We haven't had an easy time over the years, but we will always have each other, no matter what.'

Ted's breath caught in his throat as he watched the two girls. The sight of Victoria, bathed in the rainbow light from the windows, made everything else fade away. Freddie gave his shoulder a gentle squeeze, a silent gesture of support and joy.

The girls began their walk down the aisle, each step bringing Victoria closer to Ted and their future together. The dress whispered against the floor, its vintage lace telling stories of love that spanned generations. As she reached Ted, their eyes met, and in that moment, the small church seemed to hold all the happiness in the world.

The minister smiled warmly at the couple, his voice carrying to every corner of the intimate space. 'Dearly beloved...'

And so, in front of their closest friends and family, surrounded by the warmth of tradition and the promise of tomorrow, Victoria and Ted began their journey together, their love story adding another beautiful chapter to the legacy of Alice's dress and the little church that witnessed it all.

5

The soft golden light of dawn was just beginning to filter through the curtains as Victoria stirred, her eyes fluttering open. For a moment, she was disorientated, the unfamiliar weight of the ring on her finger catching her attention. Then the events of the previous day came rushing back, and a complex mix of emotions washed over her.

She turned her head to see Ted sleeping peacefully beside her, his face more relaxed than she had seen it in months. Victoria's heart swelled with love, even as she remembered the tumultuous journey to this moment.

The wedding had been far from the fairy tale she had once imagined. Ted's episode in the morning had nearly derailed everything, but her decision to stand by his side and face his demons together had turned the day around. The ceremony itself had been small and subdued, a far cry from the grand affair they had initially discussed, but somehow all the more meaningful for it.

She remembered how his hands had trembled the morning

before the wedding, how the sound of a car backfiring outside had sent him into a spiral of memories he fought so hard to keep at bay.

As she watched Ted sleep now, Victoria reflected on the vows they had exchanged. 'For better or for worse, in sickness and in health.' Those words carried so much more weight now than she could have ever imagined when they first got engaged. The war had changed Ted, had changed both of them, but their love had endured, had even grown stronger through the trials they had faced.

She thought of how steady his voice had become during the ceremony, how the tremor in his hands had stilled when she walked down the aisle. Alice's dress, borrowed and beautiful, had felt like an armour, protecting them both with its history of love and commitment. Freddie's steady presence as best man, understanding Ted's struggles better than most, had been an anchor throughout the day.

Ted stirred, his eyes opening to meet hers. For a moment, there was confusion in his gaze, then recognition, followed by a slow, warm smile that made Victoria's heart skip a beat.

'Good morning, Mrs Marsden,' he murmured, reaching out to touch her cheek.

Victoria leaned into his touch, her own smile blooming. 'Good morning, Mr Marsden.'

The simple exchange held worlds of meaning. She could see in his eyes that he remembered everything about yesterday, both the difficult moments and the beautiful ones. His thumb stroked her cheekbone, a gesture of gratitude and love that needed no words.

As they lay there, talking softly about the day ahead and the life they were embarking on together, Victoria felt a sense of peace settle over her. Yes, there would be challenges ahead. Ted's recovery was ongoing, the war was still raging, and the flu epidemic loomed over everything. But they were together now, officially and irrevocably bound to one another. Whatever came their way, they would face it as one.

The world outside their little bubble was full of uncertainty and fear, but here, in this moment, Victoria found hope. She thought of the telegram sitting unopened on the dresser, likely another casualty list that would have to be dealt with at the hospital where she had previously volunteered. A voice screamed in her head, it could be about her brother, Stephen, who was still fighting on the front line. She tried to shake the voice away, she couldn't take any more, while she didn't open it everything is as it was before the telegram arrived. For now, she would savour this moment, this beginning, with all its imperfect perfection.

Her bedroom was small and modest, but now it was their room and she had space available for him. The morning light painted everything in shades of gold, transforming the simple space into something magical. Ted's arms around her felt like home, his heartbeat under her palm a steady reminder of all they had overcome to reach this moment. The war might have changed them, but it hadn't broken them. If anything, it had forged their love into something stronger, more resilient than the naive romance they had started with when she was a young teenager.

'What are you thinking about?' Ted asked softly, his voice still rough with sleep.

Victoria smiled, tracing his jawline with her finger. 'About how some of the best things in life don't look anything like what we imagine they will.'

Ted caught her hand, pressing a kiss to her palm. 'Like

marrying a broken soldier instead of the dashing officer you met at the start of the war?'

'Like marrying the bravest man I know,' she corrected him gently, 'who fights his battles every day and still has the strength to love me so completely.' Victoria paused for a moment. 'I don't want to spoil this morning, but a telegram has arrived, and I keep putting off reading it in case it's bad news about Stephen...'

Ted pushed himself up on his elbow. 'I didn't realise, do you want me to read it?'

Victoria shook her head. 'No, but thank you, it's something I've got to do.' She swung her legs out of bed and took the couple of steps towards her dresser. Staring down at it before taking a deep breath and picking it up. She turned it over in her hands several times.

'Come back to bed so I can cuddle you as you open it.' Ted's whispered words broke the tense silence that now filled the room.

Victoria forced a weak smile and walked over to sit on the edge of the bed. She felt Ted's arm around her waist, squeezing her close to him. Frantically tearing the envelope open she pulled the telegram free, Victoria gasped.

Ted held on to her tightly. 'What is it? Is it...'

Victoria breathed a sigh of relief. 'No, it isn't, Stephen has been injured but he's being brought home.' She turned to hug Ted. 'Hopefully, we'll get to see him soon and his physical injuries won't be life changing for him. I can't wait to feast my eyes on him for myself.'

The morning stretched ahead of them, the first of many they would share as husband and wife. Outside their window, the world continued its tumultuous course, but in this room, in this moment, they had found their peace. It wasn't the perfect beginning that young Victoria had once dreamed of, but it was real, it was honest, and it was theirs.

* * *

The summer heat seemed particularly oppressive in the bookshop that day. Molly took a handkerchief out of her pocket and mopped her brow. 'I don't know if it's me but it's so hot in here today.'

Alice smiled. 'It is hot. I'm glad it wasn't this warm when Victoria got married a couple of days ago.'

Molly thrust her handkerchief back into her skirt pocket. 'I'm surprised Victoria's in work this morning, but I'm glad they managed to have a good day in the end. I must admit when I saw the state of Ted before the wedding, I wasn't sure it would, or could, go ahead.'

Alice frowned. 'I know what you mean. She certainly has a lot on her plate, but they were so happy after that. I hope they can find their way through all of the demons that haunt him.' She yawned and picked up some books. 'I expect Victoria had to come in because it's all about paying the bills with Ted not working. Anyway, I had better start work.'

The usual buzz of Foyles Bookshop was undercut by a current of unease. Customers huddled in small groups; their voices low as they discussed the latest news. Alice, restocking a shelf of popular novels, couldn't help but overhear snatches of conversation.

'...they're saying it's worse than the usual influenza...'

'...my cousin in Manchester says the hospitals are overflowing...'

'...calling it the Spanish Flu. Have you heard?'

Alice's hand trembled slightly as she placed the last book on the shelf. The war had already taken so much from them all. The idea of a new threat, an invisible enemy that couldn't be fought with guns and tanks, sent a shiver down her spine.

She made her way back to the counter where Victoria was writing up a customer's purchases. As the elderly gentleman gathered his books and shuffled out, coughing into his handkerchief, Victoria turned to Alice with wide eyes.

'Did you hear him? He said his neighbour's whole family has fallen ill. High fevers, terrible coughs... it sounds dreadful.'

Alice nodded; her brow furrowed with concern. 'I've been hearing whispers all morning. Do you think... do you think we'll be all right?'

Before Victoria could respond, Mr Leadbetter emerged from the back office, his usually jovial face sombre. 'Ladies, a moment of your time, please.'

As the staff gathered around, Mr Leadbetter cleared his throat. 'I'm sure you've all heard the rumours about this new strain of influenza. I had hoped it wasn't serious but it appears to be taking hold. I've just heard several shops have had to close due to staff illnesses. We need to be prepared.'

A murmur ran through the group. Molly, her face pale, spoke up. 'What can we do, Mr Leadbetter?'

The old bookseller sighed, running a hand through his thinning hair. 'For now, we carry on. But we'll be implementing some new procedures. More frequent cleaning of surfaces, especially the counter and door handles. If possible, it might be best to wear a face mask over your mouth and nose – not ideal but if it stops you breathing in the germs then it needs to be done. And if any of you feel unwell, even slightly, I want you to stay home, no exceptions.' Mr Leadbetter frowned as he walked away.

Alice noticed Mr Leadbetter was more hunched over than usual. A knot of fear tightened in her chest. She thought of Freddie, already struggling with the aftermath of the war, and of their two young boys. How could she protect them from an enemy they couldn't see? Alice gave herself a mental shake. Panic wasn't going to help anybody. She had to be busy, be practical. She picked up the bottle of disinfectant and her cleaning cloth and began cleaning her counter.

Molly took a breath. She'd been feeling off all morning, the usual nausea compounded by a persistent light-headedness. Feeling sure it would soon wear off, she walked over to a customer who was standing on the bottom rung of the bookshelf trying to reach a book. 'Let me help you.' She wiped her brow and began climbing the nearby ladder, her head swimming slightly. As she stretched to retrieve the desired volume, the room suddenly tilted alarmingly. Molly gripped the ladder tightly, her knuckles turning white as she fought to maintain her balance.

'Molly? Are you all right up there?' Alice's concerned voice floated up from below.

Molly tried to respond, but the words seemed stuck in her throat. The book slipped from her grasp, tumbling to the floor with a loud thud. She felt her grip on the ladder loosening, her vision blurring at the edges.

Suddenly, there were hands on her waist, guiding her down. Molly blinked, finding herself seated in a chair, Alice and Victoria hovering anxiously over her.

'What happened? It's a good job you were here to catch her, Mr Marsden.' Mr Leadbetter's worried face appeared in her field of vision.

'Please, call me Ted.' He looked worried as he studied Molly. 'Are you all right?'

Mr Leadbetter frowned. 'Should we call for a doctor? Do you feel like you are coming down with something?'

Molly shook her head, trying to clear the fog. 'No, no, I'm fine. Just a bit dizzy. It's this heat, you know.'

But as she looked up, she saw the doubt in her friends' eyes.

They'd known each other too long, too well, for such a flimsy excuse to hold water.

'Molly,' Alice said gently, kneeling beside her. 'Is there something you're not telling us? You've been... different lately. Tired, pale. And now this...'

Victoria gasped softly, her eyes widening with sudden understanding. 'Molly, are you...?'

Molly felt tears welling up in her eyes. The secret she'd been carrying for weeks, the joy and fear she'd been holding close to her heart, suddenly seemed too big to contain. She nodded, a small sob escaping her lips.

'Oh, Molly,' Alice breathed, pulling her friend into a tight embrace. Victoria joined the hug, her own eyes glistening with tears.

Mr Leadbetter looked thoroughly out of his depth. Smiling, he cleared his throat, glad it wasn't the awful flu that was going around. 'Right, well, I think perhaps Molly should have a cup of tea first and then take the rest of the day off. And maybe... maybe it's time to consider some lighter duties?'

As her friends helped her gather her things, fussing over her in a way that was both touching and slightly overwhelming, Molly felt a weight lift from her shoulders. The secret was out, at least part of it. She still had to tell Andrew, still had to face the uncertainty of bringing a child into this war-torn world. But for now, surrounded by the love and support of her friends, Molly allowed herself to feel, just for a moment, the pure joy of impending motherhood.

Later, as the three friends huddled together during their tea break, the gravity of the situation hung heavy in the air.

'It's like the war all over again,' Molly said softly. 'Only this time, we can't see the enemy coming.'

Victoria reached out, squeezing both their hands. 'We've

made it through four years of war. Whatever this flu brings, we'll face it together.' She took a breath. 'Talking of war, I had a telegram about Stephen—'

The girls gasped in unison.

'No, he's been injured and is in hospital but not in London, I don't know where but I'm hoping Stephen will write to let me know.' Victoria looked thoughtful. 'Actually, I suppose I could just write to him like I've always done and hopefully it will find him.'

Alice breathed a sigh of relief. 'I'm so glad he's... well I hope his injuries aren't too severe. I'll let Charles and Freddie know he is safe; it'll be wonderful to give them some good news.'

Molly grabbed Victoria's hand. 'You must have been terrified when you got the telegram, thank goodness it wasn't bad news.'

Victoria nodded. 'Ted was with me when I opened it, in fact he held me tight, just in case, but thankfully the news wasn't as bad as it could have been.'

* * *

Andrew paced the living room of their home in Bury Street, his brow furrowed with worry as he waited for Molly to return from work. The call he'd received at the bank from Mr Leadbetter earlier that day had left him shaken. Thank goodness Ted was there, otherwise who knows what would have happened. Molly nearly fainting at the bookshop could have had serious consequences. It confirmed the nagging suspicions he'd been harbouring for weeks about his wife's health.

The sound of a key in the lock made him stop in his tracks. Molly entered, looking pale and tired, but her face brightened with a smile when she saw him.

'Andrew, you're home early. Is everything all right at the bank?'

He moved to help her with her coat, studying her face closely. 'Everything's fine at work, love. But Mr Leadbetter called me today. He told me what happened at the shop.'

Molly's smile faltered, and she looked away, busying herself with hanging up her coat. 'It was nothing, really. I was just a bit dizzy from the heat.'

Andrew gently took her by the shoulders, turning her to face him. 'Molly, please, I know something's been going on with you. You've been tired, and sick in the mornings. I've been so caught up in my work with the veterans, I haven't... I should have been paying more attention.'

Molly's eyes filled with tears, and for a moment, Andrew feared the worst. Had she caught the flu? Was she seriously ill?

Andrew studied her closely. 'Sit down. I've made you a cup of tea and a sandwich. I hope the tea is still hot.' He watched Molly from across the dinner table, a small frown creasing his forehead. She wasn't touching the sandwich, her usual healthy appetite seemingly vanished. It wasn't just tonight; he'd noticed changes in her behaviour over the past few weeks. She seemed more tired, more emotional, and there was a new secretiveness about her that he couldn't quite understand.

'Everything all right with the food, love?' he asked gently.

Molly looked up, startled, as if she'd forgotten he was there. 'Oh yes, thank you for making it. I'm just not very hungry tonight.'

Andrew reached across the table, taking her hand in his. 'Molly, what is it? You've seemed... different lately. Is it this influenza everyone is talking about? Are you worried about getting sick?'

Molly's eyes filled with tears, and for a moment, Andrew thought she might tell him what was bothering her. But then she blinked them away, forcing a smile. 'I'm fine, really, just tired.

Things have been so busy at the shop, what with all the cleaning we're having to do, and of course there was Victoria's wedding. I do worry about her and Ted. It was quite scary to see him on the morning of the wedding, and on top of that she told us today she had received a telegram but thankfully Stephen is all right, he's injured but she doesn't know how bad yet.'

Andrew nodded, not entirely convinced. He knew there was more to it, but he didn't want to push. Ever since the rumours of the flu had been going around, he'd felt a distance growing between them. He spent so much time helping other veterans, trying to make sense of his own experiences, that he feared he'd been neglecting his wife.

'You know you can talk to me about anything, right?' he said, squeezing her hand. 'Whatever it is, it doesn't matter. Remember our vows: for better, for worse, for richer, for poorer, in sickness and in health, to love, to cherish until death do us part.'

Molly's smile wavered, and for a moment, Andrew thought she might break down in tears, even though the love she was feeling showed in her face. But then she nodded, squeezing his hand back. 'I know, Andrew. I love you so much and there's nothing I wouldn't do for you. I just... I need a little more time to sort things out in my head.'

Andrew couldn't shake the feeling that something significant was happening, something that could change their lives forever. He only hoped that when Molly was ready to share, whatever it was, their love would be strong enough to weather it.

Molly gazed across at her husband. 'I'll wash these few bits up and make you some dinner.'

As Molly busied herself in the kitchen, Andrew found himself standing by the window, looking out at the darkening street. The world outside seemed fraught with danger, what with the ongoing war, and the flu that was ravaging the city. He had thought being with Molly would make everything right again, but the scars of war ran deep, and now this new tension between them...

He turned back to watch Molly, noticing the careful way she moved, the slight tremor in her hands as she stacked the plates. There was something almost protective about her posture, as if she was guarding a secret close to her heart.

A thought struck him then, so sudden and startling that he almost gasped aloud. Could Molly be...? But no, surely she would have told him if she was expecting. Wouldn't she?

The possibility, once considered, refused to leave his mind. It would explain so much: her tiredness, her changing moods, her lack of appetite. But why would she keep such news from him? Was she afraid of his reaction? Did she think he wouldn't be happy about a child?

The idea of becoming a father sent a whirlwind of emotions through Andrew. Fear, certainly – how could he be responsible for a new life when he still struggled to make sense of his own? But there was excitement too, and a fierce, protective love for what could be their child.

'Molly,' he said, his voice softer than he intended. She turned to look at him, a question in her eyes. 'I... I want you to know that I love you. No matter what's going on, no matter what changes might be coming our way. We're in this together.'

Molly's eyes welled up with tears again, but this time she didn't try to hide them. She crossed the room to him, burying her face in his chest as he wrapped his arms around her.

'Oh, Andrew,' she whispered, her voice muffled against his shirt. 'I've been so scared.'

He held her tighter, his heart racing. 'Scared of what, love? You can tell me anything – you know that.'

Molly pulled back slightly, looking up at him with a mixture of fear and hope in her eyes. 'I'm... we're...' She took a deep breath, seeming to gather her courage. 'Andrew, I'm pregnant.'

The words hung in the air between them, momentous and life-altering.

'Are you... are you sure?' he asked, his voice barely above a whisper.

Molly nodded, tears streaming down her face now. 'I've known for a few weeks. I wanted to tell you, but I was so afraid. With everything going on – you know the war, the flu, your work with the veterans – I didn't know if you'd be happy about it.'

Andrew felt a pang of guilt as he pulled her close again. 'Molly, I couldn't love you any more.' He paused. 'I'll admit becoming a father does scare me a little.' He gave a nervous laugh as Molly pulled back. 'But that's only because I want to be a supportive husband and the best father in the world.'

Molly's tears rolled down her cheeks. She gave her husband a watery smile. 'It scares me too, because I want to be a good mother.' She wiped her hand across her face. 'I worried about telling you because you're always so busy, I didn't know if you had room for a child as well.'

Andrew stroked her damp cheek. 'Yes, I keep myself busy but there's always room for you and our child.' He lowered his head and brushed his lips over hers.

'I'm sorry,' Molly whispered, her voice choked with emotion. 'I should have told you sooner. I was just... I was scared.'

A smile slowly spread across Andrew's face. 'We're going to have a baby?'

Molly nodded, her own smile growing to match his. 'I was worried, with everything going on, that you might think it was bad timing, or—'

Her words were cut off as Andrew pulled her into a tight

embrace, tears of joy now streaming down his own cheeks. 'Bad timing? Molly, this is... this is wonderful news. A baby, our baby.'

As they stood there, holding each other, both laughing and crying, Andrew felt a surge of hope he hadn't experienced since before the war. Yes, the world was still a dangerous, uncertain place. But this, this miraculous new life, was a promise of a future worth fighting for.

6

Over the last few weeks the streets of London, once teeming with life, had taken on an eerie quietness. No one seemed to be out enjoying the early August sunshine. Alice pulled her shawl up over her mouth and nose as she made her way to Foyles, trying not to flinch every time she heard a cough or sneeze from a passer-by. The usual morning bustle of Charing Cross Road was subdued. Many shops had their shutters down, signs in the windows announcing temporary closures due to illness. Alice's heart sank as she approached Foyles, half-expecting to see a similar sign on their door.

But the bookshop was open, Mr Leadbetter's determined face visible through the window as he arranged a display. Alice steeled herself and entered, the little bell above the door chiming cheerfully, at odds with the sombre atmosphere.

'Good morning, Mrs Leybourne,' Mr Leadbetter greeted her, his voice muffled behind his mask. 'I'm glad you made it in safely.'

Alice nodded, lowering her shawl to speak. 'It's so quiet out there. I've never seen London like this.'

Mr Leadbetter's eyes, visible above his mask, were grave. 'These are unprecedented times, my dear. But books have seen humanity through countless crises. We must do our part to keep knowledge and imagination alive, even in the darkest of days.'

Alice decided to place a mask over her mouth and nose to try to protect herself from infection before beginning her morning tasks. She couldn't help but notice how empty the shop was. The few customers who did venture in moved quickly, clearly eager to complete their errands and return home. The usual leisurely browsing, the quiet conversations between book lovers, were conspicuously absent.

Victoria arrived a short while later, her face pale beneath her mask. 'I saw an ambulance on my way here,' she said in a low voice to Alice. 'They were taking away old Mrs Higgins from the bakery. It doesn't look good.'

Alice felt a chill run down her spine. Mrs Higgins had been a fixture in the neighbourhood for as long as she could remember, always ready with a warm smile and a fresh loaf of bread. The idea that the flu could take someone so vibrant, so much a part of the fabric of their community, made the threat feel all the more real and immediate.

As the day wore on, news trickled in from customers and passers-by. More shops were closing, more people falling ill. The hospitals were overwhelmed, makeshift wards being set up in school halls and churches. The war, which had dominated their thoughts and conversations for so long, suddenly seemed distant in the face of this new, invisible enemy.

During a quiet moment, Alice found herself in the medical section of the shop, pulling out books on epidemics and public health. She flipped through pages detailing the spread of diseases, the importance of quarantine and hygiene. The clinical language and stark statistics did little to quell the growing knot of anxiety in her stomach.

'Anything useful?' Victoria's voice made her jump. Her friend was looking over her shoulder at the open book.

Alice shook her head. 'Not really – it all seems so... impersonal. Numbers and data. But this isn't just about numbers. It's about people, our neighbours, our friends, and our families.'

Victoria nodded, her eyes distant. 'Ted's regiment has been called in to help at the hospitals. He says... he says it's worse than anything he saw at the front. At least in battle, you can see your enemy.'

The bell above the door chimed, and both women turned to see Molly enter, her pregnancy now visible beneath her coat. Alice felt a fresh wave of concern. Molly was more vulnerable now, both she and her unborn child at greater risk from the flu.

'Should you be out?' Alice asked, unable to keep the worry from her voice.

Molly managed a small smile behind her face mask. 'I'm being careful. I can't just stay cooped up at home. Besides, people need books now more than ever. A bit of escape, a bit of hope.'

Mr Leadbetter emerged from the back room, a stack of papers in his hand. 'Ladies, if I could have a moment of your time. We need to discuss some new procedures in light of the worsening situation.'

As they gathered around the counter, Alice couldn't help but feel a sense of déjà vu. How many times during the war had they huddled like this, adapting to new regulations, new shortages, new challenges? Yet somehow, this felt different. The war, for all its horrors, had been a human conflict. This... this was nature itself turned against them.

Mr Leadbetter outlined new cleaning regimes, mandatory masks for all staff and customers, stricter limits on the number of customers allowed in the shop at one time, and a proposed system for quarantining returned books before returning them to the shelves. As he spoke, Alice found her gaze drawn to the window, to the unusually empty street outside. Throughout history London had survived so much: a plague, fire, war. Surely it would survive this too. But at what cost?

As the meeting concluded and they returned to their tasks, Alice found herself lingering in the poetry section. Her fingers traced the spine of a volume of Tennyson, and almost without thinking, she opened it to 'Ulysses'. The final lines seemed to leap off the page:

> Tho' much is taken, much abides; and tho'
> We are not now that strength which in old days
> Moved earth and heaven; that which we are,
>   we are;
> One equal temper of heroic hearts,
> Made weak by time and fate, but strong in will
> To strive, to seek, to find, and not to yield.

In that moment, surrounded by books that had survived centuries, that had seen humanity through countless trials and triumphs, Alice felt a flicker of hope. Yes, the streets were quiet, the future uncertain. But here, in this haven of words and ideas, they would continue. They would adapt, they would persevere. They would be, as Tennyson wrote, *'strong in will to strive, to seek, to find, and not to yield.'*

The bell chimed again, and Alice turned to assist the new customer, her resolve strengthened. Whatever challenges lay ahead, they would face them as they had faced all others – with courage, with compassion, and with the enduring power of books to light their way.

* * *

Foyles Bookshop was quieter than Alice could remember it ever being in the past. Where once the aisles had been filled with the excited murmur of literary discussions, now there was a tense silence, broken only by the occasional cough or sneeze. The morning light filtering through the tall windows seemed weaker somehow, as if the very atmosphere had grown heavy with worry.

Alice stood behind the counter, surreptitiously wiping it down with a cloth soaked in disinfectant for the third time that hour. The sharp smell of carbolic soap made her nose wrinkle, but she kept at it, finding comfort in the repetitive motion. Her mind drifted to Albert, who wasn't allowed to come up from the basement for fear of him catching the flu. His absence left a noticeable void: no more learning cockney rhyming slang or his cheerful whistling as he carried his books through the aisles, no more penny sweets secretly passed to young customers when their parents weren't looking. Albert's cheerfulness had always brightened everyone's day, but keeping him safe was more important, even more so after his illness a few months ago. She made a mental note to ask Mr Leadbetter if she could take him down some tea and biscuits later.

The clock on the wall ticked loudly in the unusual quiet, marking time in a shop that seemed frozen in anxiety. Alice's gaze drifted to a pale-faced young woman browsing the poetry section, her handkerchief pressed firmly against her mouth. The woman's gloves were black mourning gloves, and her hands trembled slightly as she reached for a volume.

'Miss?' Alice called out gently, maternal instinct overriding professional distance. 'Are you feeling all right? Perhaps I could help you find what you're looking for?'

The woman turned, her eyes watery and red-rimmed. In the

wan light, Alice could see she was younger than she'd first appeared, barely out of her teens. 'Oh, I'm fine, thank you, it's just a bit of a cold.' She sniffled, then added, 'I'm looking for Rupert Brooke. My brother... he was a fan. We used to read the poems together before he...' Her voice trailed off, the unfinished sentence hanging heavy in the air.

Alice's heart sank at the use of past tense. No doubt another casualty of the war. She thought of her own brothers who had been fighting in France. Robert forever lost to them and Charles who had returned home injured. She said a silent prayer, thankful for his safe return. 'Of course,' she said softly. 'Let me help you find it. The poetry section has been rearranged recently. We've had to make room for all the new poets, like Robert Graves.'

As she guided the woman through the poetry section, Alice couldn't help but notice again how empty the shop was. Ted sat on one of the stairs nearby, his head down, concentrating on the pages in front of him. He'd been there for hours, finding solace in the words of someone who seemed to understand his experience. Mr Leadbetter hadn't the heart to ask him to buy the book or leave.

The morning light caught the dust motes dancing in the air. Mr Leadbetter had already sent two staff members home with fevers, and customers were becoming even more scarce. The usually crowded aisles between the towering bookshelves stood empty, the leather-bound volumes serving as silent witnesses to these strange and frightening times.

Later, during their lunch break, Alice and Victoria huddled in the small break room, their sandwiches barely touched. The room, with its perpetual smell of tea and old books, had always been a sanctuary of sorts. Now it felt like a confessional, where they shared their fears in hushed voices.

As Molly approached the break room, she overheard their quiet conversation through the partially open door. She paused, her hand on the doorknob, struck by the worry in their voices.

'...don't know how much longer we can stay open,' Alice was saying, absently folding and refolding her handkerchief. 'With the flu spreading so quickly... Did you see Mrs Parker this morning? She could barely stand upright, but she insisted on coming in for her order of prayer books.'

Victoria nodded, her face grave. Her engagement ring caught the light as she wrapped her hands around her teacup, seeking warmth. 'Mr Leadbetter's worried sick. Half the staff are out ill, and customers are staying away in droves. Even the soldiers home on leave have stopped coming in to escape the crowds and noise of the London streets.'

Molly felt a fresh wave of guilt wash over her as she had tried hard to not worry about the future and the potential crisis they were facing. Her hand drifted to her belly, where new life grew even as death seemed to hover over London. She forced a smile and strode into the break room. 'Thank goodness it's lunchtime. It's unusually quiet out there.'

The girls smiled at Molly as she placed her sandwiches on the table, though their eyes were shadowed with worry. The afternoon sun slanted through the small window, illuminating the dust in the air and making them all think of germs.

'Did you hear about Mrs Higgins?' Victoria asked, her voice low. 'Her whole family has come down with it. They say her youngest is in a bad way. Not even four years old...' She trailed off, unable to finish the thought.

Molly shuddered, unconsciously placing a hand protectively on her unborn child. The gesture wasn't lost on Alice. 'It's terrifying. How are we supposed to protect ourselves when we're dealing with the public every day?'

Alice reached out, squeezing both their hands. Her wedding ring was cool against their skin. 'We'll get through this,' she said, trying to inject confidence into her voice. 'We just need to be careful, follow Mr Leadbetter's precautions. The doctors say fresh air and cleanliness are our best defences.'

They all knew she was trying to convince herself as much as them. The break room fell silent except for the ticking of the clock and the distant sound of someone coughing on the shop floor.

As they returned to work, Alice caught sight of Mr Leadbetter emerging from his office, his face grave. His usually immaculate hair was slightly dishevelled, as if he'd been running his hands through it in worry. She braced herself for more bad news, wondering how much longer they could keep the doors open in the face of this invisible threat.

Behind her, she could hear Victoria helping a customer find a book on home remedies, her voice steady despite everything. Molly had retreated to the children's section, where she was carefully wiping down the story-time chairs that now sat empty; no mother would risk bringing their child to a reading now.

The afternoon stretched ahead of them, each hour marked by the methodical cleaning of surfaces, the careful distance kept from customers, and the growing whispers of a city under siege – not from German bombs, but from something far more dangerous. Through the shop windows, Alice could see people hurrying past on the street, many wearing masks, all avoiding eye contact. London itself seemed to be holding its breath, waiting to see what this epidemic would bring.

* * *

Alice's hands trembled as she held the photograph, her eyes fixed on the image of her father, arm in arm with a woman she didn't recognise. They were smiling, looking at each other with an intimacy that made Alice's chest tighten with a mix of shock and betrayal.

She had spent the last few weeks wondering what her way forward was, and whether she should tell Freddie. Alice hadn't wanted to add another worry to Victoria's day, so she had told no one, not even her sister. She thought back to the letter that had turned her world upside down, when she found it hidden in a book in the attic. She was thankful her mother hadn't come across it first. She was riddled with guilt when she made the decision to look around her father's office. That was when she had found an old photograph tucked away in her father's study, hidden between the pages of an old ledger. She'd been searching for clues about his trips to Norfolk, but this... this was more than she had bargained for. Alice stared down at the photograph. Was this the woman he had known since 1902?

The woman in the photo was attractive, perhaps a few years younger than her mother – it was hard to tell. She had a warm smile and kind eyes, and Alice couldn't help but notice how young and relaxed her father looked beside her. The happiness she saw staring back at her was a side of him she rarely witnessed at home.

Questions raced through Alice's mind. How long had this been going on? Did her mother know?

The sound of the front door opening jolted Alice from her thoughts. She quickly tucked the photo into her pocket, her heart pounding as she heard her father's voice calling out. 'Anyone home?'

Alice took a deep breath, trying to compose herself. She

couldn't confront him, not yet. Not until she had more answers. But how could she face him now, knowing what she knew?

As she stepped out of the study, plastering a smile on her face, Alice felt as though her whole world had shifted. The father she thought she knew, the family she had always relied on, suddenly, it all felt like a carefully constructed facade. And she was the one who had accidentally stumbled behind the curtain, seeing the truth that lay hidden.

'There you are, Alice,' her father said, smiling warmly at her. 'How was your day at the bookshop?'

Alice forced herself to meet his eyes, to keep her voice steady as she answered. But inside, she was screaming, demanding answers to questions she wasn't sure she was ready to ask.

'It was fine, Father,' she managed, her voice sounding strange to her own ears. 'Quiet, with the flu keeping people at home.'

Her father nodded, his face growing serious. 'Yes, it's a worrying situation. You're being careful, I hope? Washing your hands regularly?'

The concern in his voice, so genuine and fatherly, made Alice's heart ache. How could this man, who clearly cared for her well-being, be the same person who had hidden such a massive secret from his family?

'Yes, of course,' she replied, her mind racing. Should she confront him now? Demand explanations? But no, she needed time to think, to process what she had discovered.

'Good girl,' her father said, patting her shoulder as he moved past her towards his study. 'I've got some work to catch up on before dinner. Could you let your mother know I'll be down shortly?'

Alice silently nodded, watching as he disappeared into the room she had just vacated. The room where, in an old ledger, she had found the evidence of a life she had never known existed.

As she made her way to the kitchen to find her mother, Alice felt as though she was moving through a dream. The familiar hallway, lined with family photographs, suddenly seemed like a gallery of lies. In each image, her father smiled out at her, the perfect picture of a devoted husband and father. How many of those smiles had been genuine? How many had hidden guilt, or thoughts of his other family?

In the kitchen, she found her mother preparing dinner, humming softly to herself. The sight of her, so content and unaware, made Alice's throat tighten with emotion.

'Mother,' she said, her voice catching slightly. 'Father says he has work to do but he'll be down for dinner soon.'

Her mother turned, smiling warmly. 'Thank you, dear. Are you feeling all right? You look a bit pale.'

Alice forced a smile. 'Just tired, I think. It's been a long day at the shop.'

As her mother turned back to her cooking, Alice leaned against the counter, her hand unconsciously moving to her pocket where the photograph lay hidden. She thought about the woman in the picture, about the life her father had built in Norfolk. Did that woman cook dinner for him too? Did she hum while she worked, unaware that the man she loved had another family waiting for him in London?

The weight of her discovery pressed down on Alice, making it hard to breathe. She loved her father, had always looked up to him. Yes he had been stiff and unyielding at times, but he had also been a paragon of integrity and honesty. But now, every memory, every moment they had shared was tainted by this newfound knowledge.

As she helped her mother set the table for dinner, Alice's mind raced with possibilities. Should she tell her mother? Confront her father? Keep the secret to herself or tell her sister,

Lily? Each option seemed fraught with potential for pain and upheaval.

The sound of her father's footsteps on the stairs made Alice tense. In a few moments, they would sit down to dinner as a family, just as they had done countless times before. But this time, Alice would be carrying a secret of her own, a mirror image of the secret her father had carried for who knew how long.

As her father entered the kitchen, smiling at them both, Alice firmed her resolve. She would wait, gather more information, try to understand the full scope of her father's deception before taking any action. But she knew that nothing would ever be the same again. The photograph in her pocket was more than just an image, it was a key, unlocking a door to a world of secrets and lies that she was only beginning to comprehend.

The war had changed so much in their world, had forced them all to confront harsh realities and make difficult choices. But this, Alice realised, might be her greatest challenge yet: navigating the complex web of love, loyalty, and betrayal that lay at the heart of her own family.

7

Alice sat at the dressing table in her bedroom, a map of Norfolk spread out before her, various locations circled in red ink. The evening light cast long shadows across the worn paper, making the red circles look almost like bloodstains. Her heart raced with a mixture of anticipation and dread as she planned her upcoming trip, a journey that could potentially unravel everything she thought she knew about her family.

The brass lamp on her table flickered, casting an uncertain light over her father's letter. The discovery had sent her world spinning, leading to weeks of careful investigation.

She had been piecing together the puzzle of her father's secret life meticulously, studying train schedules until the numbers blurred before her eyes, and even sneaking peeks at her father's personal correspondence whenever possible. The guilt of such subterfuge weighed heavily on her, but the need to know the truth drove her forward. Now, finally, she felt ready to confront the truth head-on.

Her fingers traced the railway line from London to Norwich on the map. The Great Eastern Railway would carry her into unknown territory, both literally and metaphorically. She had already memorised the timetable: the 9.30 from Liverpool Street Station would get her to Norwich hopefully by lunchtime, leaving enough time to investigate before returning home.

As she jotted down notes and possible itineraries in her small leather notebook, Alice's mind wandered to the potential outcomes of her investigation. What if she did find proof of another family? The thought of half-siblings somewhere in Norwich terrified her. How would she confront her father, this man who had always seemed so proper, so Victorian in his morals? And perhaps more terrifyingly, how would she tell her mother, whose quiet dignity masked years of what Alice now suspected was silent knowledge?

The wooden floorboards outside her room creaked, a familiar sound that she had learned to recognise as her mother's approach. A soft knock at the door startled her from her thoughts. 'Come in,' she called, hastily covering the map with some schoolbooks and her copy of *North and South* by Elizabeth Gaskell.

Her mother entered, a basket of laundry balanced on her hip, her sleeve cuffs slightly damp from washing. The scent of lavender soap followed her into the room. 'Alice, dear, I was wondering if you could help me with... What's all this?' she asked, noticing the clutter on the table. Her eyes lingered for a moment on the corner of the map peeking out from beneath the books.

Alice felt a moment of panic before forcing a smile, her hands unconsciously smoothing her skirt. 'Oh, just some research for a project at the bookshop. Mr Leadbetter wants us to expand our travel section.' The lie tasted bitter on her tongue, but she pushed through. 'With the war making foreign travel so difficult, he thinks there might be interest in domestic destinations.'

Her mother nodded, seemingly satisfied with the explanation, though something flickered in her eyes, something that made Alice wonder again if her mother knew more than she let on. 'Oh, I almost forgot, Freddie wanted me to let you know he has taken the boys into the garden for five minutes.'

Alice nodded. 'Thank you, I've not spent much time with them lately, I'm too busy worrying about everyone else and work.'

'Trust me when I say worrying won't change anything.'

As her mother turned to leave, the light caught the silver threads in her dark hair, and Alice felt a pang of guilt so sharp it was almost physical. She hated lying to her mother, but how could she explain what she was really doing without causing pain? And if she didn't know, could she tell this woman, who had devoted her life to maintaining a respectable household, that her husband might have another family hidden away in Norwich?

Once alone again, Alice returned to her planning. She would take a day off from the bookshop next week, cite a need to visit a sick friend. The train schedules were memorised, the addresses of potential locations – gleaned from close study of her father's correspondence – carefully noted in her small notebook. She had even prepared for the possibility of needing to stay overnight, though the thought of explaining such an absence made her stomach churn.

Through her window, she could see the garden where she had spent countless hours of her childhood, watching her father tend to his beloved roses. How many times had he left them, citing business in Norfolk? How many lives had he been living, all this time?

As she finalised her plans, Alice couldn't shake a feeling of trepidation. This trip to Norwich could change everything, her relationship with her father, her mother's peace of mind, her own understanding of truth and lies, but she had come too far to turn back now. The weight of unknown siblings, of lives connected to hers by blood but separated by secrets, drove her forward. Whatever the truth was, she was determined to uncover it, for better or for worse.

With a deep breath, she circled a date on her calendar: next Thursday. In just a few days, she would embark on a journey that could redefine her understanding of family, love, and the complex web of adult relationships. The morning train would carry her towards answers, but would they be answers she could live with?

Alice glanced at the photograph on her dressing table – her father in his best suit, stern and proper, one hand resting on her shoulder at her last birthday celebration. How different would he look in other photographs, in another house, with other children? The thought made her chest tighten.

She carefully folded the map and tucked it into her copy of *North and South*, a fitting hiding place, she thought wryly, for a story about secrets and parallel lives. As she prepared for bed, Alice caught her reflection in the mirror. She looked different somehow, older perhaps, as if the weight of her investigation had aged her. Or perhaps it was simply that she was seeing herself differently now, seeing how easy it was to live a double life, to keep secrets, to become someone other than who you appeared to be.

The distant sound of her father's key in the front door made her jump. He was home late again. Would he explain it as another business meeting? Alice wondered how many more lies would be served with tomorrow's breakfast, how many more secrets were hidden behind her father's newspaper and her mother's teacup. In just a few days, she would begin to unravel them all.

* * *

Mr Leadbetter cleared his throat as he stood before the assembled staff of Foyles. Alice, Victoria, and Molly exchanged worried glances as they waited for him to speak.

'As you're all aware,' Mr Leadbetter began, his voice graver than they'd ever heard it, 'the influenza epidemic is worsening. As most of you probably already know we have sadly lost two of our colleagues to this dreadful illness that is going around, and I fear things may get worse before they get better. I've also received word that Vera won't be in as she has also succumbed to it. We must all pray that she soon makes a full recovery.'

A murmur of anxiety rippled through the group. Alice felt a chill run down her spine, thinking of Freddie out there on the streets in his work as a policeman, exposed to who knew what.

Mr Leadbetter held up his hands for silence. 'However, we have a responsibility to our community. Books provide comfort, knowledge, and escape – all things sorely needed in these trying times. So, we will remain open, but with the new, stricter safety measures in place that we discussed yesterday. Additionally,' he continued, 'we hope to implement a delivery service for our more vulnerable customers. When the time comes I'll need volunteers for this – I know it carries extra risk, but...'

Before he could finish, several hands shot up, including those of Alice, Victoria, and Molly. Mr Leadbetter's eyes misted over with emotion.

'Thank you,' he said softly. 'Your courage and dedication does you credit.'

As the meeting dispersed, the three friends huddled together.

'Are you sure about this?' Alice asked, looking at Molly with concern. 'With your... condition?'

Molly nodded firmly. 'I can't just sit by and do nothing. Besides, fresh air might do me good.'

Victoria squeezed both their hands. 'We'll be careful. We've faced worse than this, haven't we?'

As they moved to implement the new measures, transforming the familiar space of the bookshop into this new, more cautious version, Alice couldn't help but feel a sense of surreal detachment. With the war, and now this epidemic, it seemed the world was determined to test them in every way possible.

And on top of this, she was still carrying her father's secret, which in turn had become her secret. Alice knew she should talk to Freddie, her sister Lily, or at least her friends about it, but something held her back. Was it shame? Was she embarrassed her family weren't perfect, that their lives were all based on a lie? No, she had to make sure she didn't allow her imagination to run away with her. She knew she should confide in her friends. They would understand; after all, they had all been through so much together.

Victoria strolled towards Alice. 'Is everything all right? You look deep in thought.'

Colour rose in Alice's cheeks. 'Of course, just thinking about all this.' She smiled. 'How's married life treating you?'

Victoria lowered her eyelashes. 'It's good.'

Alice frowned. 'What is it? Has he had another episode since your wedding day? I know I didn't see it all, but it was hard to watch.'

Victoria shrugged. 'I think Ted's getting worse instead of better. His episodes are almost a daily occurrence; I worry about leaving him on his own in case he harms himself in some way, but we need the money to pay our bills. He doesn't seem able to relax for long. He jumps at the slightest noise. I think he was protected more in hospital, and I wasn't aware how bad it can get.'

Alice stared at her friend, realising her own problems were quite insignificant by comparison. Victoria's life had been hard since her parents died. She reached out and stroked her friend's back. 'Do you regret getting married? It's all right if you do.'

Victoria shook her head. 'No, I will always love Ted with all my heart; it's just not the romantic love story I thought it was going to be.'

'Is there someone he can see? I mean, to get help.'

'He already is but it doesn't seem to be making any difference, although it's early days.' Victoria gave a forced smile behind her mask. 'I just have to learn to be patient.'

Alice nodded. 'Perhaps you should both take a trip to Brighton to see your brother and grandparents. The fresh sea air might do you both some good.'

Victoria laughed. 'I'm not sure they've forgiven me for not having the big fancy wedding they wanted to give me.'

Alice chuckled. 'I'm sure they'll understand the reasons once they know why. Victoria, at the moment you have to think about you and Ted. You've been through a lot; allow yourself to enjoy the little moments and try not to worry about the future. None of us know what that holds.'

Victoria raised her eyebrows. 'Good job we don't.'

Alice laughed. 'But you can't forget we are the three musketeers, "all for one and one for all". We will get through everything together, just as we always do.'

Victoria laughed. 'Exactly, and are you sure you don't have something you want to discuss with us? You know we're not keeping secrets any more.'

Alice sighed. 'That's right but I don't want to discuss it here, or at home.'

Victoria raised her eyebrows. 'I'm intrigued now. Well, we can either go out for tea and cake or you can come to me, or we can go round Molly's. I'm sure she won't mind us inviting ourselves.'

Alice giggled. 'I'll talk to her when I get a chance and see what she wants to do, but not right now.'

* * *

The train compartment rocked gently as it sped through the English countryside, but Alice barely noticed the picturesque scenery flashing by outside the window. Her mind was focused on the task ahead, her stomach a knot of anxiety and determination.

She glanced down at the small notebook on her lap, open to a page filled with hastily scribbled notes. Dates, addresses, snippets of things she had overheard were the sum of her knowledge about her father's mysterious trips to Norfolk. It wasn't much to go on, but it was a start.

Alice had told Freddie she was visiting an old school friend for the day. The lie had sent a surge of guilt through her, it made her heart ache when she thought about it, but she couldn't bring herself to share her suspicions about her father – not yet, she had to be sure. Instinct told her he would say leave well alone, but she couldn't do that.

As the train pulled into the station at Norwich, Alice took a deep breath, steeling herself. She had no real plan beyond finding the address she'd discovered in her father's papers. What would she do if she actually found... what? Another family? A secret business? The possibilities made her head spin.

Stepping onto the platform, Alice was struck by how ordinary everything seemed. People hurrying about their business, porters calling out, the smell of coal smoke in the air. It was hard to believe that somewhere in this city, the truth about her father, and by extension, her entire family, was waiting to be uncovered.

She asked for directions before making her way along roads that had been bombed, and many properties had been reduced to rubble. She carried on through the bustling streets, her heart pounding as she neared the address. It was a modest house on a quiet street, not unlike Victoria's home. Alice stood across the road, watching, unsure of what to do next.

Just as she was considering turning back, convincing herself this whole idea was foolish, the front door opened. Alice's breath caught in her throat as a woman emerged. She instantly recognised her from the photograph she had found. The woman was older and was perhaps a few years younger than her mother. An animated young boy followed her.

The woman was laughing at something the boy had said, her face alight with affection. As they passed by Alice, completely unaware of her presence, she stared at the boy. The resemblance to her father was unmistakable.

Alice felt as if the ground had dropped out from beneath her feet. It was true, all of it. Her father had another family, a whole other life here in Norwich.

As she watched the woman and boy disappear around a corner, Alice was overwhelmed by a mix of emotions – shock, anger, grief, and a strange sense of relief at finally knowing the truth. But had she uncovered the truth, or was she jumping to conclusions? And if it was the truth, she had to decide what to do with it.

Alice found herself wandering the unfamiliar streets, her mind reeling from what she had just witnessed. The boy, who could be her half-brother, she realised with a jolt had looked to be about fourteen or fifteen years old. Which meant her father's deception had been going on for at least that long, possibly longer.

She thought back over the years, trying to recall any signs she might have missed. The frequent business trips to Norfolk, and the occasional unexplained absences from family events. It all made sense now.

As she walked, Alice found herself outside a small park. She sank onto a bench, her legs suddenly weak. The reality of her discovery was beginning to sink in, bringing with it a flood of questions. Did her mother know? Had she been complicit in this deception, or was she as much a victim as Alice felt herself to be?

And what about this other woman, this other family? How much did she know about Alice, her brothers and sister, and her mother? Had her father talked about them, and if so, what had he said? Had he felt stuck in London for all these years? Was this other woman living on false hope or was she in the dark about their lives together, as Alice had been until today?

Alice pulled out her notebook again, flipping through the pages of carefully gathered evidence. It all seemed so inadequate now, in the face of the living, breathing proof she had just encountered. She had come seeking answers, but instead found herself with even more questions. She knew that to discover the answers a conversation was needed with Margaret Wilson.

A group of children ran past, their laughter echoing in the quiet park. Alice watched them, wondering if her half-brother had been a happy child, like they appeared to be. They weren't worrying about the war or the flu that was killing people – that was for grown-ups. Did he have any inkling that his life, like hers, was built on a foundation of lies?

Alice knew she would have to make a decision. She could confront her father, demand explanations and accountability. She could tell her mother, potentially shattering the family she had always known. Or she could keep this secret, carrying the weight of this knowledge alone.

None of the options seemed right, none of them without the potential for devastating consequences. But as she sat there, watching the ordinary life of Norwich continue around her, oblivious to her internal turmoil, Alice knew she couldn't simply return to London and pretend nothing had changed.

The war had already altered so much in their world, had forced them all to confront harsh realities and make difficult choices. But this, Alice realised, might be her greatest challenge yet.

As the sun began to set, casting long shadows across the park, Alice stood up, her decision made. She would return to London, armed with the truth she had uncovered. But she wouldn't confront her father immediately. First, she needed to gather more information, to understand the full scope of this deception before taking any action. She realised now she should have spoken to the woman and maybe got some answers from her, but it was too late.

Walking back towards the train station, Alice felt as though she had aged years in a single afternoon. The girl who had arrived in Norwich this morning, full of nervous anticipation, was gone. In her place was a woman facing an uncertain future, carrying a secret that had the power to reshape her entire world.

The train journey back to London seemed to pass in a blur. Alice sat, staring out the window at the darkening landscape, her mind still whirling with the implications of what she had discovered. She knew that from this moment on, nothing would ever be the same again.

8

_____

Molly held on to the handrail as she stepped carefully down the stairs from the children's section. Glancing around she saw Victoria and Alice talking and wandered over to them. 'What are you two deep in conversation about?'

Alice laughed. 'Nothing new – we were talking about life and all the rubbish that keeps getting thrown at us.'

Molly peered over her mask from one to the other. 'Well, I'm here to help. Rosie and Ellen are looking after the children's books. It's so quiet now it doesn't take three of us and I think Mr Leadbetter wants me where he can see me, or at least where one of you two can.'

Victoria watched as Molly laid a protective hand across her baby bump. 'How are you feeling now?'

'I'm pleased to say the sickness seems to be wearing off now and Andrew is happy, although a little scared at becoming a father, so all is as good as it can be at the moment.'

Alice nodded. 'I expect your ma was over the moon about the prospect of having a grandchild.'

Molly chuckled. 'It's all she's talked about since Andrew and I got married, so yes it's fair to say she's very happy about it.' She glanced at Victoria. 'Talking of which, are you enjoying being married?'

Victoria raised her eyebrows. 'It's good. To be honest I can't believe we finally got married. I never thought that day would ever come with anyone let alone with Ted.'

Molly smiled behind her mask. 'I don't think it will be long before Ellen and Rosie will be setting wedding dates. They are clearly both smitten with their men, although they probably would never admit it's got that far.'

Alice giggled. 'I can remember worrying about Freddie and whether we would actually get married, especially when he went to war, but it all worked out in the end.'

Victoria chuckled. 'Are you saying love conquers all?'

Alice thought for a moment. 'I suppose I am, but it has to be true love.'

Molly squeezed Victoria's arm. 'And that's you and Ted. Your love for each other is strong and that will help you overcome what life throws at you both.'

Victoria nodded. 'I'm just not sure how much more Ted can take. He's finding life difficult, and I think it's getting worse, but I'm happy we managed to get married.'

Molly watched as Victoria's eyes looked full of sadness; maybe things were harder for them than she was letting on. Her mind drifted back to the early days when Victoria was pawning her family's things so they'd have enough money to eat, and she never told either Alice or her. Molly's lips tightened. She needed to keep an eye on her; maybe she'll talk it over with Alice. After all it was Alice who had discovered Victoria's money problems before. Alice would think about it sensibly and not go crashing in, like she was capable of doing.

Victoria cleared her throat. 'I know I'm changing the subject but I'm going to go and see how Albert's doing in the basement; he doesn't get the visitors to chat to these days.'

'Please say hello to him from us and let him know we miss our chats.' Alice paused. 'I hope he is well.'

Molly nodded. 'I hope he stays well – not that this flu is only affecting the elderly, but it's hard not to worry.'

Alice frowned. 'I know what you mean. It's not just our family, there's Mr Leadbetter too. Hopefully Albert will be all right because he's had the flu, but you never can tell. We just have to protect each other as much as we can.'

Victoria sighed. 'Which brings us back to cleaning everything in sight.' She turned and walked towards the back of the shop.

Alice glanced at Molly. 'I'm concerned about Victoria. I saw what happened with Ted on their wedding day and I understand it's almost a daily thing. I know it's difficult, but we need to keep an eye on her. Ted is much worse than Freddie.'

Molly nodded. 'And Andrew, but she says he's seeking help so let's hope he improves with time. I think it helps him coming to the shop; maybe it's to do with the peace we all find here. Mind you, from what Andrew has told me it could take a long time and some people never get over what they've experienced, apparently. They call it shell shock but now everyone has it the same.'

Alice's thoughts moved to Freddie, wondering if she would have been strong enough to cope like Victoria was. 'When we discovered your pregnancy, we talked about not having secrets any more, so I wondered if we could be cheeky and invite ourselves round to yours one evening. There's something I need to tell you both, but I don't wish to discuss it in the shop.'

Molly frowned. 'Of course, you don't need to ask. We've been friends for a long time so just turn up whenever you want.'

Alice's eyes crinkled in the corners as she smiled. 'We won't just turn up. I'll talk to Victoria; maybe we can come round tomorrow evening after I've put the boys to bed.'

Molly laughed. 'That sounds good. I'm intrigued so that means I'll be impatient to know what's going on.'

Alice shook her head. 'Nothing changes there then.' She glanced around. 'I suppose we should get on with the cleaning again.'

Molly nodded.

The girls separated to pick up their rags and collect the bowls of disinfectant to start wiping down all over again.

* * *

The atmosphere in Foyles was tense. Alice watched Mr Leadbetter lock the shop door and place a handwritten sign in the window to say the shop would be shut for the next half an hour. He gathered the staff together in the back room. The space, usually cluttered with new arrivals and returns waiting to be processed, had been cleared to accommodate the meeting. Alice, Victoria, and Molly exchanged worried glances as they took in his grave expression. The usual warmth in his eyes was dimmed, his hunched shoulders carrying the weight of responsibility.

Through the closed door, they could hear the muffled sounds of people in the street, unaware of the gravity of the meeting taking place just feet away. The sellers and their carts had slowly got fewer in number as the weeks had gone by, the sound of them calling out to sell their wares now silent. The afternoon sun slanted through the small window, catching dust motes in its beam, a sight that suddenly seemed ominous to Alice, who couldn't help but wonder if invisible virus particles danced alongside them.

'I'm afraid I have some difficult news,' Mr Leadbetter began, his voice heavy with concern. He rubbed his hand over his mouth and clean-shaven chin, a nervous habit they'd all come to recognise over the years. 'We've had word that several more of our colleagues have fallen ill with influenza. Miss Perkins, Mr Thompson, and young Jimmy are all bedridden with high fevers.'

A collective gasp went through the group. These weren't just names on a list; these were friends, people they worked with every day. Alice thought of Miss Perkins, who had trained her when she first started at Foyles, always patient with her mistakes. Victoria remembered how young Jimmy had helped her reorganise the entire history section just last week, his cheerful whistling making the tedious task almost enjoyable. Molly's hand instinctively went to her pregnant belly, thinking of Mr Thompson, who had been setting aside children's books he thought would be perfect for her baby.

Mr Leadbetter continued, his voice catching slightly, 'Given the circumstances, the owners are toying with the difficult decision to close the shop for about a week. We need to do our part to slow the spread of this dreadful disease.'

Victoria felt her heart sink. Closing the shop meant no income for a week, something many could ill afford, including her. With Ted still struggling to find consistent work due to his shell shock, they relied heavily on her wages, but she also knew it was necessary. The flu had been ravaging London, and Foyles – with its steady trickle of customers handling books and brushing against each other in narrow aisles – must be a perfect breeding ground for the virus.

Near the back of the group, young Elsie Peters began to cry softly. Her father had lost his job the month before, and Victoria knew the family was already struggling to make ends meet. Ellen put an arm around her shoulders.

'What about our customers?' Victoria asked, ever practical,

trying to keep her voice steady despite her own fears. 'Many of them rely on us for information, for comfort even, especially during these trying times.'

She was thinking of Mrs Aldridge, the elderly widow who came in twice a week for new novels, and old Mr Owen who reads to his blind wife from their poetry section. For so many of their regular customers, Foyles was more than just a bookshop, it was a lifeline to the world.

Mr Leadbetter nodded, a small smile breaking through his worried expression. 'An excellent point, Mrs Marsden, which is why I now want to move forward with the limited delivery service we talked about a few weeks ago, mainly for our elderly and infirm customers who can't risk going out. I know several of you volunteered to help then but I understand if there has been a change of heart. I won't ask anyone to put themselves at risk.'

Before he'd even finished speaking, Alice, Victoria, and Molly had stepped forward, just as they had previously. They'd faced the dangers of war together; they would face this new threat the same way. Several other staff members joined them, including Ellen, who still had her arm around Sarah.

Albert also stepped forward. 'I could drive the van. We could load it up with different types of books and one of the youngsters 'ere could jump out to offer 'em to the customers.'

'That's a good idea. We would have to pick the books carefully and when we've been there once it will be easier to take orders for what they would like next.' Mr Leadbetter's eyes misted over at their immediate response. 'I don't know what I'd do without you all,' he said softly. Then, squaring his shoulders, he continued more briskly, 'Right then, let's work out the logistics. Those who volunteer will need to take precautions, masks at all times, careful handling of books, maintaining distance from customers and maybe even wearing gloves until you can wash your hands.'

As they began to plan the details of their makeshift delivery service, Molly was determined to do her bit despite her condition. Yes, there was risk involved, but books had power – the power to comfort, to distract, to inspire. In delivering them, they would be bringing more than just pages and ink to their customers. They would be bringing hope.

'We should prioritise our most vulnerable customers,' Alice suggested, already making notes in her small notebook. 'Perhaps we could arrange a schedule, make sure no one falls through the cracks, and it would be a good way of checking they are all right at the same time.'

Victoria nodded, adding, 'And we should quarantine returned books for several days before handling them. I read something about that in the medical journal Mr Thompson was showing me last week.' Her voice caught slightly at the mention of their ill colleague.

Mr Leadbetter beamed at them with pride, though his eyes remained worried. 'This is exactly why Foyles has survived the war, shortages, and now this. It's not just the books that make this place special; it's the people who care for them and for each other.'

As the meeting continued, with staff members offering suggestions and volunteering for various tasks, Alice looked around the cramped back room. So much had changed since she'd first started working at Foyles. The war had altered everything, and now this new threat was forcing them to adapt once again. But one thing remained constant: the sense of family and community.

Later, as they were preparing to leave the shop, not knowing when it would be open to the customers again, Alice found herself lingering by the shelves. She ran her fingers along the spines of the books, these old friends that had been a constant in her life through all the upheavals of war.

Molly came up beside her, placing a gentle hand on her arm. 'It feels wrong, doesn't it?' she said softly. 'Closing the shop – it's like we're giving up. And how will Ted cope? He's in here most days.'

Alice shook her head. 'We're not giving up. We're just... changing tactics. We will be in here every day sorting out a selection of books to be delivered to the people who need them most. I'm sure Mr Leadbetter will allow Ted to come in with Victoria.'

The process of closing the shop was more emotional than any of them had anticipated. As they moved through the familiar rooms, covering displays and securing valuable first editions, each of them was lost in thought, remembering the countless moments that had made Foyles more than just a workplace; it was a second home.

Alice paused in the poetry section, her hand resting on a volume of Rupert Brooke's works. She thought of all the soldiers who had come through the shop before shipping out, many buying poetry to take with them to the front. How many of those young men would never return? The thought made her throat tight with unshed tears.

Victoria was in the children's section, carefully arranging the stuffed animals that usually sat on top of the shelves. 'Do you remember,' she said softly to no one in particular, 'the first story time we held here after the war started? All those children, so scared and confused, finding comfort in fairy tales and adventures.'

Molly, moving more slowly due to her advancing pregnancy, was at the counter, running her hand along its smooth surface. 'Do you remember Andrew dressing up as Father Christmas for the children?' she said, a wistful smile on her face. 'He loved

giving the books to the children, and the joy it gave them.' She
giggled. 'Then we thought the bombs were dropping and ended
up spending most of the evening in the basement.'

Victoria nodded. 'I believe that's when I told you and Alice
that I had proposed to Ted.'

Molly chuckled. 'I couldn't believe you'd done that.'

Mr Leadbetter cleared his throat, drawing their attention. 'I
know this is difficult,' he said, his voice thick with emotion.
'Foyles has been a constant in all our lives, a beacon of normalcy
in these troubled times. But we must remember, it's not the
building that makes Foyles special. It's the people. The books, the
ideas, and those... those we carry with us, wherever we go.'

As they gathered their things, preparing to leave, Alice
noticed Mr Leadbetter lingering by the front door. She
approached him quietly. 'Are you all right, sir?'

He turned to her, his eyes misty. 'You know, Alice, I've never
known a life without Foyles. To see it closed, even temporarily... it
feels like the end of an era.'

Alice placed a comforting hand on his arm. 'Not an end, Mr
Leadbetter, just an intermission. We'll be back before you know
it, ready to start a new chapter.'

They walked out into the eerily quiet streets of London with
their masks securely in place and locked the door behind them.
Alice felt a strange mix of sorrow and determination. Yes, closing
the shop was a blow. But in the face of this new threat, they would
adapt. They would find new ways to bring books to people, to
keep the flame of knowledge and imagination burning bright.
She felt a renewed sense of purpose. The world outside might be
growing darker by the day, but here in Foyles in their own small
way they could still bring light. One book, one delivery, one act of
kindness at a time.

The war had taught them resilience, had shown them that

they were capable of facing challenges they never could have imagined. Now, in the face of this invisible enemy, they would draw on that strength once again. Foyles might be closed, but its spirit, the love of books, the power of words to comfort and inspire, that would live on through them, no matter what the coming weeks might bring. Thanks to the dedication of the shop staff who volunteered to be out and about visiting customers with their choice of books, the heart of Foyles would continue beating, delivering stories and knowledge to those who needed them most.

* * *

The late afternoon sun filtered through the net curtains of Molly's front room, casting delicate patterns on the dark green carpet. Alice perched on the edge of an armchair, her hands twisting nervously in her lap, while Victoria and Molly shared the settee. The usual sounds of London drifted in through the open window, children laughing, cartwheels on cobblestones, distant voices, the occasional clip-clop of horses, but inside tension filled the air.

'Would anyone like more tea?' Molly asked, one hand resting on her pregnancy bump.

'No, sit, please,' Alice said quickly. 'I... I need to tell you both something. Something I've discovered about my father.'

Victoria and Molly exchanged concerned glances. They had noticed Alice's distraction over the past weeks, the way she would sometimes stare into space at the bookshop, lost in her own thoughts; they had assumed it was to do with the flu that was going around.

'Lily, and I, have often wondered over the years why my father keeps going to Norfolk,' Alice continued, her voice barely above a whisper. 'Anyway, after the last time we talked about it I felt compelled to find out. After all those suspicious business trips, I just had to know.'

'Oh, Alice,' Victoria breathed. 'What did you find out?'

Alice pulled a photograph from her handbag, her hands trembling slightly as she passed it to her friends. 'I found this photo hidden in his study, which is what made me decide to go to Norwich. It's my father with... with another woman.'

Molly and Victoria bent their heads together over the photograph. In it, a younger version of Alice's father stood with his arm around a pretty woman, both of them smiling at the camera with obvious affection.

Molly shook her head. 'This is an old photograph, so it doesn't mean anything on its own.'

'No, but that's not all. I was in the loft going through some bits with my mother when I found a letter he had written but never posted. It was tucked inside a book,' Alice continued, her voice catching. 'The letter talks about a baby boy being born and how happy my father was about it and whether it looked like him.'

The girls stared at Alice, watching the conflict travel across her face, while letting her words sink in.

Alice took a breath. 'Anyway, I told Freddie I was spending the day with a friend and took the train to Norwich. I saw her, the woman from the photograph and... and a boy. He must have been about fourteen or fifteen and he looks like my father.'

A heavy silence fell over the room. Molly's hand had gone to her mouth in shock, while Victoria sat perfectly still, the photograph still held between her fingers.

'Are you saying...' Molly began carefully, 'that your father has another family?'

Alice nodded, tears finally spilling onto her cheeks. 'A whole other life with a son we never knew existed. He's been living this double life for years, probably since before I was old enough to remember.'

Molly shook her head. 'Did you speak to this woman and are you sure your mother knows nothing about it?'

Alice wiped away her tears. 'No is the answer to both of those questions – it has the potential to tear everyone's lives apart.'

Victoria set the photograph aside and moved to kneel beside Alice's chair, taking her friend's hands in hers. 'Oh, Alice. I'm so sorry. What a terrible burden to carry alone. Why didn't you tell us sooner?'

'I couldn't... I couldn't make it real by speaking it out loud, and I suppose I was embarrassed. I haven't even mentioned the letter or the photograph to Freddie or Lily, I did try to talk to Freddie about the possibility of my father leading a double life in Norfolk, but he dismissed it out of hand,' Alice said, her voice breaking. 'And I didn't want to burden you both. With the flu epidemic, and Molly's pregnancy, and Ted's situation, Victoria...'

'Stop that right now,' Molly said firmly, pushing herself up from the settee to join them. 'We're your friends. Your burdens are our burdens, just as our joys are your joys. That's what friendship means.'

Alice looked at her friends through tear-filled eyes. 'I don't know what to do. Should I tell my mother? Confront my father? Pretend I never discovered any of it?'

'Do the woman and her son know about you?' Victoria asked gently. 'About your mother?'

Alice shook her head. 'My father mentioned us in his letter, but that didn't get posted so I'm not entirely sure what she knows.' She paused. 'I watched them for a while, from a distance. They seemed... happy. Normal, like we always seemed, I suppose.' She gave a bitter laugh. 'What a family we make, a half-brother and all of us living in ignorance of each other.'

Molly waddled back to the settee, sinking down with a sigh. 'The question isn't just whether to tell your mother,' she said thoughtfully. 'It's whether that boy deserves to know the truth about his father too, or has his mother already told him? If she hasn't that's a difficult conversation to have with his mother because to blurt it out to him on his own could have dreadful consequences.'

'That's what keeps me awake at night,' Alice admitted. 'If I expose my father's deception, I'm not just shattering my own family, I'm destroying that boy's world too. What if he looks up to Father, just like I always did.'

Victoria squeezed Alice's hands. 'Perhaps... perhaps there's a way to handle this that doesn't destroy everything. Your father has done wrong, yes, but he's still your father. And that boy is your brother, even if he doesn't know it yet.'

'The war has already taken so much from everyone,' Molly added softly. 'Maybe what's needed here isn't more destruction, but a careful kind of... reconstruction. Of building something new from the pieces of truth you've uncovered.'

Alice looked between her friends, drawing strength from their steady presence. 'I don't know if I'm strong enough for that.'

'Of course, you are,' Victoria said firmly. 'And you're not alone. Whatever you decide to do, we'll be right here with you just like you have been there for us.'

Molly nodded in agreement. 'We've faced a war together, haven't we? We can face this too.'

As the afternoon light began to fade, the three friends sat together, talking through possibilities and options. No clear answers emerged, but Alice felt the crushing weight of her secret begin to lift. Here, in this house, with these two women who had stood by her through childhood years, the war and the hardship that brought into their lives, she felt stronger. Whatever path she chose, whatever consequences followed, she would not have to face them alone.

'Thank you,' she said finally, looking at her friends through fresh tears. They were not of despair now, but of gratitude. 'I don't know what I'd do without you both.'

'Well, you'll never have to find out,' Molly said, patting the space beside her on the settee. 'Now come here, both of you. I know it's too early and it's probably wind, but it could be the baby moving, and I want you to feel it.'

As Alice and Victoria rushed to place their hands on Molly's belly, feeling the miraculous flutter of new life, Alice felt a spark of hope. Yes, her world had been shaken to its foundations. But perhaps, like this baby growing within Molly, something new and beautiful could emerge from all this upheaval. She just had to find the courage to face whatever came next.

The rest of the evening passed in gentler conversation, punctuated by cups of tea and the sharing of small confidences. When Alice finally left Molly's house, walking home through the darkening streets of London, she felt steadier than she had in weeks. The truth she had discovered was still painful, the path ahead still uncertain, but she was no longer carrying it alone.

9

Victoria sat on the edge of the bed, her hand resting gently on Ted's back as he hunched over, his breathing ragged. The late afternoon light filtered through the crack of the roughly drawn curtains. She had heard Ted's screams as soon as she got home from work. He had been jolted awake from his afternoon nap by another nightmare, leaving him shaking and disorientated.

'It's all right, love,' she murmured soothingly. 'You're home. You're safe. It was just a dream.'

Ted nodded jerkily but didn't lift his head. Victoria could feel the tension in his muscles, the way he seemed to be fighting to bring himself back to the present.

These episodes had been happening even more frequently lately. The rumours of the war's end, while bringing hope to many, seemed to have intensified Ted's struggles. It was as if the possibility of peace had unleashed all the memories and fears he'd been holding at bay.

'Do you want to talk about it?' Victoria asked gently, though she already knew the answer.

As expected, Ted shook his head. 'No,' he said, his voice

hoarse. 'No, I... I can't. I'm sorry, Vic. I know this isn't what you signed up for when you married me.'

Victoria felt a pang in her heart at his words. She moved closer, wrapping her arms around him. 'Ted, look at me,' she said firmly.

Slowly, he raised his head, his eyes meeting hers. The pain and shame she saw there made her want to cry, but she held it back. Ted needed her strength now.

'I married you,' she said slowly, clearly, 'for better or for worse, in sickness and in health. I knew what I was signing up for, and I have never, not for one moment, regretted it. Do you understand me?'

Ted nodded, a ghost of a smile flickering across his face. 'I don't deserve you,' he murmured.

Victoria shook her head, a wry smile on her lips. 'None of that now. We deserve each other. We've earned each other, through all of this.'

She stood up, holding out her hand. 'Come on. Let's go downstairs and have some tea. I'll read to you for a bit. How about that?'

As they made their way to the kitchen, Victoria's mind was racing. She knew Ted needed more help than she could provide alone. The nightmares, the anxiety, the way he flinched at loud noises – it was all getting worse, not better.

Tomorrow, she decided, she would talk to Alice and Molly. Surely among the books at Foyles, there must be something about helping returning soldiers. And maybe it would help Ted to see Dr Harrison more often. Seeing him once a fortnight didn't seem to be helping, but she had a feeling that Ted would think that was a waste of time.

For now, though, she would do what she could. She would make tea, read aloud from one of Ted's favourite books, and remind him with every word and gesture that he was loved, that he was not alone in this struggle.

As the kettle began to whistle, Victoria sent up a silent prayer. *Let the rumours be true,* she thought. *Let this war end, so that the real work of healing can begin.*

Victoria moved about the kitchen with practised ease, preparing the tea just the way Ted liked it. As she worked, she couldn't help but reflect on how much their life had changed since the early days of their courtship. They had been so young, so full of hope and dreams for the future. The war and her parents dying had changed all that, had forced them to grow up faster than they should have had to.

She glanced over at Ted, who sat at the kitchen table, his eyes distant. In moments like these, she could almost see the carefree young man he had been before the war, overlaid like a ghost on the haunted veteran he had become. The contrast made her heart ache. She forced herself to smile. 'I almost forgot to tell you; I got a letter from Stephen today, he had received mine so he knew all the latest news about Molly being pregnant and us getting married.'

Ted nodded. 'That's good, how is he doing?'

Victoria beamed. 'He sounds well and sends his congratulations on our wedding, He's going to be in hospital for quite a while, apparently, one of his legs was injured and from what he says it's going to take a while to sort out, so he obviously isn't telling me the whole truth.'

Ted grinned. 'I'm so pleased he is relatively well, perhaps we'll see him soon.'

Alice nodded. 'Here we are,' she said brightly, setting the tea tray on the table. 'I thought we might read some Dickens tonight. How does *Great Expectations* sound?'

Ted managed a small smile. 'That sounds nice,' he said, his

voice still rough from the nightmare. 'You know, I've been thinking...'

Victoria sat down beside him, her heart quickening. Ted rarely initiated conversations about his feelings or experiences. 'What is it, love?'

He took a deep breath, his hands curling around the warm teacup. 'These rumours about the war ending... I should be happy, shouldn't I? But instead, I feel... I don't know. Scared, I suppose.'

Victoria reached out, covering his hand with hers. 'That's perfectly natural, Ted; it's a big change. And that can be frightening, even when it's change for the better.'

Ted nodded slowly. 'It's just... what if I can't adjust? What if I can't be the man I was before this war?'

Victoria felt tears pricking at her eyes, but she blinked them back. 'Oh, Ted,' she said softly. 'You're so much more than the man I first met. You're stronger, braver, more compassionate than you ever were before. Yes, you're carrying wounds – we all are. But that doesn't make you less. It makes you human.'

She saw a glimmer of hope in Ted's eyes, a spark of the old confidence he used to have. It was moments like these that made all the difficult nights worthwhile.

'Now,' she said, opening the book. 'Shall we see what Pip is up to?'

As Victoria began to read, her voice steady and soothing, she felt Ted gradually relax beside her. She knew that this moment of peace was fragile, that the nightmares and anxiety could return at any time. But for now, in their cosy kitchen, with the familiar words of Dickens flowing between them, there was a calmness. They were together. And really, Victoria thought, that was all that mattered.

The war might be ending out there in the world, but here, in this small house in London, a different kind of battle was being fought, a battle for healing, for understanding, for a return to normalcy. It was a battle Victoria was determined to win, one cup of tea, one chapter, one moment of connection at a time.

* * *

Alice stepped off the train in Norwich, her heart pounding with a mix of anticipation and dread. The quaint streets and historic buildings she had found charming on her previous visit now felt ominous, hiding secrets that could shatter her family forever.

She clutched her small notebook, filled with addresses and snippets of information she'd gleaned from going through her father's papers as she walked along the streets to Margaret Wilson's house. With memories of her previous visit rushing around her head, she was determined to speak to her this time.

As Alice approached the house, she saw a woman in the front garden, tending to a bed of roses. Her heart nearly stopped when the woman looked up, her features startlingly similar to those of the woman in the photograph with her father.

'Can I help you?' the woman called out, noticing Alice hovering by the gate.

Alice swallowed hard, her carefully prepared speech deserting her. 'I... I'm looking for information about Luke Taylor,' she managed to say, her voice barely above a whisper.

The woman's face changed instantly, a mix of recognition and wariness crossing her features. 'Who are you?' she asked, her voice tight.

'My name is Alice,' she replied, then, taking a deep breath, added, 'Luke is my father.'

The silence that followed was deafening. The woman's face paled, her hands gripping her gardening tools so tightly her knuckles turned white. Just as Alice thought she might turn and flee, the front door of the house opened, and a young boy came bounding out.

'Ma, have you seen my...' the boy started, then stopped short when he saw Alice.

Alice felt as though she'd been punched in the stomach. The boy was the spitting image of her father at that age, a fact she knew from old family photographs. There was no doubt in her mind, this was her half-brother.

The woman seemed to make a decision, her shoulders squaring as she turned to the boy. 'Peter, go back inside please. I need to speak with this lady.'

As Peter reluctantly went back into the house, the woman turned to Alice. 'I'm Margaret Wilson. You'd better come in,' she said, her voice a mix of resignation and defiance. 'I suppose we have a lot to talk about.'

Alice nodded numbly, following the woman into the house. She stepped across the threshold, into the narrow hall, shutting the front door behind her before following Margaret into a small sitting room.

Peter walked in behind Alice. 'Ma, what's going on? Who is this lady?'

Alice turned to face the young man. 'My name's Alice, and... and I'm not from around here so I've got myself lost and your ma has offered to help me.'

Peter smiled. 'That sounds about right, well, I'll leave you to it but take it easy – you look a little pale.' He turned to leave the room. 'It's nice to meet you and I hope you get to where you want to go. Ma, I'll be downstairs polishing my shoes but shout if you need me.'

Margaret peered at Alice after he had gone. 'Thank you, thank you for not saying anything to him.' She moved the palms of her hands down her black skirt. 'I always knew this day would come but it's still caught me by surprise. I have nothing rehearsed...' Her gaze shifted towards the door as she listened to her son moving around. 'I'm not sure we should talk about it here; I don't want Peter finding out things before I have chance to talk to him properly and in private.'

Alice nodded.

'I'm sorry...' Margaret took a breath '...forgive my bad manners, it must be the shock of seeing you. Please take a seat.'

'No, I won't, thank you. I think you're right; it wouldn't be wise to talk here.' Alice paused. 'Please know I'm not here to cause trouble – perhaps we should meet somewhere else so we can talk freely.'

Margaret gave a faint smile. 'I would appreciate that but it's not something I can do today because I'm expected at the tea table at the station. It's for the soldiers who are coming home from the front. It's not much but at least I feel like I'm doing something to help.'

'My ma does the same thing; the war has left a lot of terrible things in its wake.'

Fear flicked across Margaret's face. 'Yes, I sit with several of the men at the hospital, and some are in a bad way, and it's not just physical injuries. I'm praying it will be over before Peter is of the age to get called up.'

Alice frowned as her thoughts flew to Ted. 'I hope so too. It's terrible to see the carefree innocence lost. My eldest brother, Robert, died and my younger brother, Charlie, was badly injured. I used to drive an ambulance and take the injured soldiers from the train station to the hospital. It was heart breaking. I don't do it now because I'm afraid I have my hands full with family and work, and the hospitals are now so busy with this influenza that's making people so ill, having small children I don't want to take any unnecessary risks.'

Silence rested between them.

Alice cleared her throat. 'I should leave but I would still like to have a talk with you about...' She glanced over her shoulder. 'About... things.'

Margaret nodded. 'I'll write down the address of a café where we could meet.'

'Thank you, maybe we can meet in a couple of days?'

Margaret picked up a pen and scrawled an address on a piece of paper before passing it to Alice.

After staring down at the elegant handwriting, Alice thrust the paper into her handbag.

With the final arrangement made Alice left the house, knowing her life would never be the same. Whatever answers she found here would change everything. Her relationship with her father, her understanding of her family, and perhaps even her view of love and betrayal. But she had come too far to turn back now. It was time for the truth, no matter how painful it might be.

* * *

Victoria stood at the kitchen window, a cup of tea cooling in her hands as she watched the early morning light creep over the rooftops of London. The house was quiet, Ted still asleep upstairs, exhausted from another night plagued by nightmares.

She sighed, running a finger over the gold band on her left hand. Married life, she was quickly learning, was not quite the fairy tale she had imagined as a young girl. The realities of war, of Ted's ongoing struggles with shell shock, and the ever-present threat of the flu epidemic cast long shadows over their newlywed bliss.

But there were moments of joy too, unexpected and all the more precious for their rarity. Like last night, when Ted had managed to laugh, really laugh at a silly joke she'd made over dinner. Or the quiet moments in the evening when they sat together, reading or simply enjoying each other's company, the horrors of war temporarily held at bay.

Her mind drifted to the shock of Alice's news; they had always seemed the perfect family to her. Her own mother and father had held on to their secret, so she had no right to judge; perhaps all families had things they were too afraid to share.

Victoria sipped her tea, knowing she needed to ask Alice what she intended to do next. Her thoughts took her back to when she discovered she had family in Brighton. She knew it wasn't the same but there was still the anguish of what to do about it. Alice and Molly had been a great support to her then and she must now return the favour to her childhood friends, but she wasn't sure how she could help except to listen when they wanted to talk. Things were changing all around her. She had got caught up with Ted, and that made it easy to forget to support her friends.

Victoria was pulled from her reverie by the sound of footsteps on the stairs. She turned to see Ted enter the kitchen, his hair messy from sleep, dark circles under his eyes testament to another restless night.

'Good morning, love,' she said softly, moving to pour him a cup of tea.

Ted gave her a wan smile, accepting the cup gratefully. 'Morning, I'm sorry if I woke you last night. The dreams—'

Victoria shook her head, cutting him off with a gentle kiss. 'You have nothing to apologise for. We're in this together, remember?'

Ted eyed Victoria for a moment before peering into his cup of tea. 'You know I've been thinking about Molly being pregnant... We've never discussed whether we would have children or not.'

'Do we need to discuss it?'

Reaching out to take Victoria's hand in his, Ted studied Victoria. 'Would you like to have children?'

Victoria took a breath. 'Maybe, but there's no rush. Let's not worry about it right now. Let's just enjoy what we have.'

Ted gave a faint laugh. 'It's just that I'm not sure I'd be a good father.'

Victoria smiled at him. 'Or I a good mother. That's what everyone worries about – just ask Andrew and Molly.' She squeezed his hand. 'Now stop worrying and finish your tea.'

As they sat at the small kitchen table, discussing their plans for the day, Victoria felt a surge of determination. This wasn't the married life she had envisioned, but it was theirs. And she would fight against the nightmares, against the lingering shadows of war, against anything that threatened their happiness with everything she had.

The road ahead might be difficult, but as she looked at Ted across the table, and saw the love and gratitude in his eyes, she knew it was a road worth travelling. Together, they would build a life filled with love, understanding, and hopefully, in time, peace.

10

Mr Leadbetter stood in the middle of Foyles; it was uncharacteristically quiet. There were no shouts of good morning, along with the normal chatter and laughter from the staff in the break room, or the click as everyone clocked on when they first arrived. He would be glad when the shop reopened, and he could talk to them and the customers again.

Alice and Victoria knocked on the shop door and waited for Mr Leadbetter to let them in.

He turned the key and pulled the door open. The ring of the bell above the door chimed as he did so. 'Sorry, ladies, I have to keep it locked – otherwise customers will start wandering in, and I know I would find it hard to turn them away.'

Alice nodded. 'It's a difficult time but hopefully it won't last long.'

Victoria took off her jacket. 'It's already warm out there, and it's not even nine o'clock.' She glanced at Mr Leadbetter. 'I don't know if Albert told you, but we got stopped quite a lot yesterday with people asking us if we could deliver them some books.' She took a notepad out of her handbag and opened it. 'Word of our delivery service has definitely got out. I have pages of requests, so maybe we should take a payment pad with us to give out as receipts when people pay us.'

Alice smiled. 'It was a busy day. I wrote down all the addresses we stopped at, what their book request was and if any payments were made because we had the book in the van.' She opened her handbag and pulled out a purse and shook it. The coins chinked together. 'I emptied my money out so I could keep theirs separate.'

'My, it sounds like you were busy.' Mr Leadbetter smiled. 'It's certainly proving to be popular.' He walked to the counter and picked up several bits of paper and waved them in front of him. 'When I came in this morning customers had pushed their book requests through the letter box.'

Victoria reached out for the notes he was holding. 'It looks like we're in for another busy day.'

Alice looked thoughtful. 'I'm not sure this delivery service is going to be easy to stop when we reopen.'

Victoria nodded in agreement. 'We can't worry about that now; we've got books to find and get into the van.' She looked at Mr Leadbetter. 'We're getting better at separating the orders so we're not rummaging around looking for them and keeping the customers waiting.'

Alice smiled. 'Some of the older customers have even asked us to pick up a couple of bits of shopping for them; maybe I shouldn't have agreed to that, but it feels like we're doing something good.'

Mr Leadbetter laughed. 'I don't mind. Our aim has always been to be there for people and that's what you are doing now when people need you the most.' He ran his hand over his chin. 'How is Albert doing? I hope you're keeping an eye on him? I worry about him; at his age he should be at home with his wife.'

Victoria chuckled. 'You can't keep a man like Albert down, but he's being sensible, probably because he's already had the flu and has no desire to catch it a second time.'

Alice giggled. 'He keeps us entertained but he's not getting out of the van to talk to anyone.'

'That's good to hear.' Mr Leadbetter nodded.

'Don't worry, we're keeping a close eye on him.' Victoria smiled. 'I suppose we had better get these orders together. There's a lot of them and we have to try and find the books.'

'Don't let me hold you up, ladies; in fact if you let me know what books you are looking for, I can help.' Mr Leadbetter looked around him. 'It's strange being in here with no customers or staff, so I'd rather be busy and help where I can.'

Victoria laughed. 'We won't say no to any offers of help. You know when we came up with the idea of a delivery service, I didn't expect it to be as popular as it is, but I suppose more people are confining themselves to the house, unless they have to go out for food.'

* * *

Alice intertwined her fingers in front of her, squeezing them tight. She stepped forward and nervously peered out of the window into the darkness. Turning, she watched Molly light candles in her front room, the flickering light bringing dancing shadows and giving the room a cosy feel.

Victoria had made tea, and the familiar ritual of pouring and passing cups provided a moment of normalcy before Alice's world-changing revelation. Alice moved to perch on the edge of an armchair, her hands wrapped tightly around her teacup, the warmth spreading its heat. She loosened her grip as she peered at Molly and Victoria sharing the settee.

'I met them,' Alice said finally, her voice barely above a whisper. 'Margaret Wilson and... and, Peter, my father's other son.'

The silence that followed was heavy with tension. Victoria and Molly exchanged glances, having suspected something was weighing on their friend since her return from Norwich.

'Tell us what happened,' Molly said gently, one hand resting on her swollen belly. 'From the beginning, and don't leave anything out.'

Alice took a shaky breath. 'She was working in her garden – it's not very big, but she had some roses that she was cutting back. The street wasn't that different from Percy Street. The house was similar to yours, Victoria. It's not that far from the cathedral. Peter seemed quite caring and showed concern for his mother.' A bitter laugh escaped her. 'She helps out on the tea table at the station, like my mother does. It seems my father has a type: women who care about others; maybe that's how he's got away with it for so long.'

'What are they like?' Victoria asked softly, reaching out to squeeze Alice's hand.

'Margaret is... kind. Dignified. She was visibly shocked when I introduced myself outside her house. I'm not sure she wanted to meet me at first, but when I explained who I was...' Alice's voice caught. 'She knew about us. About mother and the family.'

'Oh, Alice,' Molly breathed.

'And Peter?' Victoria prompted gently.

Alice's eyes filled with tears. 'He looks so much like Father, and Robert, it took my breath away. He has the same way of tilting his head when he's thinking, the same habit of running his hand through his hair. He... he doesn't know about us.'

'That sounds very difficult,' Victoria said, moving to sit on the arm of Alice's chair.

'The worst part was watching them together. Peter clearly

adores his mother.' Alice's voice broke. 'All those years, I thought I knew my father. I thought we were all special to him. But he's been living this whole other life, being a father to another child, loving another woman...'

'Your father's choices don't diminish his love for you,' Molly said firmly. 'A person can love more than one child, more than one life.'

'But he lied,' Alice said, anger finally breaking through her sadness. 'He's been lying to all of us for years. To Mother, to all of us in London, and to Peter... How can love exist alongside such deception?'

Victoria and Molly shared another look, both remembering their earlier conversations about Alice's suspicions.

'What did Margaret say about it all?' Victoria asked. 'About the situation?'

Alice shrugged. 'We didn't really talk about it. She was naturally worried Peter would overhear and she didn't want him to find out that way.' She paused. 'I'm going up there again and we'll meet in a café where we can openly talk. I think she's worried about what I'll do with the information. She didn't say but I got the impression she wants me to think about what I do with it, because of Peter.'

'And have you?' Victoria asked. 'Thought about what you're going to do? Are you going to at least tell Lily?'

'I can't stop thinking about it,' Alice admitted. 'Every time I see Mother, or Father comes home. It's consuming me but I don't want to put Lily through the same anguish I'm going through, so when things are clearer I might tell her but not yet.'

'And Freddie?' Victoria asked.

Alice shrugged. 'I don't know, I'm worried about the children, about how discussions could easily get out of hand and frighten them, especially Arthur. Freddie thinks the whole idea of my father having another life is ludicrous so he might think I've been snooping in things that don't concern me.'

Molly shifted on the settee, making room. 'Come here,' she said, patting the space beside her. 'And you, Victoria.'

Alice and Victoria moved to join her, and for a moment, the three friends sat in silence, drawing strength from each other's presence.

'Whatever you decide,' Molly said finally, 'we're here for you. If you choose to tell your mother, we'll help you through the aftermath. If you decide to keep this secret, we'll help you carry it.'

'And Peter?' Alice asked, her voice small. 'What about my brother who doesn't know he's my brother?'

'Perhaps,' Victoria suggested carefully, 'there's a way to build a relationship with him, gradually. If you can find out about what interests him, you might be able to find a connection, maybe without necessarily exposing everything at once.'

Alice considered this. 'Maybe, I'll have to see how we get on the next time I see Margaret; after all, she will have had time to think about my turning up on her doorstep.'

'Well, it's one step at a time,' Molly advised, taking Alice's hand. 'You don't have to figure everything out all at once and certainly not tonight.'

As the night deepened outside Molly's windows, the three friends continued to talk, working through possibilities and implications. They spoke of family and betrayal, of love and lies, of the complex web of relationships that made up their lives. They spoke of the war, and how it had changed their understanding of what was important, what could be forgiven, what must be preserved at all costs.

Finally, as midnight approached, Alice felt something settle within her. 'Thank you,' she said simply, looking at her friends through tears. 'For listening, for understanding, for… for everything.'

Molly pulled her into a hug, her pregnancy bump pressing between them. 'That's what family is for,' she said softly. 'The family we choose, as well as the family we're born into.'

* * *

Victoria woke to the sound of humming coming from the kitchen. For a moment, she lay still, disorientated. It had been so long since she'd heard Ted make any sort of cheerful noise, especially in the early morning hours, which were usually dominated by his nightmares.

Curious and a little apprehensive, she slipped out of bed, pulled on her dressing gown, and made her way downstairs. The sight that greeted her in the kitchen made her pause in the doorway, her heart swelling with a mixture of joy and cautious hope.

Ted stood at the stove, his back to her, carefully flipping pancakes. The table was set for two, with a small vase of wildflowers as a centrepiece. As Victoria watched, Ted turned, a smile spreading across his face when he saw her.

'Good morning, love,' he said, his voice lighter than she'd heard it in months. 'I hope you're hungry.'

Victoria moved towards him, hardly daring to believe the change she was seeing. 'Ted, this is… What's the occasion?'

Ted set down the spatula and took her hands in his. 'I wanted to surprise you. To thank you for… well, for everything. But mostly for standing by me through all of this.'

He took a deep breath, his eyes meeting hers with a clarity that had been missing for so long. 'I saw Dr Harrison again yesterday, and for the first time I felt able to talk about… about everything – you know, the nightmares, and the anxiety. Victoria, for the first time, I feel like there might be a way through this. A way to live with what happened without letting it control me.'

Victoria felt tears welling up in her eyes. 'Oh, Ted, that's wonderful. I'm so proud of you for talking to Dr Harrison. I know how hard that must have been.'

Ted nodded, a flicker of his old pain crossing his face. 'It was. It is. But I realised something yesterday. If the rumours I keep hearing about the war being over soon are true, then I don't want to keep fighting it in my head for the rest of my life. I want to live, Victoria. I want us to have the life we dreamed of.'

'Ah, Victoria, you're up.' Daisy rushed into the kitchen. 'I'm running late because I was giving your husband a cooking lesson.' She giggled. 'I'm only sorry I can't stop to taste the delights he has put together.'

Victoria chuckled. 'If Freddie's the desk sergeant I'm sure he'll understand when you explain the reasons.'

Daisy leaned in and kissed her sister on the cheek before moving to Ted and doing the same.

Victoria smiled. 'Please go carefully, Daisy. I want you home in one piece.'

Daisy shook her head. 'Victoria, you say that to me every day; I've really got to go.' Running to the front door she shouted out, 'Enjoy.'

Ted carried a plate of pancakes over to the table. 'I'm not sure what they'll be like.'

Victoria forced a smile as she studied the overcooked pancakes.

Ted laughed. 'You are so sweet. You're determined to encourage me, but I didn't mean my cooking.' He looked down at the plate of food. 'Although they do look a bit brown, or maybe I should say black in places. Anyway, I meant because we didn't have all the ingredients, or not enough of them.'

They both chuckled as they sat down to breakfast.

'That's the war for you; we just have to make the most of what we have.' Victoria couldn't stop smiling.

'I couldn't have put it better myself.' Ted lifted his cup of tea. 'Cheers.'

They talked and laughed in a way they hadn't in far too long. Victoria felt a sense of hope blooming in her chest. She knew there would still be difficult days ahead. Recovery wasn't a straight line, and the scars of war wouldn't disappear overnight. But this moment, this breakthrough, felt like the start of something new. A chance to rebuild, to heal, to look towards the future with hope instead of fear.

And as Ted reached across the table to squeeze her hand, his eyes bright with a determination she hadn't seen since before the war, Victoria silently thanked God for giving them the strength to get to this moment. The road ahead might still be long, but for the first time in a long time, she truly believed they would walk it together.

11

Alice's heart pounded as she approached the small café in Norwich. This was it, the moment she had been both dreading and anticipating ever since she'd uncovered the first clues about her father's secret life. Her breath caught in her throat as her chest tightened. She stopped walking and took a couple of calming breaths. Perhaps she should have brought Lily with her, or one of her friends – after all she didn't have to do this alone – but it was too late now.

As she entered the café, her eyes immediately fell on a woman sitting alone by the window. On the journey to Norwich Alice's mind had been jumping around all over the place, worrying about seeing Margaret Wilson again, even down to whether she would recognise her, which she knew was ridiculous and she should have known better. Alice studied her, as though seeing her for the first time. She guessed Mrs Wilson was in her late forties. Her eyes looked kind, but she appeared nervous as she glanced around her. Her hands were wrapped around a teacup, and Alice noticed they trembled slightly as she lifted it to her lips.

'Mrs Wilson?' Alice asked tentatively as she approached the table.

The woman looked up, her eyes widening slightly as she took in Alice's appearance. There was something in her expression that made Alice's stomach clench. 'Yes, please sit down.'

Alice slid into the seat across from Margaret. 'My married name is Alice Leybourne.' She paused. 'Thank you for agreeing to meet with me. I know it is difficult for you.'

Margaret nodded, her fingers nervously toying with her teacup. 'It's difficult for all of us. Luke... your father, he's always been so careful.'

Alice felt a chill go through her at the casual way this stranger referred to her father. 'So, it's true then? He has... another life here?'

Margaret's eyes filled with sympathy. 'Oh, my dear. I'm so sorry. I thought... I assumed you knew and that's what's brought you here.'

Alice fought back her tears. 'I've suspected it for a while. But I needed to know for sure. Please, Mrs Wilson, can you tell me... Does Peter have... have any siblings I haven't met yet?'

Margaret reached across the table, gently taking Alice's hand in hers. 'Your father is a good man, Alice. He's tried his best to balance his responsibilities, to cause as little pain as possible, but there's only Peter. He's fifteen now.'

'Does... does Peter know about us? About the family in London? I mean, have you had a chance to talk to him yet?' Alice asked, her voice barely above a whisper.

Margaret shook her head. 'No, love, I haven't. When I fell pregnant, Luke told me about his life in London. I was hurt but I couldn't give up my son. Your father has always done his best to look after us.'

Alice shook her head. 'I don't understand. How did you meet him in the first place?'

Margaret gave a faint smile. 'I was in domestic service. I worked for his father. It all seems a long time ago now.'

'It must have been hard for you, especially as people like to gossip. Someone I worked with, her friend, went through something similar and I get the impression they made her life hell. I knew your name was Margaret Wilson, but I assumed you took my father's name when you had Peter.'

Margaret nodded. 'Your father did suggest it, to save my honour against the gossips.' She laughed. 'But it was a bit late for that and I survived. We're all tougher than we realise; besides I wasn't his wife, so I didn't want to pretend otherwise.' She took a breath. 'Peter thinks his father is a widower who travels for business. It's... it's not been easy, for any of us.'

A waiter approached their table, and Alice gratefully used the interruption to compose herself, ordering tea with hands that shook only slightly. When he left, she turned back to Margaret, studying the woman who shared her father's life in ways Alice was only beginning to understand.

'How long?' she managed to ask. 'How long has this been going on?'

Margaret's face softened with remembered pain. 'I met your father sixteen years ago. I was a widow myself then, struggling to make ends meet. He was... kind and understanding. We fell in love before I knew he was married. By the time I found out, it was too late. I was already carrying Peter. Your Father wanted to do the honourable thing by me and the baby; divorce was never mentioned. That would have been too difficult and the shame it would have brought on your mother would have been too much for me to bear anyway. I think he wanted to live here and look after us, but I couldn't let him do that;

after all I should have known better.' Margaret wiped her eyes. 'I had no desire to break up another family. So, we created this… this elaborate fiction instead. I always knew it would all unravel at some point.'

Alice absorbed this information, her mind racing. It had been at least sixteen years. She would have been just a child herself when her father started his double life. How many family dinners, how many bedtime stories, how many moments she had treasured – how many of them had been shadowed by this secret?

'He's always been a good father to Peter, especially when Peter's friend died in one of the bombings. My son was distraught, and to be honest, I didn't know how to help him through it, but your father sat with him for ages talking about the friend he had lost. I think that helped Peter to come to terms with it all; until then he had been relatively untouched by the bad things that can happen in life,' Margaret continued softly. 'Just as I'm sure your father has always been there for you and your brothers and sister. He loves all of you, Alice. I know that might be hard to believe right now, but it's true.'

Alice felt tears spilling down her cheeks. Her heart went out to Peter, to experience loss at such a young age. She remembered getting the news of Robert dying in action and the grief they all felt; it had been an awful time. She shook away the memories and studied Margaret. 'How? How can he love us all? How can he live this lie?'

Margaret's own eyes were damp with unshed tears. 'Love isn't always simple, dear. Sometimes it's messy and complicated and painful. Your father… he made choices, years ago, choices that he's been living with ever since. Not always good choices, perhaps, but he's tried to do right by everyone.'

'By lying to everyone?' Alice asked bitterly.

'By protecting everyone,' Margaret corrected gently. 'Or at

least, that's what he tells himself. But now you know the truth, and that changes everything, doesn't it?'

Alice nodded slowly, feeling the weight of responsibility settling on her shoulders. What would she do with this knowledge? Could she return to London, to her life, pretending she didn't know about Peter, about Margaret?

'I don't know what to do,' she admitted. 'I don't know how to live with this truth.'

Margaret squeezed her hand. 'You don't have to decide anything right now. Take time to process it all. And, Alice... know that none of this is your fault. You've done nothing wrong by seeking the truth.'

As they sat there in the quiet café, two women bound together by their love for the same complicated man, Alice felt a strange sort of connection forming. They were all, in their own ways, victims of her father's choices. And perhaps Victoria was right, Alice thought, maybe they could find a way forward together.

'Would you...' Alice hesitated, then pressed on. 'Would you tell me about Peter? What's he like?'

Margaret hesitated for a moment before taking a breath. 'He works after school and at weekends in a local bookshop. It's only small but he loves it.'

Alice gave a faint smile. 'I can understand that as I work in London's Foyles Bookshop, and I wouldn't give it up for anything.'

'I think that's how Peter feels.' Margaret's face lit up with pride as she began to share stories about the brother Alice had never known. Alice listened with a mixture of pain and fascination. Here was a whole other world, a life that had been running alongside her own for all these years. And now that she knew about it, she could never unknow it.

The afternoon light was fading by the time they finally parted, having shared more tears and even a few laughs. As Alice watched Margaret walk away, she felt both lighter and heavier: lighter for having finally learned the truth, heavier with the knowledge of what she must do next.

The war had taught her that sometimes the hardest battles were fought not on distant battlefields, but in the quiet moments of ordinary life. This would be such a battle, a fight for truth, for understanding, for some kind of resolution that wouldn't destroy everything she held dear.

As she made her way back to the train station, Alice squared her shoulders. She would face this challenge as she had faced all others – with courage, with honesty, and with the hope that something good could emerge from even the most painful truth. That would mean trying to protect her mother while separately confronting her father, but it was all about choosing the right time, and then there was Freddie and Lily. She wondered how they would all react to her news; something told her it wasn't going to be good.

* * *

The train pulled into the station, its whistle piercing the evening air. Alice stepped onto the platform, her mind still reeling from her trip to Norfolk. The weight of the information she'd uncovered pressed heavily on her shoulders, making her usual brisk walk more of a weary trudge.

As she made her way home, the streets of London seemed different somehow. The same buildings, the same cobblestones under her feet, but everything felt altered by the knowledge she now carried. Her father, the man she'd looked up to her entire life, had another family. A son she'd never known about. A whole other life he'd kept hidden from them.

Approaching her family's house, Alice paused. Through the

window, she could see her mother in the front room, reading her latest book. The sight, once so comforting, now filled her with a mix of love and heartache. How could she tell her mother what she'd discovered? How could she keep it from her?

Taking a deep breath, Alice pushed open the front door. As she did, she heard her father's voice from inside the house, calling out a greeting to her mother. The sound made her freeze. For a moment, she considered turning around, fleeing back to the station, to anywhere but here where she'd have to face the reality of her family's fractured foundation.

But no, she'd come this far. She owed it to herself, to her mother, to see this through. With a trembling hand, Alice reached for the door handle. Whatever came next, whatever difficult conversations and painful truths lay ahead, she would face them. For better or worse, the life she'd known was about to change forever.

As Alice stepped into the house, the familiar scents of home – her mother's lavender sachets, the polish her father used on his shoes – enveloped her. For a moment, she was transported back to her childhood, to a time when her world was simple, and her father was an infallible hero. The contrast with her current reality was stark and painful.

'Alice, darling, you're back.' Her mother's voice, warm and welcoming, cut through her thoughts. Alice plastered on a smile as her mother embraced her. Over her mother's shoulder, she saw her father enter the room, his face lighting up at the sight of her.

'How was your trip, Alice?' he asked, moving to hug her as well. 'Did you have a nice time with your friend?'

The lie she'd told to cover her true destination in Norwich now felt like ash in her mouth. As she returned her father's embrace, Alice couldn't help but wonder if he'd hugged his other child, Peter, with the same affection. Did he whisper the same terms of endearment to both his families? The thought made her stomach churn.

'It was... enlightening,' Alice managed, pulling away perhaps a bit too quickly. She saw a flicker of concern cross her mother's face.

'Are you all right, dear? You look pale. Was the journey very tiring?'

Alice nodded, seizing the excuse. 'Yes, I think I'll turn in early if you don't mind.'

As she climbed the stairs to her room, Alice could feel her parents' worried gazes on her back. She knew they could sense something was amiss, but how could she even begin to explain? Alice pushed open the boys' bedroom door, holding her breath as the hinges grated. Stepping inside, she walked over and gave each of her sleeping boys a light kiss on the forehead before straightening their bedclothes. Sighing, she knew her mother would have a good reason for putting them to bed in the bedroom instead of the basement; she just had to hope they wouldn't have any bombs dropping that night. She fleetingly wondered where Freddie was, she guessed it was either work or helping returning soldiers. She realised she should have asked her mother, but she was too exhausted to go back downstairs and face her.

In the safety of her own room, Alice finally allowed the tears she'd been holding back to fall. She thought of Margaret, the woman she'd met in Norwich, her father's other... wife? Partner? Mistress? What term could possibly encompass the complexity of their relationship? Margaret had been kind, if wary, willing to talk once Alice had explained who she was. And Peter... seeing her half-brother had been like looking at a younger version of her father. The resemblance was undeniable, as was the bond between Peter and their father – evident in the photos Margaret had shown her.

Alice's mind raced with questions. How had her father managed to maintain two separate lives for so many years? And perhaps most painfully, had any of his love for her and her mother been real, or was it all part of an elaborate charade?

As she changed for bed, moving on autopilot, Alice caught sight of herself in the mirror. The woman staring back at her looked older, wearier than she remembered. The war had aged them all, but this, this personal betrayal, seemed to have etched new lines of worry and sorrow onto her face overnight.

She knew she would have to make a decision soon. Confront her father? Tell her mother? Reach out to Peter? The weight of these choices pressed down on her, making sleep seem like an impossible luxury. But as she lay in bed, staring at the familiar shadows on her ceiling, Alice felt a resolve forming within her. The war had taught her strength she never knew she possessed. Now, it seemed, it was time to put that strength to the test in her own home.

* * *

Alice was in her bedroom, arranging books on her shelf, when she heard the sharp rap of knuckles on her door. Before she could respond, Lily burst in, closing the door firmly behind her. One look at her sister's face told Alice everything she needed to know.

'When were you going to tell me?' Lily demanded, her voice low but intense. 'Or were you planning to keep me in the dark just like Father's been doing to all of us?'

Alice felt the blood drain from her face. 'How did you—'

'Mrs Henderson saw you at Norwich station,' Lily cut in. 'Her son's stationed there, and she was visiting him. She said she was quite sure it was you, though she thought it was strange you didn't acknowledge her greeting.' Lily's eyes narrowed. 'Of course, you were probably too preoccupied with spying on Father to notice anything else.'

Alice sank onto her bed, her legs suddenly weak. 'Lily, I...'

'Don't.' Lily held up a hand. 'Don't you dare make excuses. All these years, I was the one who first suspected something wasn't right. I was the one who noticed the patterns in his trips, the way he'd get so defensive if anyone mentioned Norfolk. And now you've gone investigating without even telling me?'

There was hurt beneath the anger in Lily's voice, and it made Alice's heart ache. She patted the space beside her on the bed, a peace offering. After a moment's hesitation, Lily sat down.

'I couldn't tell you,' Alice said softly. 'I couldn't tell anyone. I needed to be sure before I...' She swallowed hard. 'Before I upended everyone's lives.'

'And are you?' Lily asked, her voice smaller now. 'Sure?'

Alice nodded, feeling tears prick at her eyes. 'Her name is Margaret Wilson. She lives near the cathedral. And there's...' She took a shaky breath. 'There's a boy, Peter. He's fifteen.'

Lily's sharp intake of breath was the only sound in the room for a long moment. 'A brother,' she whispered finally. 'We have another brother.'

'Half-brother,' Alice corrected automatically, then wondered why it mattered.

'What's he like?' Lily asked, turning to face her sister fully. 'Does he... does he look like Father?'

'And Robert, so much so it hurts to look at him,' Alice admitted. 'He has Father's mannerisms too. The way he runs his hand through his hair when he's thinking, the way he...'

'Tilts his head when he's reading,' Lily finished, her voice catching. 'Oh, Alice.'

The sisters sat in silence for a moment, both lost in thought. Outside, they could hear their mother moving about downstairs, humming as she prepared dinner, blissfully unaware of the conversation taking place above.

'Does he know about us?' Lily asked finally.

Alice shook her head. 'He thinks Father is a widower. That his first wife, our mother, died years ago.'

'How convenient for him,' Lily said bitterly. Then, more softly: 'And Margaret? What's she like?'

'Kind,' Alice said, surprising herself with how quickly the word came to her. 'She's... she didn't have to meet with me, didn't have to tell me anything. But she did. She said she thought... she thought we had a right to know our brother, even if he can't know we're his sisters. At least not yet anyway.'

Lily absorbed this, her fingers plucking at Alice's bedspread. 'And now what? We just... what? Keep Father's secret? Pretend we don't know about our brother? Watch Mother continue to believe in a marriage that's been a lie for years?'

'I don't know,' Alice admitted. 'I've been going round and round with it in my head. Every option seems wrong somehow. Tell the truth and destroy two families or keep the secret and be complicit in Father's deception.'

'Does anyone else know you went to Norwich?'

'Just Victoria and Molly – they've been helping me... to process it all.'

Lily's face hardened slightly. 'So, you could tell your friends but not your own sister?'

'Oh, Lily.' Alice turned to face her sister fully. 'It wasn't like that. I just... I needed to work through it myself first. And then find a way to tell you that wouldn't...' She gestured helplessly. 'That wouldn't make it worse somehow.'

'Make it worse?' Lily gave a hollow laugh. 'How could it be worse? Our father has another family. Another child. He's been living a lie for longer than we can imagine. What could possibly make that worse?'

'Losing you,' Alice said quietly. 'Having you hate me for being the one to confirm all your suspicions, for making it real.'

Lily's face softened. She reached for Alice's hand, squeezing it tightly. 'I could never hate you; you fool. You're my sister. My only sister... shame Peter wasn't born a girl.'

Despite everything, they both laughed at that. There was a slightly hysterical edge to it. When they calmed, Lily asked, 'Will you take me next time? To Norwich? I'd like to... I'd like to see them for myself.'

Alice nodded, relief flooding through her at not having to carry this burden alone any more. 'Yes, though we'll have to be careful. If Mrs Henderson spotted me once...'

'We'll be careful,' Lily assured her. 'We've had plenty of practice keeping secrets in this family, haven't we?'

The bitterness was back in her voice, and Alice squeezed her hand. 'It won't be forever. Just until we figure out the right way to handle it all.'

'And Mother? What do we do about Mother?'

Before Alice could respond, they heard their mother's voice calling them down to dinner. Both sisters froze, the familiar summons now laden with new meaning.

'We should go down,' Alice said finally. 'Before she comes looking for us. I don't think we should say anything to anybody yet, not even Freddie.'

Lily nodded but didn't move. 'Promise me something?'

'Anything.'

'There'll be no more secrets between us. Whatever we decide to do about all of this, we do it together.'

Alice pulled her sister into a fierce hug. 'I promise, no more secrets. I've found this whole business so difficult and believe it or not I did wish I had taken you with me.'

The thud of the front door shutting and Arthur laughing told Alice Freddie was home.

Mrs Headley's voice rang out. 'Someone is pleased to see you Mr Leybourne, and you're just in time for dinner.'

'Thank you, Mrs Headley, but please call me Freddie.'

As the girls made their way downstairs, both sisters squared their shoulders, preparing to face another family dinner full of careful conversations and hidden truths. But something had shifted between them, a new understanding, a shared purpose.

12

The grey early October morning cast its chilly breeze across Charing Cross Road as Alice made her way to Foyles. For the first time in weeks, she noticed more people on the streets, shop-keepers sweeping their storefronts, delivery boys on their rounds, even a few early-bird customers window-shopping.

As she approached the bookshop, she saw Mr Leadbetter outside, taking down the sign that had warned customers about the influenza precautions. He beamed at her as she drew near.

'Good morning, Mrs Leybourne, I'm so pleased to have the shop open again. I know it was only for just over two weeks and everyone worked hard at looking after our customers, but I love being in this shop. It's my home. It certainly feels like a wonderful day.'

Alice couldn't help but smile back. 'It is indeed, sir, and it's good to see you taking down the warning sign.'

He nodded, his eyes twinkling. 'My friend, Dr Thompson, was telling me the worst of the epidemic has passed. We'll still need to be cautious, of course, but it seems the tide is turning.'

As they entered the shop together, Alice was struck by how

much lighter the atmosphere felt; it had been replaced by a cautious optimism.

Victoria and Molly arrived soon after, and the three friends gathered around the counter all pleased to be back in the shop they loved, sharing news they'd heard about recovering patients and reopening businesses.

'My neighbour's daughter is finally out of bed,' Molly said, her hand resting on her baby bump. 'First time in three weeks she's been well enough to leave her room.'

Victoria nodded. 'Ted's regiment is standing down their emergency medical unit. They say the number of new cases has dropped dramatically.'

As they prepared to open the shop, more good news arrived. A telegram for Mr Leadbetter announced that two of their colleagues who had been seriously ill were on the mend and hoping to return to work within the fortnight.

The bell above the door chimed as the first customer of the day entered. The three women exchanged glances, a mix of excitement and apprehension in their eyes. It felt like the first day of school, or perhaps more accurately, like the first tentative steps into a new world.

Mr Leadbetter stepped forward to greet the customer, his voice warm and welcoming. 'Good morning, sir, welcome to Foyles. How may we assist you today?'

As the customer began to browse, Alice found herself straightening books on a nearby shelf, her hands trembling slightly. The familiar task grounded her, reminding her of why she loved working at Foyles. Books had been a constant comfort through the dark days of war and the epidemic, a reminder that there was still beauty and knowledge to be found in the world, even in its darkest moments.

Throughout the day, a steady trickle of customers came

through the doors. Many were regulars, their faces lighting up at the sight of familiar shelves and the comforting smell of books. Others were new, perhaps drawn in by the promise of escape or understanding that books could provide in these tumultuous times.

Alice found herself recommending books with a new perspective. Titles that once seemed frivolous now felt important – reminders of joy and normalcy in a world that had been turned upside down. History books were in high demand, as people sought to understand the events that had shaped their world. And poetry... poetry seemed to speak to something deep within the souls of many customers, offering solace and expression for emotions too complex for everyday words.

As the day wore on, Alice noticed a change in the atmosphere of the shop. Conversations between customers and staff, once hushed and hurried, now lingered. People seemed hungry for connection, for the exchange of ideas and experiences that had been put on hold by fear and isolation.

Victoria appeared at her elbow, a stack of books in her arms. 'Penny for your thoughts?' she asked, noting Alice's pensive expression.

Alice smiled, gesturing around the shop. 'Just thinking about how much has changed. And yet, here we are, still surrounded by books, still connecting people with stories and ideas. It's... comforting, isn't it? To know that some things endure, even in the face of such upheaval.'

Victoria nodded, her eyes shining with understanding. 'It is. And perhaps that's our real job here, isn't it? Not just selling books, but helping people find hope, find meaning, find a way forward in whatever is going on in their lives.'

As they returned to their tasks, Alice felt their world had changed, and yes, there were still challenges ahead, both personal and collective, but they had all discovered a strength they didn't know they had.

Surely, the four years of war must come to an end soon. The epidemic was fading, but the need for stories, for understanding, for connection – that would never end. And as long as there were books and readers to bring together, Alice knew she had a role to play, as they all did, in shaping the world that would emerge from the ashes of the old.

* * *

Alice paced the length of her bedroom, her heart pounding with a mixture of determination and dread. The weight of the knowledge she'd gained in Norwich pressed heavily on her conscience. Every interaction with her father since her return had been strained, every family dinner an exercise in maintaining a facade of normalcy.

But tonight, that would end. She couldn't bear the secrecy any longer. The papers were full of talk of how the war might be ending soon. Would the Germans really surrender? Could this be the beginning of the end of the bloodshed? Will it finally bring peace into everyone's lives? It was all everyone was talking about but they were too scared to hope it was true. But her battle – the battle for truth within her own family – was just beginning. Alice and her family had a different kind of fight, the struggle to rebuild trust, to redefine their relationships in light of this long-hidden truth.

Taking a deep breath, Alice smoothed down her skirt and made her way downstairs. She found her father in his study, as she knew she would. He was at his desk, poring over some papers, a familiar sight that now seemed tainted by what she knew.

'Father,' she said, her voice steadier than she felt. 'I need to speak with you.'

Luke looked up, a smile crossing his face at the sight of his daughter. But as he took in her serious expression, the smile faded. 'Of course, Alice. What is it?'

Alice closed the door behind her and moved to stand in front of his desk. For a moment, she hesitated. This was her last chance to turn back, to pretend she didn't know, to preserve the family as it had always been.

But she couldn't. She owed it to herself, to her mother, even to the half-brother she didn't really know, to bring the truth into the light.

'I know about Norwich,' she said, her voice barely above a whisper. 'About your... your other family.'

The colour drained from her father's face. For a long moment, he said nothing, his eyes searching hers as if hoping to find some hint that he had misunderstood.

'How...' he finally managed, his voice hoarse. 'How did you find out?'

Alice felt a surge of anger at the question. Not a denial, not an apology, but concern for how his secret had been uncovered. 'Does it matter?' she shot back. 'What matters is that it's true. You've been lying to us, to Mother, for years.'

Her father slumped in his chair, suddenly looking older than Alice had ever seen him. 'Alice, please... you have to understand. It's complicated. I never meant to hurt anyone.'

'But you did,' Alice said, tears pricking at her eyes. 'You've hurt us all. Mother, Lily, me... and them. Your other... your son. How could you, Father? How could you live this double life? If Robert was alive, he'd be devastated. He idolised you and what he thought you stood for. I'm not sure how Charles will react when he finds out. You picked on him so much when he was growing up while all the time leading this secret life. There's a lot of explaining and making up to do.' Alice watched as anxiety ran across her father's face.

Her father's mouth dropped open, and then shut again as he struggled to know what to say. His eyes widened. 'Does Lily know?'

'Yes, she has suspected something for years, but when she knew I had been to Norwich and it was confirmed, she was angry.'

Luke shook his head as his gaze darted from left to right and back again. 'I'm amazed she hasn't confronted me.'

'I asked her not to because of Ma.'

'It's not how you think. I made mistakes, but I've only ever tried to protect my family here.'

Alice studied her father as he quoted Margaret's words to her.

As her father began to speak, to try to explain years of deception and divided loyalties, Alice listened with a mixture of anger, sorrow, and a strange sort of pity. The man before her, the father she had idolised for so long, suddenly seemed small and flawed.

But as she listened, she also felt a sense of relief. The truth, painful as it was, was finally out. Whatever came next, whether forgiveness or irreparable fracture, at least it would be based on honesty. It would be difficult, painful even, but as Alice stood there, facing her father's confession, she knew it was necessary. For only through truth could they hope to find a way forward, into whatever future awaited them all.

As her father's words washed over her, Alice found her mind drifting to the day in Norfolk when she'd first laid eyes on Peter, her half-brother. The shock of recognition, seeing her father's features mirrored in a boy she'd never met, had been overwhelming. Now, looking at her father, she could see traces of Peter in him too.

'Did you ever plan to tell us?' Alice asked, cutting through her father's explanations. 'Or were you content to live this lie forever?'

Luke sighed heavily, running a hand through his greying hair. 'I... I don't know, Alice. I told myself that keeping the two worlds separate was best for everyone. That no one would get hurt if—'

'If the truth never came out?' Alice finished for him. 'But secrets have a way of surfacing, Father. Surely you must have known that.'

Her father nodded, a look of defeat on his face. 'I suppose I did. But I was a coward. I couldn't bear the thought of losing any of you, your mother, or... or Peter and Margaret.'

The casual use of their names sent a jolt through Alice. To hear her father speak of his other family with such familiarity made the reality of the situation hit home once again.

'What happens now?' she asked, suddenly feeling very young and unsure.

Luke looked up at her, his eyes filled with a mixture of regret and hope. 'That... that depends on you, Alice. And on your mother. I know I have no right to ask for forgiveness, but...'

Alice held up a hand, stopping him. 'I can't speak for Mother. She deserves to hear the truth from you, not from me. As for me... I need time, Father, as I expect Lily and Charles will. Time to process all of this, to figure out how I feel.'

She turned to leave but paused at the door. 'And Peter deserves the truth too. He has a right to know about us, about his... his other family.'

As she left the study, closing the door softly behind her, Alice felt as though a great weight had been lifted from her shoulders, only to be replaced by a different kind of burden. The truth was out now, at least between her and her father. But the ripple effects of this revelation were only beginning.

Making her way back to her room, Alice's mind raced with

questions and possibilities. How would her mother react? Would Peter want to know the family in London? Would he hate her for bringing it all to a head? Could their fractured family ever be whole again, or would this secret tear them apart forever?

As she sat on her bed, Alice's eyes fell on a photograph on her nightstand, a family portrait taken before the war. They all looked so happy, so untroubled. She picked it up, tracing the outline of her father's face. The man in the photograph suddenly seemed like a stranger.

But as she set the picture down, Alice felt a flicker of something unexpected: hope. Yes, their family had been built on a lie. Yes, there would be pain and difficult conversations ahead. But there was also the possibility of something new, something honest. A chance to rebuild their relationships on a foundation of truth.

* * *

The usual bustle of Foyles Bookshop took on a feverish quality that morning. Alice had noticed it the moment she stepped through the doors, an electric current of excitement running through the customers, hushed conversations punctuated by exclamations of disbelief and hope.

As she arranged a display of newly arrived novels, she couldn't help but overhear snippets of conversation.

'I can't believe my brother could be home soon,' a young woman was saying to her companion. 'He's been in France for so long. I hope the rumours are true and there is talk of an armistice.'

'I'm keeping my fingers crossed,' her friend replied, though her voice quivered with barely suppressed hope. 'After all this time...'

Alice's hands trembled slightly as she placed the last book on the display. Could it be true? After four long years of war, of loss and sacrifice, could peace finally be within reach?

She made her way to the counter where Victoria was checking a payment slip for a customer's purchases. As the elderly gentleman gathered his books and shuffled out, coughing into his handkerchief, Victoria turned to Alice with wide eyes. 'Have you heard?' she whispered urgently. 'There are rumours...'

Before Alice could respond, Mr Leadbetter emerged from his office, his face etched with an odd mixture of excitement and apprehension as he strolled towards Alice and Victoria. 'I'm struggling to believe it, but if everything I keep hearing is true, we could have an official announcement within days.'

Molly, who had silently joined them, placed a protective hand over her growing bump. 'Is it really possible?' she breathed. 'After all this time?'

Mr Leadbetter nodded solemnly. 'Maybe, but we mustn't get our hopes up too much; after all, these are still just rumours, and we don't want to spread false hope. But we should be prepared. People will be looking for information, for understanding. We need to be ready to provide it.'

As they dispersed to their various tasks, Alice felt a strange mixture of emotions washing over her. Joy, certainly – the prospect of peace after so many years of conflict was almost overwhelming. But there was fear too, and uncertainty. What would a post-war world look like? She thought about Ted, Andrew and Freddie and she couldn't help wondering how other returning men would settle back into their home lives. Would everyone adjust to peace after becoming so accustomed to war? Women had become more independent, working hard to keep the country's war effort going. Would they be expected to go back to the way things were before as well?

Throughout the day, the atmosphere in the shop grew increasingly charged. Customers lingered longer than usual, discussing the rumours in hushed tones. The newspaper stand was constantly surrounded, people poring over every word, searching for confirmation of what they desperately hoped to be true.

During a quiet moment, Alice found her mind drifting back to all those years ago, hearing Lily at the suffragette demonstration and the trouble it had caused at home, how her father had wanted to marry the troublesome Lily off. It wasn't long after that everyone had rushed to the palace to see the king standing on the balcony. The excitement four years ago was great. Alice remembered the distress Victoria's brother and hers caused when they sneaked off to war by lying about their ages. They had thought it was an adventure and it would be over by Christmas in 1914, but it wasn't. So much death, so much destruction, and for what? As the possibility of peace loomed, these questions seemed more pressing than ever.

'You can almost touch the hope here today. Are you all right?' Victoria's voice broke through Alice's reverie. She looked up to see her friend watching her with a mixture of concern and understanding.

Alice smiled wryly. 'I suppose I'm trying to remind myself of the cost. Even if the war ends tomorrow, there's so much healing to be done.'

Victoria nodded. 'You're right, of course. But perhaps that's where we come in. The array of books we have here, and new publications, may help us understand, help us remember. Maybe that's part of the healing process.'

As they stood there, surrounded by the words of poets and historians who had seen the worst of the wars in the past, Alice felt a renewed sense of purpose. Yes, the prospect of peace was thrilling, but the work of understanding, of remembering, of moving forward – that work was just beginning. And Foyles, with its wealth of knowledge and ideas, would have a crucial role to play in that process.

Victoria eyed Alice. 'You've been very quiet. Your ready smile has been missed. Is everything all right at home?'

Alice's lips tightened. 'I'm sorry. I should leave my home life at home.'

Victoria shook her head. 'We all know it isn't as simple as that.'

Alice sighed. 'I've told my father I know about Norwich.' She gave a faint smile. 'I think he was more concerned that Lily knew.'

Victoria studied her friend. 'Knowing Lily as I do, I think I'd be more worried too; you are more controlled and like to think things through, whereas Lily is more impulsive.'

Alice laughed. 'That's true.'

'Can I ask, how did your father take it?'

Alice shrugged. 'He was quite visibly shocked. He said he had made mistakes, but he was only trying to protect us, which is what Margaret had said so she obviously knows him very well.'

An elderly customer approached them. 'No news yet. I do hope it's going to happen soon.'

Smiling, Victoria stepped forward. 'We are all hoping for the same news.' She laughed. 'I don't think any of us will get much sleep tonight.'

13

Victoria stood in front of the military history section, reorganising the books that had become dishevelled during the shop's closure. As she worked, her mind wandered to the conversation she'd had with Mr Leadbetter some weeks ago.

Victoria gasped as it suddenly dawned on her she hadn't told Mr Leadbetter she wanted to accept the position he had offered her. She had got so caught up with Ted, the wedding and the flu, it had totally left her mind. She hoped she hadn't missed her opportunity. Looking around her, she realised she needed to talk to him and apologise for not letting him know earlier.

As she shelved books, Victoria's thoughts, as always, turned to Ted. His recovery was slow, the nightmares and anxiety still a daily struggle but he did seem to be more positive and there was no doubt in her mind he had been over the moon about her promotion.

Alice sidled up to Victoria. 'You seem deep in thought, is everything all right?'

'I was just thinking some weeks ago, Mr Leadbetter offered me a promotion,' she said softly. 'A managerial position.'

Alice frowned. 'I remember us talking about it. Is there a problem?'

Victoria gave a humourless laugh. 'You could say that; I forgot to tell Mr Leadbetter I wanted to accept the position. I'm worried I've missed my chance.'

Alice shook her head. 'You shouldn't worry. He knows better than most of us the load everyone has been carrying. Just talk to him and see what he says.'

Victoria took a deep breath. 'I will, thank you.' Her mind raced with possibilities as she considered the potential of her new role. She thought about the changes she could implement, the ways she could help Foyles adapt to the post-war world that was slowly taking shape around them.

Perhaps they could expand their selection of books by female authors, highlighting the voices that had emerged during the war years. Or maybe they could create a special section dedicated to understanding the conflict that had shaped their generation, featuring not just military histories but also personal accounts, poetry, and analyses of the war's social impact.

And what about the returning soldiers? Victoria thought of Ted and the struggles he faced. Could Foyles play a role in helping veterans reintegrate into civilian life? Perhaps they could host reading groups or writing workshops, providing a space for men to process their experiences through literature.

As these ideas took shape in her mind, Victoria felt a growing sense of purpose. This wasn't just about advancing her own career or proving herself capable. It was about using her position to make a real difference, to help Foyles become not just a book-shop, but a centre of healing and understanding in a world still reeling from the effects of war.

'You know,' she said to Alice, who was still listening attentively, 'I think this could be more than just a job. It could be a calling.'

Alice smiled, reaching out to squeeze Victoria's hand. 'I think you're right. And I think you're exactly the person Foyles needs right now. You understand what people have been through, what they're still going through. You can help guide the shop into this new era.'

Victoria nodded, feeling a surge of confidence. 'You're right. And it's not just about me, is it? It's about all of us – you, me, Molly, everyone who's worked so hard to keep Foyles going through these difficult years. We've all grown, all changed. Maybe it's time we embraced those changes.' She took a deep breath. 'I need to speak to Mr Leadbetter. I just hope I haven't left it too late.' She glanced around and saw him talking to a customer.

Alice squeezed her arm. 'Good luck.'

Victoria nodded before turning to walk in his direction just as the customer smiled and moved away from him. 'Mr Leadbetter.'

He glanced in her direction. 'What is it, Mrs Marsden? Has something happened?'

Colour rushed into Victoria's cheeks. 'Yes... no... sorry. I feel such a... anyway, I've only realised today that I didn't accept the promotion you offered me. I'm so sorry but I'm hoping I haven't missed my chance, because I really would like to.'

Mr Leadbetter held up his hand. 'Slow down, and please stop worrying.' He smiled. 'I assumed you would want it and organised for you to receive a pay rise. I admit because the shop has been very quiet and then closed, until recently, you may not have received it yet.'

Victoria beamed at him. 'I could hug you, but I know that's not very professional. Thank you, sir, for having faith in me, despite everything.'

Mr Leadbetter smiled. 'I appreciate you talking to me about it, and I will chase up your pay rise.' He turned and walked in the direction of his office before looking back. 'I forgot to say – Vera will be back tomorrow.'

Victoria beamed. 'That's wonderful news. I'm so glad she is fit enough to come back to work.'

As the day wore on, Victoria found herself observing the shop with new eyes. She noticed the way customers lingered in certain sections, the books that seemed to draw the most attention. She listened to the conversations around her, picking up on the themes and concerns that seemed to preoccupy people in these uncertain times.

By closing time, Victoria had filled several pages of her notebook with ideas and observations. As she locked up the shop alongside Mr Leadbetter, she felt a mixture of excitement and nerves.

'Sir,' she said, her voice steady despite her racing heart, 'I've been thinking about this new role and I have lots of ideas to take forward. I'm ready for the challenge.'

Mr Leadbetter's face broke into a wide smile. 'My dear, nothing makes me happier. Foyles is entering a new chapter, and I can think of no one better to help write it than you.'

As Victoria walked home that evening, her steps were light despite her fatigue. She knew there would be challenges ahead – balancing her new role with her responsibilities at home, navigating the changing dynamics of the workplace, helping to guide Foyles through the uncertain post-war years. But for the first time in a long while, she felt truly excited about the future.

The war had changed her, had changed all of them. But perhaps, Victoria thought, those changes had prepared them for this moment – a moment of renewal, of possibility, of hope. And she was ready to embrace it with open arms.

* * *

Molly stood at the kitchen window, absent-mindedly stirring a pot of soup as she watched the street outside. The November chill saw everyone wrapped up in their winter coats, but it hadn't stopped them lingering to discuss the news that the war could be coming to an end. It had thrown London into a frenzy of celebration, but here in their home, a different kind of anticipation filled the air.

The sound of the front door opening pulled her from her reverie. 'Molly?' Andrew's voice called out. 'Are you home?'

'In the kitchen,' she replied, turning to greet her husband with a smile.

Andrew entered, his face flushed with excitement. 'Have you heard anything? I can't believe the war's really going to be over.'

Molly nodded, her hand moving instinctively to rest on her swollen belly. 'I heard it was going to be done soon. It's the news everyone is waiting for. It's... it's almost hard to believe, isn't it? After all this time...'

Andrew crossed the room in two strides, gathering Molly into his arms. For a long moment, they simply held each other, the reality of peace washing over them.

'I've been thinking,' Andrew said softly as they parted, 'about the baby and our futures.'

Molly felt a flutter of nerves. They hadn't talked much about the practicalities of parenthood, both of them too caught up in the day-to-day struggles of wartime life. 'Oh?' she managed, trying to keep her voice light. 'What about it?'

Andrew took her hand, leading her to sit at the small kitchen table. 'I know I haven't been... as present as I should have been,' he began, his voice tinged with regret. 'I've been so focused on helping other veterans, on trying to make sense of my own experiences, that I haven't given our future the attention it deserves. But, Molly, I want you to know... I'm here now, fully and completely.'

Molly felt tears pricking at her eyes. 'Oh, Andrew—'

'No, let me finish,' he said gently. 'This baby, our child... it's a new beginning, not just for us, but for the whole world. I want to be the father our child deserves, the husband you deserve. I want us to plan for this future together.'

As Andrew began to talk about his ideas, converting one of the spare rooms into a nursery, his hopes and dreams for their child, Molly felt a wave of love and relief wash over her. He had told her he was really happy about their unborn child but for so long, she had felt something was missing. She had carried the weight of her pregnancy almost alone, uncertain of how to bridge the gap that had been growing between them.

But now, as they sat in their small kitchen, making plans and sharing dreams, that gap seemed to close. The war had changed them both, had forced them to grow and adapt in ways they never could have imagined. Here, in this moment, Molly realised that it had also strengthened them. They had survived, together, and now they would build this new life, this family, together too.

As the sun began to set outside, casting a warm glow through the window, Molly and Andrew continued to talk and plan. The world outside was hoping to celebrate the end of one era and the beginning of another. And here, in this cosy kitchen, Molly and Andrew were doing the same, looking forward to a future bright with possibility, love, and the promise of new life.

Andrew's eyes shone with a mixture of excitement and nervousness as he spoke of their future. 'I've been thinking,' he said, reaching into his pocket, 'maybe we could start a little savings account for the baby. Put aside a bit each week. It's not much, but...'

He pulled out a small, cloth-bound book, a child's savings account book from the bank where he worked. Molly's heart swelled at the sight. It was such a small thing, but it represented so much hope, planning, a future they were building together.

'Oh, Andrew,' she breathed, taking the book in her hands. 'It's perfect.'

As they bent their heads together over the kitchen table, discussing how much they could afford to save each week, Molly felt a sense of normalcy she hadn't experienced in years. This was what she had dreamed of during those long, lonely evenings when Andrew was out working for the many veterans he wanted to help. It wasn't about grand gestures or heroic deeds, but the simple, profound intimacy of planning a life together.

'What do you think about names?' Andrew asked suddenly, a shy smile playing on his lips. 'I know it's a bit early to talk about it, but...'

Molly laughed, a sound of pure joy that seemed to brighten the entire kitchen. 'I've been thinking about names for months. What do you think about Elizabeth for a girl? After my grand-mother and your sister?'

Andrew nodded vigorously. 'That's a wonderful idea. And if it's a boy?'

A flush of colour filled Molly's cheeks. 'I was toying with Andrew, the determined man who wouldn't give up on me at the beginning when I thought you were the boss man flirting with the hired help.'

Andrew chuckled. 'Yes, you did make it hard for me, but it was all worth it.' He reached out and tenderly stroked her cheek. 'Remember, you never gave up on me either. I love you, Mrs Greenwood.' He leaned in and gently kissed her lips.

* * *

Alice sat on a bench in the small park near her home, her mind whirling with the aftermath of her confrontation with her father. The truth she had uncovered in Norwich, the confession she had wrung from him – it all seemed too enormous to process.

She had walked there with Mrs Headley and Arthur in the hope the distraction would clear her head; he had giggled as Alice had gently pushed him on a swing and run around the park chasing him. Guilt rushed through her, he hadn't had much of her time recently, she realised it wasn't fair on her children, she had to move forward and make some decisions. Mrs Headley had finally taken a tired Arthur home while Alice stayed to try to straighten out her confused thoughts. She watched as children played on the nearby swings, their laughter a stark contrast to the turmoil in her heart. Somewhere out there, she had a half-brother who didn't even know she existed. A boy named Peter, who shared her blood but not her life.

'Alice?' A familiar voice broke through her reverie. She looked up to see Victoria approaching, concern etched on her face. 'Your mother said I might find you here. Is everything all right?'

Alice let out a bitter laugh. 'All right? No, I don't think anything is all right any more.'

Victoria sat beside her, waiting patiently for Alice to continue.

'I can't sleep for worrying about how my mother is going to cope with the news of my father's double life.' She took a deep breath. 'The worst part is, I don't know what to do now. Do I tell my mother? Do I try to contact Peter? Or do I just... pretend I never found out, let things go on as they have been?'

Victoria was quiet for a moment, considering. 'I can't tell you what the right thing to do is,' she said finally. 'But I can tell you this: secrets have a way of coming out eventually. And when they do, they often cause more pain than if the truth had been told from the start.'

Alice knew her friend was right, but the thought of causing such pain to her mother, of upending Peter's world, made her feel physically ill. 'How did it come to this?' she whispered. 'How could my father live this lie for so long?'

Victoria took her hand, squeezing it gently. 'People do complicated things for what they think are good reasons. It doesn't make it right, but... well, the world isn't as black and white as we might wish it to be.'

As they sat there, watching the children play as the evening drew in, Alice felt a resolve begin to form within her. The truth was out now, at least partially. She couldn't unknow what she had learned, couldn't go back to the blissful ignorance of before. The only way forward was through... through the pain, through the difficult conversations and hard choices that lay ahead.

'I have to tell my mother,' she said finally. 'And... and I think I need to meet Peter. He deserves to know the truth too.'

Victoria's lips tightened. 'Now you've spoken to his mother won't she tell him the truth? I mean, if I was in her position, I would rather my child heard the truth from me.'

Alice nodded. 'She said she would but to be honest I don't know who I can trust any more, and how long do I give her before I make contact again?'

Victoria nodded, a small, sad smile on her face. 'I'm sorry, I don't have the answers. It's all about what you can live with, but it won't be easy for any of you. I want you to know you won't be alone. Whatever happens, whatever you decide to do, Molly and I will be right here with you.' Victoria frowned. 'Are you going to tell your mother?'

'That's his job not mine. I don't think he has so I might have to tell her, but I was hoping he would do it.'

Victoria reached out and squeezed Alice's arm. 'That wouldn't surprise me. Sometimes I think men are emotionally weaker than women. They don't always like facing the truth.' She paused. 'Be gentle with her. It might not come as a shock to her. They say women know when something isn't right in their marriage, although that may not be the case here, but if it is, don't judge her because she'll have her reasons for keeping the secret – that is, if she knows.'

Alice nodded. 'I'll do my best.'

As they stood to leave, Alice felt a strange mix of dread and determination. The war might be over, but this battle – the battle for truth, for understanding, for a new kind of family – was just beginning. But with friends like Victoria by her side, Alice felt ready to face whatever lay ahead.

14

———

The bell above Foyles' door chimed incessantly as customers streamed in and out, their voices a jumble of excitement and disbelief. Alice, stood behind the counter, could barely keep up with the constant chatter of the men coming home and the possibility of the war being over. Not many customers seemed to actually want to buy anything; they just wanted to share their excitement of life possibly returning to normal.

'Is it true?' an elderly gentleman asked breathlessly as Alice wrote out his payment slip. 'I haven't had a chance to buy a newspaper yet. Are the Germans really surrendering?'

Alice offered a cautious smile. 'I haven't seen a newspaper yet but there are certainly strong rumours to that effect, sir. But as of now, I don't think anything's been officially confirmed.'

The man rushed to the payment kiosk before coming back to collect his book. 'I need to find a newspaper boy.' He hurried out, clutching his book under his arm.

Molly sidled up to Alice, her eyes wide. 'Have you ever seen anything like this?' she whispered. 'It's as if the whole of London's gone mad with hope.'

Alice shook her head, stealing a glance at the clock. It was barely noon, and already the shop felt like it had been open for days. The air buzzed with a mix of hope and anxiety.

Victoria emerged from the back room, her arms laden with copies of the day's newspapers. 'I've got these from the newspaper seller along the street – I've been asked so many times if we have any. Write them on a purchase note if anyone wants one.' She shuffled them out of her arms and onto the counter. 'Mr Leadbetter's just got off the phone with his contact at the War Office,' she said in a low voice. 'They wouldn't confirm anything officially, but he said to be prepared for a "significant announcement" in the coming days.'

The three friends exchanged excited looks of optimism. They'd lived with the reality of war for so long, the prospect of peace seemed almost unreal.

'Do you think it's really happening?' Molly asked, her hand unconsciously moving to her swollen belly. 'Could the war really be ending?'

Before either of her friends could answer, a commotion outside drew their attention. Through the shop window, they could see a group gathering around a man shouting, 'It's nearly over; it's nearly over.' Everyone around him cheered and chorused. 'It's nearly over.'

As the growing excitement continued around them, the three friends stood in their small circle, each lost in thought. The war had shaped their lives in countless ways, had changed them in ways they were still discovering. Now, with peace almost tangible, they would face a new challenge: learning to live in a world without war.

The bell above the door chimed again, and they broke apart, ready to face whatever this new chapter might bring. The war might be close to ending, but their story, and the stories of all those whose lives had been touched by the conflict, was far from over.

As the day wore on, the atmosphere in Foyles shifted from jubilant celebration to disappointment that there had been no news. Customers lingered, sharing stories and memories, their voices a mixture of laughter and tears. Alice found herself listening to tales of loved ones on the front, of years spent in anxious waiting, of hopes for reunions long deferred.

Mr Leadbetter emerged from his office, his eyes misty. 'In all my years,' he said, his voice trembling, 'I never thought I'd see a day like this. To think, after all this time... the anticipation of peace is so great.'

Victoria squeezed his arm gently. 'It's thanks to you we're here to see it, sir. You kept Foyles going through it all.'

As the afternoon light began to fade, casting long shadows through the shop windows, Alice found herself in a quiet corner, surrounded by shelves of worn second-hand books. She ran her fingers along the spines, thinking of the stories they could tell, and wondering how many had been at the front with their previous owners.

'What do you think happens now?' Molly asked, joining her. 'To all of us, I mean. We've been living with this war for so long...'

Alice shook her head, at a loss for words. 'I don't know. It's like... like we've been holding our breath for years, and soon we'll be able to finally breathe. But what comes after that?'

Victoria joined them, her face thoughtful. 'We rebuild, I suppose. We heal. We try to make sense of it all.'

'Whatever comes next,' Alice said, looking at her friends, 'we'll do it together. Just like we always have.'

Molly nodded. 'Like the three musketeers.'

They all smiled before chiming together, 'All for one and one for all,' and hugging each other tightly.

As the last customers left and they began to close up the shop, Alice couldn't shake the feeling that they were standing on the threshold of a new world. The war had changed everything, had reshaped society in ways they were only just beginning to understand. But here, in this beloved bookshop, surrounded by the wisdom and stories of countless generations, she felt ready to face whatever the future might bring.

The bell chimed one last time as they locked the door, stepping out into a London already alive with hope. Tomorrow would bring new challenges, new questions, new fears and dreams but above all else the possibility of peace would be realised.

* * *

The atmosphere in Foyles was electric. Customers crowded around the newspaper stand outside, their voices a chorus of anticipation and disbelief as they pored over the latest headlines. The usual library-like hush had once again given way to an urgent buzz of conversation, punctuated by the rustle of newspaper pages and exclamations of hope and growing impatience. Alice, Victoria, and Molly exchanged glances as they tried to keep up with the surge in demand for news and books.

The dull, grey morning light streamed through the shop windows, catching the dust stirred up by the unusual activity. Even the familiar smell of books and polish seemed charged with anticipation. A group of office workers in their neat suits huddled around a shared copy of the *Daily Telegraph*, while two women in nursing uniforms clutched each other's hands as they read.

'Is it true?' an elderly gentleman asked breathlessly, clutching a copy of *The Times*. His hands trembled slightly, and Alice noticed he wore a veteran's pin from the Boer War on his lapel. 'Are the Germans really surrendering?'

Alice offered a cautious smile, remembering too many false hopes over the years. 'The rumours certainly seem to be growing stronger, sir, but as of now, there's still been no official confirmation.' She watched as he nodded and hurried away, no doubt to share the news with others.

As she arranged a fresh stack of newspapers Victoria had got from the newspaper boy on the corner, Alice caught snippets of conversations around her, 'They say the kaiser's fled to Holland...' 'My boy at the front wrote that the Germans are exhausted...' 'Could it really be over?'

Molly sidled up to Alice, her eyes wide with excitement. Could she possibly hope that her baby will be born into peace and not war? 'I've never seen anything like this,' she whispered. 'It's as if the whole of London's holding its breath.'

Victoria nodded, adjusting a display of books. 'I heard someone say they knew someone who knew someone at the War Office and they said there'd been increased activity. They're preparing for... something.' She didn't mention that Ted had been particularly agitated lately. She didn't want everyone worrying about her and Ted.

A young boy in a telegram messenger's uniform burst through the door, making the bell jangle discordantly. He headed straight for Mr Leadbetter's office, and the shop fell momentarily silent, everyone aware that such messages could still bring devastating news.

Minutes later, Mr Leadbetter emerged from his office, his face a mix of excitement and apprehension. 'Everyone, a word if you please.'

The three friends gathered around him, conscious of the curious glances from customers. Even Albert had crept up from the basement, sensing the importance of the moment.

'I've just had word from a reliable source,' Mr Leadbetter said in a low voice, his usual formality cracking slightly with emotion. 'It seems the armistice negotiations are in their final stages. We could have an official announcement within days.'

A collective gasp went through the small group. They'd lived with the reality of war for so long: the casualty lists, the rationing, the blackout curtains, the constant fear for loved ones, that the prospect of peace seemed almost unreal. Alice thought of her brother who died in France, Victoria of Ted's ongoing struggles, Molly of her unborn child who might now know a world without war.

'What should we do?' Alice asked, always practical, even as her heart raced with possibilities.

Mr Leadbetter's eyes twinkled. 'We prepare, my dear. If, when, the announcement comes, people will want to celebrate, to understand, to remember. We need to be ready with appropriate books and materials.' He paused, emotions threatening to overcome his usual reserve. 'Foyles has been more than a bookshop during this war; we've been a source of information, of comfort, of connection. We must be ready to serve that role in peace as well.'

They began to plan, discussing which titles to prominently display, considering special orders, and even talking about a possible commemoration event. Alice suggested creating a display of peace treaties throughout history. Victoria thought about poetry collections that spoke of hope and renewal, knowing Ted could help with that. Molly proposed a section dedicated to rebuilding and new beginnings.

As they worked, more customers streamed in. A mother with three children asked for books about France. 'Their father's been stationed there so long, they need to understand where he's been.' A young woman in mourning black requested poetry about healing. An elderly professor wanted histories of previous peace negotiations.

Alice felt a surge of emotion as she helped each one. The war had shaped their lives in countless ways, had changed them all. Some changes were visible: Ted's trauma, the empty chairs at family tables, the women who had found new independence in war work. Others were subtle: the way they all flinched at sudden noises, the careful way they opened telegrams, the strange mix of guilt and relief when someone else's loved one died instead of their own.

Now, standing on the precipice of peace, she realised that their work at Foyles was more than just selling books. They were helping people make sense of history as it unfolded, providing words for experiences too overwhelming to process alone. Each book was a tool for understanding, for remembering, for distracting, and for hoping.

The bell above the door chimed again, and they broke apart to attend to customers. But as Alice moved through the shop, recommending titles and discussing the latest news, she felt a sense of anticipation building. Change was coming again, not the violent rupture of war this time, but the challenging transition to peace.

She caught sight of her reflection in the shop window, older now than when the war began, more serious perhaps, but stronger too. Beyond her reflection, she could see people hurrying along the street outside, many carrying newspapers, all wearing expressions of cautious hope. The world was changing once again.

Victoria was already making lists of books that returning soldiers might need, not just celebrations of victory, but works on finding civilian work, on healing from trauma, on rebuilding lives. Molly was quietly adding books about child-rearing to their orders, thinking ahead to the world her child would inherit. And Mr Leadbetter stood in the centre of his shop, watching his staff and customers with proud satisfaction, knowing that Foyles would continue to be a lighthouse in changing times.

As the afternoon light began to fade, the excitement showed no signs of diminishing. If anything, the shop grew more crowded as people stopped in on their way home from work, eager for the latest news. Alice found herself reaching for her fob watch, checking the time again and again, wondering if each moment might be the one when the official announcement came.

The war had begun with the chiming of church bells, which then turned to warning signals. Soon, perhaps very soon, those same bells would ring for peace. And here in Foyles, among the books that had helped them all survive and understand these dark years, they would be ready to help London turn the page to a new chapter.

* * *

The morning of 11 November dawned grey and misty, but there was an undercurrent of anticipation in the air as Alice made her way to Foyles. The rumours that had been swirling for days had reached a fever pitch, and everyone seemed to be holding their breath, waiting for news.

As she approached the bookshop, Alice saw a crowd gathering around a newsboy on the corner. Her heart began to race as she heard snatches of excited conversation.

'It's over!' someone shouted. 'The armistice has been signed!'

Alice broke into a run, bursting through the doors of Foyles to find Mr Leadbetter, Victoria, and Molly already there, gathered around a newspaper Ellen had brought in. They had done a late-night run to bring the latest news.

'...the armistice was signed at five o'clock this morning,' Mr Leadbetter announced, his voice crackling with emotion but unmistakably jubilant. 'Hostilities will cease on all fronts at eleven o'clock today. The war is over.'

For a moment, there was stunned silence. Then, as if a dam had burst, the silence was suddenly full of cheers, sobs, and exclamations filling the air. Mr Leadbetter pulled out a handkerchief and dabbed at his eyes. Victoria and Molly embraced, tears streaming down their faces.

Alice felt rooted to the spot, overwhelmed by a tidal wave of emotions. Joy, relief, disbelief, and a strange sort of grief for all that had been lost, for the innocence of the world before the war.

'Alice?' Victoria's voice broke through her thoughts. 'Are you all right?'

Alice nodded, suddenly aware of the tears on her own cheeks. 'Yes, I... I can hardly believe it. It's really over.'

Mr Leadbetter cleared his throat. 'Well, my dears, I think this calls for a celebration. But first...' He moved to the door, flipping the sign to 'Open' with a flourish. 'I have a feeling we're going to be very busy today.'

He was right. As news of the armistice spread, people flooded into the bookshop. Some were looking for newspapers that customers often left lying around, eager to understand the terms of the peace. Others sought out poetry or novels, looking for words to express the tumult of emotions they were feeling.

Victoria, in her new role as assistant manager, orchestrated the chaos with remarkable poise. She'd organised an impromptu reading corner where local authors and poets were sharing works both old and new, their words of hope and renewal resonating deeply with the emotional crowd.

Alice found herself engaging in a lively discussion with a group of university students about how the war would be remembered. 'It's our duty now to ensure that the sacrifices made are never forgotten, but also to look forward, to build a better world from the ashes of the old.'

Molly, her advanced pregnancy preventing her from moving too much, had set up court by the children's section. She was surrounded by a group of wide-eyed youngsters, reading them stories of far-off lands and grand adventures, planting seeds of imagination in minds too young to fully grasp the significance of the day's events.

Mr Leadbetter moved through the crowd, shaking hands, offering congratulations; his eyes were misty with emotion. He paused by the poetry section, picked up a volume of Rupert Brooke. 'So many bright young minds lost,' he murmured almost to himself. 'But their words, their spirit, will live on through these pages.'

As the afternoon wore on, someone produced a gramophone, and soon the strains of popular tunes filled the air. Couples began to dance between the bookshelves, their laughter and the rustle of pages creating a symphony of joy and relief.

In a quiet moment, Alice, Victoria, and Molly found themselves together near the back of the shop, watching the scene before them.

'Can you believe it?' Molly said softly, her hand resting on her swollen belly. 'After all this time, all we've been through... it's really over.'

Victoria nodded, her eyes shining. 'It feels like... like we can finally breathe again. Like the whole world is taking its first deep breath after years of holding it in.'

As evening fell and they finally closed the shop, the sounds of celebration could be heard from the streets outside. Pubs were overflowing, impromptu parades were forming, and everywhere people were embracing, laughing, crying.

The four of them – Mr Leadbetter, Alice, Victoria, and Molly – stood in the doorway of Foyles, looking out at the jubilant scene.

'Well, ladies,' Mr Leadbetter said softly, 'we've seen it through, from the darkest days to this moment of triumph. I couldn't be prouder of you all.'

As they locked up and prepared to join the celebrations, Alice felt a sense of profound gratitude. For her friends, for Foyles, for the books that had been a constant comfort through the long years of war.

15

Victoria stood before the assembled staff of Foyles, her heart pounding with a mixture of excitement and nerves. Mr Leadbetter stood beside her, a proud smile on his face as he addressed the group.

'As you all know, the past few years have brought unprecedented challenges to our beloved bookshop. We've weathered war, epidemic, and personal losses. But we've also shown remarkable resilience and adaptability. It's in that spirit of moving forward that I'm delighted to announce a change in our management structure.'

He gestured to Victoria. 'Mrs Marsden has shown exceptional dedication and leadership skills, particularly during the recent crises. As such, I've asked her to take on the role of assistant manager, with a view to increasing her responsibilities over time.'

A murmur of approval ran through the assembled staff. Victoria felt a blush creep up her cheeks as she stepped forward.

'Thank you, Mr Leadbetter, and thank you all for your support. I know change can be daunting, especially after everything we've been through. But I truly believe that together, we will not only restore Foyles to its former glory, before the war and the epidemic, but take it to new heights.'

As the meeting dispersed and the staff returned to their duties, Victoria found herself surrounded by well-wishers. Alice and Molly were among the first to congratulate her, their faces beaming with pride.

'Oh, Vic,' Molly exclaimed, pulling her into a hug. 'This is wonderful news! You'll be brilliant at it.'

Alice nodded in agreement. 'Absolutely, if anyone can help guide Foyles into this new era, it's you.'

Victoria felt a surge of gratitude for her friends' unwavering support. 'Thank you both. I couldn't have done this without you, you know – your friendship and your encouragement... it's meant everything.'

As the day progressed, Victoria threw herself into her new role with enthusiasm. She found herself looking at the bookshop with fresh eyes, noting areas for improvement, considering new initiatives they could implement.

During a quiet moment, she found herself in the military history section, her fingers tracing the spines of books detailing the war they had just emerged from. Her thoughts turned to Ted, to his ongoing struggle to adjust to civilian life. In a way, she realised, they were both embarking on new chapters of their lives. Ted, learning to live with the scars of war, and she, stepping into a role she never would have imagined for herself before the war began.

The sound of the shop bell jolted her from her reverie. Straightening her shoulders, Victoria moved to assist the new customer, a sense of purpose infusing her steps.

As she recommended titles to the customer, her mind was already racing with ideas for the future of Foyles. Book clubs for returning soldiers, perhaps, or a section dedicated to the emerging 'new woman' of post-war society. The possibilities seemed endless, and Victoria felt genuinely enthusiastic about the future.

* * *

Alice found her father in his study, where he sat in his leather armchair by the window, reading the evening paper. The familiar scene, one she'd witnessed countless times throughout her childhood, now seemed like a cruel mockery of domestic tranquillity. She closed the door behind her with deliberate care.

'Father,' she said, her voice steadier than she felt. 'Have you told Mother about your other life in Norwich yet?'

Luke Taylor lowered his newspaper slowly, his face carefully composed, though Alice noticed his hands tighten on the paper's edges. 'Alice, I—'

'It's been two weeks since I last spoke to you about Margaret and Peter,' she pressed on. 'Two more weeks of lies, of watching Mother go about her day, trusting you, loving you, while you continue this... this deception.'

Her father set the newspaper aside, running a hand through his greying hair, a gesture so familiar it made Alice's heart ache. She'd watched Peter make the same movement in Norwich.

'It's not that simple, Alice,' he said finally. 'Your mother... she's been through so much already, with the war, with everything else. I need to find the right moment, the right way to—'

'To tell her you've been living a double life for sixteen or seventeen years?' Alice cut in, her voice sharp. 'That you have another family? Another child? Tell me, Father, when exactly is the right moment for that?'

Luke stood, moving to his desk as if the physical distance

might help him manage this conversation. 'You don't understand the complexity of the situation. Margaret and I—'

'Don't.' Alice's voice cracked. 'Don't you dare try to justify this. I've met them, remember? I've seen the life you've built there.'

'I love that boy,' Luke said quietly. 'Just as I love you.'

'And Mother? Do you love her too? Or has that been another lie?'

'Of course I love your mother!' Luke's composure finally cracked. 'Everything I've done, all these years of... of managing this situation, it's been to protect her, to protect all of you.'

Alice laughed bitterly. 'Protect us? By living a lie? By letting Peter believe his father is a widower? By watching Mother wait faithfully for your return from your "business trips" while you play house with another family?'

'Alice, I won't allow you to talk to me like that. I am your father and deserve some respect, so please—'

'No, respect is earned – it's not a right.' She stepped closer to his desk, planting her hands firmly on its surface. 'I've given you two weeks to do the right thing. Two weeks to be the honourable man I always thought you were. But you're a coward, Father.'

Luke flinched at the word. 'I would expect that kind of talk from Lily because she has no understanding of how things can be but—'

'The war has taught us all about courage, about facing hard truths. Well, here's a truth for you: if you don't tell Mother about Margaret and Peter by the end of this week, I will.'

'You wouldn't,' Luke said, but there was uncertainty in his voice.

'Wouldn't I? I'm not the dutiful little girl you can pat on the head any more, Father. I've seen too much, learned too much. Mother deserves the truth, and Peter... Peter deserves to know who he really is.'

'And what about Margaret?' Luke demanded. 'Have you thought about what this will do to her and to Peter?'

'I have. Every day since I discovered your secret, I've thought about nothing else. But the alternative is to continue with this… this lie, watching Mother live in ignorance, knowing Peter has siblings he doesn't even know exist…' Alice shook her head. 'I won't do it. I won't be part of your deception any longer.'

Luke sank into his desk chair, suddenly looking old and tired. 'Alice, please, just give me more time. Let me find a way to—'

'You've had at least sixteen years,' Alice cut in, her voice gentler now but no less firm. 'Time's up, Father – tell her, or I will.'

She turned to leave but paused at the door. 'You know what the worst part is? When I was in Norwich, I remembered the father from my childhood. The man who read me poetry, who taught me to love books, who I thought was the most honest, honourable person I knew.' She looked back at him, tears finally spilling onto her cheeks. 'Was any of it real? Or was it all just another performance?'

Luke stood, reaching out to her. 'Alice, everything with you, and your mother was real. It is real.'

'Then prove it,' she said softly. 'Tell her the truth. Be the father I thought you were.'

With that, she left the study, closing the door quietly behind her. She could hear her mother humming in the kitchen downstairs, preparing dinner as she did every evening, unaware that her world was about to change forever.

Alice leaned against the wall, letting out a shaky breath. She'd done it, laid down the ultimatum she'd been rehearsing for days. Now all she could do was wait, and hope that somewhere inside her father, there was still the honourable man she'd once believed him to be.

The sound of her father's heavy sigh carried through the door, followed by the creak of his chair as he sat back down. Alice pushed herself away from the wall and headed to her room. She had letters to write, one to Margaret, warning her of what was coming, and one to Victoria and Molly, asking them to be ready for whatever fallout might come.

The war had taught them all about courage, about standing up for what was right even when it hurt. Now it was her father's turn to learn that lesson.

16

The interior of Foyles had been transformed around noon on armistice day. Gone were the sombre displays of war literature and maps of the front lines. In their place, festive bunting in the colours of the Allied nations draped the bookshelves, and a hastily made banner proclaiming 'Peace at Last!' hung above the main counter. No one had the heart to take it all down now the celebrations were over.

Mr Leadbetter wanted to leave it up to remind everyone to hold on to the good feeling and the joy they had all felt when they found out the war was over.

Alice smiled as she remembered the impromptu celebration, and it seemed all of London had decided to join. The shop had been packed with a jubilant crowd – regular customers, soldiers on leave, and passers-by drawn in by the festive atmosphere. As she thought about the celebrations, she had felt the weight of the past four years lifting, replaced by a cautious hope for the future. The war had changed them all, had changed the world, but here in this beloved bookshop, surrounded by the accumulated knowledge and imagination of countless authors, they felt ready to turn the page and begin a new chapter.

Victoria wandered over to Alice. 'You look deep in thought.'

Alice leaned against the counter. 'It's strange,' she said softly. 'I keep thinking about that summer day in 1914 when we first heard about the assassination in Sarajevo. We had no idea then, did we? No idea how our lives would change.'

Victoria nodded, her eyes distant. 'I remember thinking it would all be over by Christmas. That Stephen, Charles and Robert would soon be home, and we'd all get married and have children. Life would go on as it always had.' She gave a rueful laugh. 'How naive we were.'

Molly chuckled. 'I need to stop coming to Foyles every day as if I still work here; otherwise I'll end up having this baby in one if the aisles.' She shifted in her chair, her hand resting on her rounded belly. 'We've all changed so much,' she mused. 'The girls we were then... I wonder if we'd even recognise them now.'

A thoughtful silence fell over the group as each woman reflected on her journey through the war years.

Alice thought about the shy, bookish girl she'd been, content to live life through the pages of novels. The war had forced her out of her shell, had shown her the strength she possessed. She'd faced looking after injured soldiers on Victoria Train Station before putting them in an ambulance and driving them to hospital. There was also the discovering of family secrets, taking on new responsibilities at the shop, and learning the true meaning of friendship. The Alice of 1914 could never have imagined standing up to her father, uncovering family secrets, or finding the courage to reach out to an unknown brother.

Victoria's mind turned to the societal expectations she'd once taken for granted. She'd entered the war years anticipating a life as a traditional wife and mother, admittedly thinking it wouldn't be with Ted. Now, she found herself in a management position at Foyles, her ambitions awakened. She thought of how finding Ted in hospital had scared her, but she knew she wasn't going to give up on him without a fight this time. They had challenges to face and overcome together. Their love had been tested by war, by his struggles with shell shock, but it had emerged stronger, more equal. The Victoria who had lost her mother and father was no longer around; she was stronger than she ever thought she could be.

* * *

Alice was brushing her hair before bed when Lily burst into her bedroom, not bothering to knock. Alice raised her eyebrows. 'Have you not heard of knocking? It's lucky Freddie's on nights.'

Lily frowned. 'I obviously knew Freddie was at work.'

Their mother had already retired for the evening, and their father was, as usual, in his study. Lily closed the door with barely controlled force and leaned against it, her eyes bright with barely suppressed anger.

'Well?' she demanded in a fierce whisper. 'Has he told her yet? Or is he still playing the devoted husband while his other family waits patiently in Norwich?'

Alice set down her hairbrush with a sigh. 'Lily, please lower your voice.'

'Why should I?' Lily crossed the room to sit on Alice's bed, her movements sharp with frustration.

Alice sighed. 'Now the war is over, and the threat of being bombed in the middle of the night has gone, the children are back sleeping in their bedroom next door. I could do without you waking them up, it's bad enough I worry about Freddie's nightmares doing it but so far, they've slept through them. Let alone mother coming in wondering what we're arguing about.'

'Sorry,' Lily whispered. 'But it's not as if we're the ones with something to hide. Though I suppose we are now, aren't we? Keeping his dirty secret for him.'

'I've given him an ultimatum,' Alice said, turning to face her sister. 'He has until the end of the week to tell Mother himself, or I will.'

'The end of the week?' Lily's voice rose again before she caught herself. 'Why are we giving him any time at all? Mother deserves to know now, today, this minute.'

'It should come from him,' Alice insisted, though she couldn't help but notice how tired she sounded. 'He's the one who needs to face what he's done.'

'What he's done,' Lily repeated with a bitter laugh. 'You make it sound so simple. As if he just made a mistake, like forgetting an anniversary or missing dinner. He has another family, Alice. A whole other life, a son who thinks his father is a widower. It's... it's monstrous.'

Alice moved to sit beside her sister on the bed. 'I know, Lily. Believe me, I know. I'm the one who went to Norwich, remember? I'm the one who saw them.'

Lily pressed her hands to her ears. 'I know but I can't bear how he's created this whole other perfect little family while we...' She dropped her hands, tears spilling onto her cheeks. 'While we've been here, thinking we were enough for him.'

Alice pulled her sister into a hug, feeling Lily's shoulders shake with suppressed sobs. 'We were enough,' she whispered fiercely. 'We are enough. Father's choices don't reflect on us.'

'But they do,' Lily pulled back, wiping angrily at her tears. 'Every memory I have of him now is tainted. Every time he missed something important because of a "business trip", every time he spoke about honesty and integrity... it was all lies.'

'Not all of it,' Alice said, though she wasn't sure if she was trying to convince Lily or herself. 'The love was real, at least.'

'Was it?' Lily stood up, pacing around the small room. 'How can you love someone and lie to them for sixteen years? How can you claim to love your children while denying them knowledge of each other?'

'It's complicated—'

'No!' Lily whirled to face her. 'That's what he wants us to believe, but it's not complicated at all. He made choices – selfish, cruel choices. And now Mother is in bed no doubt planning his favourite meal for tomorrow, completely unaware that her whole marriage is a lie.'

'Lily.' Alice stood, catching her sister's hands. 'I understand. I feel the same anger, the same betrayal. But rushing in and blurting out the truth won't help anyone.'

'It would help Mother,' Lily insisted. 'She could stop living a lie.'

'And then what? Have you thought about what comes next? Where she'll go? What she'll do? We need to be prepared to support her when the truth comes out.'

Lily pulled her hands away. 'You're starting to sound like him, making excuses, talking about protecting people...'

'I am nothing like him.' Alice's voice was sharp. 'I'm trying to handle this in a way that causes the least amount of damage to everyone involved, including Peter and his mother.'

'Peter and his mother,' Lily repeated mockingly. 'Listen to yourself! Why should we care about protecting them?'

'Because they're victims in this too,' Alice said quietly. 'Margaret didn't know Father was married when she fell in love with him. And Peter... Peter is as innocent in all this as we are.'

Lily sank back onto the bed, the fight seeming to drain out of her. 'I hate this,' she whispered. 'I hate what he's done to us, to Mother, to our family.'

'I know,' Alice sat beside her again. 'But we have to be better than him. We have to think about more than just our own hurt and anger.'

They sat in silence for a moment, listening to the familiar sounds of their father moving about in his study below.

'The end of the week?' Lily asked finally.

Alice nodded. 'If he hasn't told her by then, we'll do it together. Agreed?'

Lily took a shaky breath. 'Agreed. But Alice—'

'Yes?'

'What if... what if Mother already knows? What if she's suspected all along, like we did?'

Alice had considered this possibility more times than she could count. 'Then we'll support her in any way we can.'

Lily leaned her head on her sister's shoulder, a gesture reminiscent of their childhood. 'Remember when we were little, and Father used to say we could face anything as long as we stood together as a family?'

'Another lie,' Alice said softly.

'No.' Lily took her hand. 'He just didn't realise he wasn't part of the "we" any more.'

The sisters sat together in the growing darkness, each lost in their own thoughts about the days ahead. Outside their window, London continued its evening routines, unaware that in this quiet bedroom, two sisters were preparing for a storm that would change their family forever.

'Have you discussed it with Freddie?'

Alice took a deep breath. 'No, at first I wanted to be sure of the facts. I know that's a conversation I need to have, but it's not one

I'm looking forward to. I suppose, thinking about it, I'm carrying our father's shame, so I keep putting it off. When I think about how he interrogated Freddie when he asked for my hand in marriage, and all that time he had another life we knew nothing about. Remembering how he told you off for bringing shame on the family when the police brought you home after the suffragette meeting and me for having one of their leaflets in my pocket. The lies and the shame run deep, but I'm hoping Freddie will ask if we're all right, and if we are then he won't worry any more than that; however, it's all unknown and it doesn't stop the shame of what we have become.'

'Whatever happens,' Lily said finally, 'we stick together, right?'

Alice squeezed her hand. 'Always.'

They both knew there would be more arguments in the days ahead, more clashes between Lily's fierce desire for immediate justice and Alice's more measured approach. But in this moment, they were united in their love for their mother and their determination to right their father's wrongs, whatever the cost.

* * *

The church hall was dimly lit by the late afternoon sun filtering through stained-glass windows, casting coloured shadows across the worn wooden floor. Molly and Andrew sat in the back row of hastily arranged chairs, his hand gripping hers tightly enough to hurt, though she wouldn't dream of mentioning it. Around them, other couples and individuals filtered in, some speaking in hushed tones, others maintaining a tense silence.

Molly could feel Andrew's tension mounting as more people arrived. His breathing had become shallow, and she noticed the slight tremor in his right leg, signs she had learned to recognise since his recovery from the munitions factory explosion. She ran her thumb soothingly over his knuckles, remembering how long it had taken to persuade him to come here.

'We can still leave,' she whispered, though she prayed he wouldn't take her up on the offer. 'No one would think any less of you.'

Andrew shook his head, his jaw set with determination. 'No, we need to do this, for us, and for the baby.' His free hand moved briefly toward Molly's growing bump before dropping away. 'I need to learn how to... how to be present again. How to be the father our child deserves.'

Before Molly could respond, the creaking front door echoed around the hall. She peered over and saw Ted slip in and sit in the back row away from everyone else. She moved to tell Andrew just as a tall man in his forties stepped to the front of the hall. Dr Harrison, she presumed, the specialist recommended by Ted. He looked around mid-forties and had kind eyes; he seemed a steady presence and appeared to calm the restless energy in the room.

'Welcome, everyone,' he began, his voice warm and measured. 'I'm glad to see so many new faces here today. This group is a safe space for veterans and their loved ones to share experiences, fears, and hopes as we all learn to adjust to life after fighting this dreadful war.'

Molly felt Andrew's grip on her hand ease slightly. She glanced around the room, taking in the others present. A young man with visible burn scars sat alone, his cap pulled low over his eyes. An elderly couple supported a son who couldn't stop twitching. A woman about her own age, also visibly pregnant, sat beside a man who stared fixedly at the floor. The sight made Molly's throat tight. They were all fighting their own battles, all trying to find their way back to some semblance of normalcy.

'Would anyone like to begin?' Dr Harrison asked. 'Perhaps share what brought you here today?'

The silence stretched for several long moments. Then, to Molly's surprise, Andrew cleared his throat.

'I'll speak,' he said, his voice rough but clear. When Dr Harrison nodded encouragingly, Andrew continued, 'My name is Andrew. I served in France for two years before being injured in an explosion. I came home, worked at the munitions factory in Silvertown until...' He swallowed hard. 'Until that exploded too. Sometimes I feel like I'm still fighting, still waiting for the next explosion, the next disaster. My wife is expecting our first child, and I'm terrified that I'll... that I won't be the father I need to be.'

Molly blinked back tears as murmurs of understanding rippled through the group. She noticed several other veterans nodding, their faces reflecting the same fears, the same struggles.

'Thank you, Andrew,' Dr Harrison said. 'That fear you speak of, the waiting for the next disaster, it's something many of our veterans experience. Would anyone else like to share their experience with similar feelings?'

The pregnant woman raised her hand hesitantly. 'My husband, James... he can't handle loud noises. The other day, our neighbour's child dropped a pan in their kitchen, and James... he...' She trailed off, looking at her husband, who had finally lifted his gaze from the floor.

'I ducked under the table,' James finished, his voice barely audible. 'In front of everyone at our Sunday dinner. I couldn't help it. In my mind, I was back in the trenches, waiting for the shells to fall.'

More voices joined in, each story different yet somehow the same. The fear, the flashbacks, the struggle to reconcile the person they had been before the war with who they were now. Molly listened, her heart aching for all of them, but especially for Andrew, who had begun to relax slightly as he realised he wasn't alone in his struggles.

Dr Harrison listened to each story with careful attention, offering gentle suggestions and coping strategies. 'The first step,' he explained, 'is understanding that these reactions are normal responses to abnormal experiences. You're not weak, you're not failing, you're human beings who have endured more than any human should have to endure.'

As the session progressed, Molly noticed a subtle shift in the atmosphere. The tension began to ease as people shared their stories, their fears, their small victories. A veteran spoke of finally being able to walk through the market without panicking. A wife described how she had learned to recognise her husband's triggers and help him through difficult moments.

Andrew participated more than Molly had expected, asking questions, even offering his own suggestions when another veteran spoke of struggling with nightmares. It was a side of him she hadn't seen in months: engaged, helpful, almost like his old self.

Near the end of the session, Dr Harrison asked them to pair up with someone they hadn't spoken to before. 'Share one hope,' he instructed. 'One thing you're working toward, no matter how small it might seem.'

Andrew turned to the scarred young man who had been sitting alone. After a moment's hesitation, they began to talk quietly. Molly found herself paired with the other pregnant woman – Eileen, she learned.

'It helps, doesn't it?' Eileen said softly, glancing at their husbands. 'Knowing we're not alone in this?'

Molly nodded, her hand resting on her bump. 'I've been so worried about the baby,' she admitted. 'About bringing a child into this... situation, but seeing everyone here, working so hard to heal—'

'It gives you hope,' Eileen finished. 'That's my hope, by the way. That our child will know their father as the man he truly is, not the shadow the war left behind.'

As they prepared to leave, Molly noticed Ted slip outside. He hadn't shared his experiences, but maybe he wasn't ready for that right now. Dr Harrison approached each person, offering words of encouragement and information about the next meeting. When he reached Molly and Andrew, he smiled warmly.

'Thank you for talking today, Andrew. Will we see you next week?'

Andrew glanced at Molly, then nodded firmly. 'Yes, I think you will.'

Outside, the evening air was cool on their faces. Andrew stopped on the church steps, turning to face Molly. 'Thank you,' he said softly. 'For believing in me. For not giving up.'

Molly reached up to cup his cheek. 'Never,' she promised. 'We're in this together.'

As they walked home, hand in hand, Molly felt a flutter of movement from the baby. Despite everything, despite the long road still ahead, she felt something she hadn't felt in a long time: hope. They weren't alone in this journey. And maybe, just maybe, that would make all the difference.

17

Alice paced around the kitchen. The deadline she had set her father had passed. He had said nothing to her, neither had her mother. Freddie had gone to work and Alice had asked Mrs Headley to watch the children, which she always loved doing so she was happy to help. As Alice moved around the kitchen the photograph was burning a hole in her pocket as it waited to be set free. Her mother bustled about, preparing tea, oblivious to the turmoil raging within her daughter. Lily sat at the kitchen table, her fingers drumming an anxious rhythm on the worn wood. They had agreed to do this together, though Alice could see her younger sister's hands trembling slightly.

'Ma,' Alice began, her voice shakier than she'd like, 'I need to talk to you about something, about father.'

Her mother turned, a slight frown creasing her brow. 'What about your father, dear? Is everything all right?'

Lily's drumming stopped abruptly. The silence felt deafening.

Alice took a deep breath, then pulled out the photograph. 'I found this,' she said, placing it on the kitchen table. 'In Father's study.'

She watched as her mother's face went through a range of emotions, confusion, shock, and then, to Alice's surprise, a deep sadness tinged with resignation.

'Oh, Alice,' her mother sighed, sinking into a chair. 'I had hoped... I had hoped you'd never have to know about this.'

'You knew?' Lily burst out, her voice sharp with disbelief. 'All this time, you knew?'

Their mother reached across the table, trying to take Lily's hand, but Lily pulled away, standing so abruptly her chair scraped against the floor.

'How could you keep this from us?' Lily demanded. 'Let us go on thinking everything was perfect when all along—'

'Lily,' Alice warned softly, seeing the pain flash across their mother's face.

Their mother nodded, her eyes fixed on the photograph. 'Your father... he's not a bad man, Alice, Lily. But he's made mistakes. We both have.'

'Both?' Lily's voice cracked. 'What mistake did you make, Mother? Being too forgiving? Too understanding?'

As their mother began to speak, telling a story of a marriage strained by the pressures of work and societal expectations, of a moment of weakness that led to ongoing deception, Alice found herself watching both her sister and her mother. Lily paced the kitchen like a caged animal, while their mother seemed to age before their eyes, the weight of her long-held secret finally lifting but leaving visible marks in its wake.

'There's more,' Alice said softly, once her mother had fallen silent. She glanced at Lily, who had finally stopped pacing and stood gripping the back of her chair. 'I went to Norwich. I met her and her son. He looks just like father.'

Their mother closed her eyes, a single tear slipping down her cheek. 'I suspected as much. Your father doesn't know that I know about the child. I've never confronted him about it.'

'But why?' Lily exploded. 'How could you just live with this? Let him come and go as he pleased, playing father to another family while we...' Her voice broke, and Alice moved to put an arm around her sister's shaking shoulders.

Their mother reached out, taking both her daughters' hands in hers. 'Because, my dears, life is complicated. Love is complicated. Your father may have strayed, but he always came home to us. And I made a choice to forgive, to keep our family together.'

'It wasn't your choice to make alone,' Lily whispered fiercely. 'We deserved to know. That boy, our brother, he deserves to know.'

'Half-brother,' Alice corrected automatically, then wondered why it mattered.

Their mother's grip tightened on their hands. 'Perhaps you're right. Perhaps I was wrong to keep this secret, to let you believe in a perfect family that never existed. But I did what I thought was best at the time.'

'And now?' Alice asked gently. 'Now that we know?'

Their mother looked between her daughters, seeing not the little girls she had sought to protect, but the strong young women they had become. 'Now... now we decide together, as a family.'

'We're not a family,' Lily said bitterly. 'We're just pieces of one, scattered between London and Norwich.'

'Lily.' Their mother's voice was firm now. 'Whatever your father's choices, whatever my mistakes in handling them, we are a family. Different from what we thought, yes, but still bound together by love – complicated, imperfect love.'

Alice felt Lily sag slightly against her. 'I don't know how to forgive this,' her sister admitted.

'Neither do I,' Alice said. 'But maybe we don't have to figure it out all at once.'

Their mother stood, pulling both her daughters into an embrace. For a moment, they stood there in the kitchen, three women bound together by secrets and love and pain, each processing the truth in her own way.

The kettle whistled, startling them apart. Their mother wiped her eyes and moved to tend to it, her habitual actions a stark contrast to the life-altering conversation they'd just had.

'He'll be home soon,' she said quietly, her back to them as she prepared the tea.

Lily tensed. 'What do we do?'

Their mother turned, her face showing a strength Alice had never fully appreciated before. 'We have tea. We continue on. And tomorrow... Tomorrow, we begin the work of building something new from the truth we all now share.'

As they sat around the kitchen table, the photograph still lying between them like a challenge, Alice looked at her sister and mother. They were all changed by this knowledge. Lily's innocence shattered, their mother's mask of contentment cracked, her own understanding of love and forgiveness challenged. But they were together, and maybe that would be enough to face whatever came next.

* * *

The Taylor family dinner table, once a place of warmth and lively conversation, now sat shrouded in a tense silence. Alice, thankful her boys were tucked up in bed, pushed her food around her plate, stealing glances at her mother, who hadn't spoken more than a few words since the truth about her father's double life had come to light. Beside her, Lily sat rigid in her chair, her fork gripped so tightly her knuckles had turned white. Their brother Charles appeared to be oblivious to the atmosphere, although he did keep glancing at their mother. Alice noticed Freddie kept peering at everyone around the table, she wondered if his police intuition had kicked in, but he said nothing.

The only sounds were the gentle clink of cutlery and the ticking of the grandfather clock in the hall, the same clock that had marked so many happy family dinners, now counting down the seconds of this excruciating meal.

The clank of Charles letting his knife fall on to his dinner plate startled the girls. 'All right, I know I'm always the last to know what's going on because, despite going to war, I'm deemed to be the baby of the family – but even I can sense something is wrong, so what is it?'

Luke Taylor cleared his throat, the sound startlingly loud in the quiet room. 'Perhaps... perhaps we should discuss this,' he began hesitantly.

'Discuss what, Luke?' Sarah set down her fork with a clatter. 'How you've lied to us for years? How you have another family? Another child?'

The pain in her mother's voice made Alice wince. She had known the revelation would be difficult, but seeing the toll it was taking on her family was almost unbearable.

Charles stared open-mouthed at his mother and father. 'What?'

Freddie held his loaded fork mid-air for a moment before lowering it and looking straight at Alice, who didn't meet his gaze.

'I never meant to hurt anyone,' Luke said, his voice low. He stared at his dinner plate, unable to meet the eyes of his children. 'I thought... I thought I could keep the two worlds separate.'

'Separate?' Lily's voice cut through the air like a knife. 'Like we're some sort of experiment you could keep in different jars? How convenient for you, Father.'

'Lily,' Sarah warned softly, though there was no real reproach in her tone.

Alice couldn't hold back any longer. 'But they were never really separate, were they, Father? Not for you, and certainly not for Peter and his mother.'

At the mention of Peter's name, Sarah let out a small sob. Alice reached out, taking her mother's hand, while Lily pushed back from the table abruptly, her chair scraping against the floor.

Charles and Freddie stared at each other. Freddie lifted his hands and shrugged.

'How old is he?' Sarah asked suddenly, her voice barely above a whisper. 'Your... your son?'

Luke's face crumpled. 'Fifteen,' he admitted. 'He's fifteen.'

'Fifteen years,' Lily said, her voice shaking. 'Fifteen years of lies. Every birthday, every Christmas, every family dinner like this one, all of it a lie.'

'Not all of it,' Luke protested. 'My love for you, for all of you—'

'Don't you dare!' Lily shouted, tears streaming down her face. 'Don't you dare talk about love when you've been living a whole other life, loving a whole other family.'

'I'm so sorry, Mother,' Alice said, squeezing her mother's hand. 'I... I didn't want to cause you pain. But I couldn't keep living with this secret.'

Sarah squeezed Alice's hand back, her eyes filled with a mixture of hurt and gratitude. 'No, my dear, you did the right thing. The truth... the truth hurts but lies will poison everything they touch.'

Freddie frowned at Alice. 'Why didn't you tell me?'

Alice shook her head. 'There never seemed to be a good time plus you thought the idea of another family was ridiculous, remember?'

Freddie nodded. 'Sorry, I was clearly wrong about that.'

Lily spoke with suppressed anger. 'Yes Freddie, father clearly doesn't have the moral standing you thought he had.'

'Does he know about us?' Sarah asked, looking directly at her husband. 'This boy, Peter, does he know he has sisters and a brother?'

Luke shook his head, unable to meet her gaze. 'He thinks... he thinks I'm a widower.'

The silence that followed this revelation was deafening.

Lily let out a sound that was half-laugh, half-sob. 'So, you didn't just lie to us,' she said. 'You've lied to him too. Made him believe his father was a tragic figure instead of a... a...'

'Coward,' Alice finished quietly. 'That's what you are, Father. A coward who couldn't face the consequences of his choices.'

Luke looked up, hope flickering in his eyes. 'Can you... can you ever forgive me?'

The question hung in the air, heavy with years of deception and the weight of an uncertain future. Alice held her breath, waiting for her mother's response.

Sarah took a deep breath, her voice steady as she replied, 'I don't know, Luke. Forgiveness... forgiveness takes time, and then there's trust. I don't know if I can trust you any more, but I do know this: we can't go back to the way things were. If there's any hope for this family, we need to move forward with complete honesty.'

'And Peter?' Lily asked, finally sinking back into her chair. 'What about him? Doesn't he deserve the truth too?'

'He does,' Sarah said firmly. 'That boy, whatever the circumstances of his birth, he's innocent in all this. He deserves to know he has sisters and a brother, a... a whole other family.'

Luke blanched. 'Margaret, his mother, she won't want—'

'Margaret doesn't get to decide,' Alice cut in. 'Not any more, none of us do. The truth is out now, and we all have to deal with the consequences.'

As the conversation continued, painful, raw, but necessary, Alice felt a strange mix of sorrow and relief. The comfortable illusion of their perfect family was shattered, but in its place, something new was emerging. Something built on truth, as difficult as that truth might be.

'I've written to Peter,' Alice admitted finally, deciding not to say she hadn't posted the letter yet. 'I've not told him everything, just introduced myself, suggesting a connection through our mutual interest in books.'

Lily's head snapped up. 'You have? When were you going to tell me?'

'I was waiting for the right moment,' Alice said softly. 'Everything's been so raw...'

Sarah nodded slowly. 'Perhaps... perhaps that's the way forward. Slowly, carefully, building bridges instead of burning them.'

They all looked at Luke, who sat with his head bowed, the weight of his deceptions finally fully visible on his shoulders.

Charles shook his head before pushing his chair back and going to stand next to his mother. He rested his hands on her shoulders. 'When I asked what had happened... well, I certainly hadn't expected all of this.' He glared at his father. 'You are such a hypocrite. When I think of all the times you picked on me, bullied me, you know I grew up always thinking I wasn't good enough for you and then I find out you have this secret. You should be ashamed of yourself.'

'Whatever happens next,' Sarah said, her voice gaining strength, 'it happens on our terms now. No more lies, no more secrets.'

Later that night, as Alice lay in bed, she thought about Peter, about the letter she hadn't yet sent. Whatever happened next, she realised, their family would never be the same. But perhaps, just perhaps, it could become something stronger, more authentic, than it had ever been before.

Freddie placed his arm around his wife. 'I'm so sorry you didn't feel able to talk to me, I should have been there for you, we should have dealt with it together, and I should have listened to your concerns.'

Alice squeezed his arm. 'I can't pretend it hasn't been hard trying to decide what is the best thing to do and I did want to talk to you about it, I just didn't know how because you had been so adamant, I was wrong.'

'I'm truly sorry, I've thrown myself into work and helping others at the detriment of being there for you and my family. It won't happen again, I promise.'

In the room next door, she could hear Lily crying softly.

'It's done now, we can only hope we can get through it as a family.' Alice gave Freddie a kiss. 'I'm sorry but I need to go to Lily.'

Freddie nodded. 'I hope she's all right, she's not as tough as she makes out.'

Alice got up and went to her sister, slipping into bed beside her as they had done as children. They held each other, sharing their pain and their hope for what might come next.

The war had taught them all about surviving impossible situations, about rebuilding from ruins. Now they would have to apply those lessons to their own family, piecing together something new from the fragments of truth that had finally come to light.

* * *

The frost on the ground glistened on Charing Cross Road as the murky grey day began with Alice walking slowly to Foyles. She was deep in thought, reliving the conversation with her mother and Lily. It had been hard to hear that her mother already knew about Margaret. At the last moment, Alice managed to side-step a baker setting out his wares on his barrow. Glancing around, she noticed life was getting back to how it was before the war started. There were more people on the streets, vendors were out with their barrows, shouting to sell their wares. The aroma of freshly baked bread and hot soup wafted around, enticing customers to buy. As Alice walked along the perfume of cut flowers followed her.

As she approached the bookshop, she saw Mr Leadbetter pulling the rack of books outside. He beamed at her as she drew near.

'Good morning, Mrs Leybourne, isn't it a wonderful day?'

Alice couldn't help but smile back. Mr Leadbetter's cheerfulness was infectious. 'It is indeed, sir.'

As they entered the shop together, Alice was struck by how much lighter the atmosphere felt. The heavy cloud of fear that had hung over them all for so long had disappeared, and optimism was the order of the day.

Victoria arrived soon after, and the two friends walked with Mr Leadbetter to the back room to collect their cards to clock on.

'It's like waking from a long nightmare,' Alice murmured, voicing what they were all feeling.

Mr Leadbetter nodded solemnly. 'Indeed, it is, my dear. We've all been through so much – the war and the flu – but look at us now. Still standing, still moving forward.'

As the day progressed, Foyles was as busy as ever. People seemed no longer concerned about the flu. They were relaxed, lingering over books rather than rushing in and out as they had during the height of the epidemic.

Molly arrived at lunchtime, and during their lunch break the three friends sat in the small back room, sharing a pot of tea and reflecting on the changes they were seeing.

'It's strange just popping in to have lunch with you both,' Molly said, absently rubbing her belly. 'For so long, it felt like the world was ending. The war, then the flu... But now, with the war over and the epidemic fading, it's like... like the world is beginning again.'

Victoria nodded, her eyes distant. 'I know what you mean. Ted said something similar the other day. He said it feels like he's learning how to live again, not just survive.'

Molly wondered whether to tell Victoria she had seen Ted at the church hall meeting, but would she question her on the things he might have talked about or heard? Molly decided against it, after all she didn't know how much detail he told Victoria, and she didn't want to be put in an awkward position. If Ted wasn't ready for her to know everything, she couldn't break his trust by telling her.

Alice listened to her friends, a mix of emotions swirling within her. The lessening of the flu epidemic was undoubtedly good news. The weight was lifted from all their shoulders. But it also meant that she could no longer put off dealing with her family situation. The crisis that had consumed everyone's attention was passing, and the personal struggles she had pushed aside were now demanding to be addressed.

'Alice?' Molly's voice broke through her thoughts. 'You've gone quiet. Is everything all right?'

Alice managed a small smile. 'Yes, just... Thinking about what comes next, I suppose, for all of us.'

Victoria studied Alice for a moment. 'Did you talk to your mother about Norwich?'

Alice tightened her lips. 'Yes, my father didn't have the courage to come clean but as it turned out my mother had already guessed about his other life, although she didn't know about the son.' She shook her head. 'It was a hard conversation round the dinner table, which Charles accidentally started, but at least it's all out in the open now. Even Freddie knows now, he was shocked, but it wasn't planned to discuss it at dinner, and we've talked about it since. If I'm honest I feel worn out with it all.'

Molly nodded. 'As hard as it was, you did the right thing.'

Alice closed her eyes for a moment. 'I know, but the lies and the shame don't seem to want to leave my mind.'

Victoria leaned forward. 'That will take time. Don't be hard on yourself. You've faced something you never thought you would have to do.'

Alice smiled. 'Thank you, I'm glad it's out but the healing and the forgiveness need to begin and that's not so easy.'

Victoria stood up. 'Nothing worthwhile ever seems to be easy, but remember we are always here if you want to talk, rant, or cry.'

Alice laughed. 'Thank you and the same goes for you two.'

Victoria nudged Molly. 'Well, it's lovely seeing you look so well but some of us have to get back to work. Don't feel you have to rush off, though.'

Molly chuckled. 'Thanks, but I've got to make a move. It takes me ages to waddle home these days.'

As they returned to the shop floor, Alice found herself looking at her friends with a new appreciation.

The bell above the door chimed as a customer entered, and Alice moved to assist them, pushing her worries aside for the moment. There would be time to deal with her family issues. For now, she would focus on this moment, on the simple joy of helping a reader find the perfect book, on the comfort of routine in a world that was slowly but surely returning to normal.

As she recommended titles and discussed favourite authors with the customer, Alice felt a spark of hope ignite within her. The world was healing, changing, moving forward, and so, she realised, must she.

18

Victoria stood on a small stepladder, carefully hanging a banner across the front window of Foyles. 'Books for a New Era' it proclaimed in bold letters. Around her, the bustle of preparation filled the air as staff members arranged displays and set up chairs for the evening's event.

'A little higher on the left, Victoria,' Alice called from outside, squinting up at the banner as she pulled at the collar of her thick winter coat.

Victoria adjusted it, then climbed down, surveying their work with satisfaction. 'What do you think?' she asked, turning to Mr Leadbetter who had just emerged from his office.

The old bookseller's eyes crinkled with a smile. 'It's perfect, Mrs Marsden. This event of yours... it's exactly what we need right now.'

Victoria felt a flush of pride. When she'd first proposed the idea of an evening of readings and discussions focused on hope, renewal, and moving forward after the war she'd been unsure how it would be received. But Mr Leadbetter had embraced the concept wholeheartedly, and the response from authors and the community had been overwhelming.

As evening approached, Victoria found herself growing nervous. This was her first major initiative in her new role as assistant manager, and she wanted everything to be perfect.

Molly waddled over. 'Stop fretting,' she said softly, squeezing Victoria's arm. 'It's going to be wonderful.'

The bell above the door chimed as the first guests began to arrive. Victoria took a deep breath, straightened her dress, and moved to greet them.

The evening unfolded better than she could have hoped. Local authors read passages from their works, some poignant, some humorous, all touching on themes of resilience and new beginnings. A professor from a nearby university gave a short talk on the cultural shifts they could expect in the post-war world. And throughout it all, the atmosphere in the shop was one of cautious optimism, of people coming together to make sense of the changing world.

During a brief intermission, Victoria found a quiet moment with Alice and Molly.

'This is amazing, Victoria,' Alice said, her eyes shining. 'Look at everyone talking and sharing ideas. It's like... it's like the whole city is waking up.'

Molly nodded in agreement. 'You've done something special here, given people a place to hope again.'

Victoria felt a lump form in her throat. 'I couldn't have done it without you both and everyone here at Foyles.'

As they turned back to the crowd, Victoria caught sight of Ted pushing the shop door wide open. The bell rang out as he stepped inside, the door slammed shut behind him. He was agitated, his coat open and slightly dishevelled, his gaze darting around the crowded shop. She noticed his hands trembling

slightly, a sign Alice had warned her about. It was one of Freddie's
shell shock symptoms.

'I should check on Ted,' Victoria murmured, frowning at her
husband's distress, wondering what had happened; he had
seemed to be making such progress.

But before she could move, a car backfired loudly outside the
shop. The sound echoed through the quiet street like a gunshot.

Ted's reaction was immediate and violent. In his mind, he was
no longer in Foyles but back in the trenches. He lurched forward,
shouting a warning about incoming fire. 'Come on, it's not safe
here. You've got to take cover.' His powerful frame moved with
military training rather than conscious thought. He pulled open
the door and ran outside.

Victoria, standing near the stepladder, had no time to react as
Ted screamed at them to follow him, his mind not seeing his wife
but a threat in the darkness of No Man's Land. Victoria ran
towards door, shouting, 'Ted, Ted.'

There was a screech of brakes and a man shouting, 'Help,
someone call an ambulance.' His desperation carried in the air.
'He just ran out in front of me. I couldn't stop in time.'

The next few moments were chaos. Screams filled the air as
Ted lay motionless on the ground. Victoria rushed towards him,
collapsing to her knees, shaking violently as reality slowly
returned to her eyes. Alice knelt beside Victoria, her medical
training from the war taking over.

'Someone get an ambulance.' Mr Leadbetter's voice cut
through the chaos. But even as he spoke, those with medical
experience in the crowd could see it was too late. Ted's eyes stared
sightlessly upward, blood pooling beneath his head, the ghost of
his last fearful expression still on his face.

Molly put her arm around Victoria as the realisation of what
had happened washed over her.

Victoria shook his body. 'Ted, Ted it's Victoria. Come on, wake up. Everything is going to be all right.'

Molly watched helplessly as tears slowly began to flow down her own cheeks.

The horror dawned in Victoria's eyes as she stared at Ted's still form, as she understood what his war-haunted mind had done. 'No,' she whispered, her voice breaking. 'No, please God, no...' Her sobs suddenly filled the air as they racked through her body.

Alice sat back on her heels, tears streaming down her face as she shook her head slightly at Molly. The crowd had gone deathly quiet. The only sound was Victoria's sobs.

The banner Victoria had hung earlier fluttered in the shop window as the cold air rushed through the open doorway, its message of hope now seeming like a cruel joke. One moment of war-induced terror had shattered not just a life, but the very future they had been working to build.

* * *

Later that night, after the police had come and gone, after Ted's body had been taken away, and the shocked guests had filed out into the London night, Alice sat with Victoria in her home, which had evidence of Ted everywhere she looked. Victoria hadn't spoken since the incident, her eyes fixed on her trembling hands.

'It wasn't your fault,' Alice whispered, though the words felt hollow even to her. 'The shell shock... the war...'

'He had come to support me,' Victoria said, her voice raw. 'Ted, who survived the whole bloody war, who was building something beautiful... he's gone because of me and my dreams of a new beginning.'

Alice shook her head. 'I'm not having that, Victoria. You

weren't to know that Ted was going to come to Foyles, or that a car would backfire, and he would react the way he did.' She took a breath. 'He struggled to leave the war behind.'

Victoria had no response to that.

Alice thought of Victoria's excitement about the evening, about her plans for Foyles, about the future that may never come to pass. She thought of Ted and realised if Victoria had been a few seconds quicker running out the door they would have been together. Her throat tightened as her thoughts ran round her head. If only one of them could have survived, he wouldn't have coped if she had gone first. He was a war-damaged soul and could have cost her friend her life.

The sudden thud of the front door slamming shut startled Alice.

Daisy came rushing into the front room, breathless in her bid to get home quickly. 'Victoria, I've only just heard. I'm so sorry.' She threw her arms around her sister before glancing at Alice. 'Freddie is on his way. He'll take you home; obviously I'll be here with Victoria and I'm not going to work tomorrow, so I'll make sure she's all right.'

Alice nodded. 'It's such a shock. It all happened so quickly.' She blinked rapidly to stop the tears from falling.

Daisy stood up. 'I'll go and make you a cup of tea.' She strode out of the room before Alice could say anything.

Tears began to stream down Victoria's cheeks. Alice silently wrapped her arms around her friend and pulled her in close.

* * *

Alice's first thoughts when she woke up were about Victoria. She wondered if she had managed to get any sleep at all. Her hand trembled as she held the letter, the address in Norwich staring back at her accusingly. She had written and rewritten this letter countless times over the past week, struggling to find the right words to introduce herself to a brother who didn't know she existed. She'd had many arguments with herself about sending the letter at all or posting it to Margaret instead of Peter, but she didn't want to risk waiting and then regretting it because something else had happened. She had no desires to cause more conflict but Ted going so unexpectedly had emphasised that none of them knew how long they had in this world, even in peacetime. Taking a deep breath, she read through it one last time.

Dear Peter,

My name is Alice Taylor, and I'm writing to you because… well, because I recently discovered that we share a father. I know this must come as a shock, and I'm sorry to burden you with this information. But I believe you have a right to know the truth about your family, our family.

I don't know how much you know about our father's life in London, but I want you to know that I'm not writing out of anger or to cause trouble. I simply want to reach out, to maybe get to know the brother I never knew I had.

I'll tell you a little bit about me. I have a love of books and I work in Foyles bookshop in London's Charing Cross Road. During the war I also did the odd shift driving an ambulance to get injured soldiers returning from the front to hospital. Thankfully, with the war over, that work has lessened.

I have a younger sister, Lily, who can be a bit fiery and impulsive, but she's been working in the police since the war began. I have a younger brother – Charles. He lied about his age to sign up and be a soldier and we're thankful he came back in one piece. I had an older brother – Robert. He died on the front line. My mother is a kind and supportive woman who will do anything for anyone.

If you're willing, I'd very much like to meet you. We could talk, share stories about our lives, our experiences with Father. But I understand if this is too much to process right now. If you need time, or if you'd prefer not to meet at all, I will respect your wishes.

Whatever you decide, please know that I'm glad to know of your existence, Peter. In a world that has seen so much loss and sorrow these past years, finding a new family member feels like a gift.

I hope to hear from you soon.

Your sister,

Alice

With a mixture of trepidation and resolve, Alice stared at the envelope before sealing it. Margaret Wilson's name was above the address, she hoped she would understand and pass the letter on to her son. Sighing, she stood to leave for the post office. As she walked through the streets of London, her mind raced with possibilities. Would Margaret want the truth to come out and give the letter to Peter? How would he react? Would he be angry, hurt, curious? Would he want to meet her, or would he reject this unexpected intrusion into his life?

At the post office, Alice hesitated one last time before dropping the letter into the box. There would be no going back after this. The truth, once shared, could not be un-shared. But as she watched the letter disappear into the box, Alice felt a weight lift from her shoulders. Whatever happened next, she had taken the first step towards honesty, towards a new understanding of family and identity.

As she turned to leave, Alice caught sight of her reflection in a nearby window. The woman looking back at her seemed different somehow, older, perhaps, or simply more resolved. The war had ended, the flu epidemic was fading, and now this last great secret of her life was finally coming to light.

Walking towards Foyles, her mind drifted back to Victoria who had waited so long to marry the love of her life and now he was gone. She knew Molly would be waiting to hear how the talk with her mother went, but Victoria was now her priority as she knew she would be Molly's. The world was changing, healing, moving forward, and so, she realised, was she but Victoria would take a lot longer.

Whatever response came from Norwich, whether it led to a new relationship with her half-brother or simply brought closure to this chapter of her life, Alice knew she had done the right thing. The truth, painful as it might be, was always preferable to a comfortable lie.

* * *

The early December morning brought a chill mist to London's streets, wrapping Foyles' windows in the greyness of the day. A hastily written notice had been placed on the door explaining the shop would be closed that day due to a family bereavement. Without knowing what had happened the previous evening, the staff began to arrive as usual. The banner hung limply in the window, its message of hope now a bitter reminder of all they had lost. Inside, the chairs were still arranged for an evening that had ended in tragedy. While the newly arrived Christmas display stood half-finished, paper chains and holly sprigs a jarring contrast to the sombre mood within.

Victoria stood in Ted's favourite corner of the shop, where the poetry section met the window. He'd chosen it carefully when he first started visiting, quiet, but with a clear view of both exits, a soldier's instinct for situational awareness never quite leaving him. Now, his absence felt like a physical thing, heavy and real in the morning light.

'He was getting better,' she whispered, more to herself than to Alice and Molly, who stood nearby. 'The new doctor was helping. He'd started talking about the future...'

Alice moved closer, placing a gentle hand on Victoria's arm. She remembered how Ted would nod quietly to Freddie whenever they passed each other, a silent acknowledgement between two men who understood the weight of war memories. Her husband had been one of the few who truly understood Ted's struggles, who recognised the signs of an impending episode and knew when to simply sit in companionable silence.

'The cold weather was always harder for him,' Molly said softly, remembering how Andrew had mentioned seeing Ted walking the streets late at night, trying to escape the dreams that the winter chill seemed to intensify. 'Andrew never talked much about his torment, but he once told me the damp reminded him of the trenches, which made the nightmares worse.'

Mr Leadbetter appeared from his office, looking uncertain, a rare expression for the usually confident bookseller. He had never quite known how to interact with Ted, this quiet man who seemed most at peace among his books. 'Mrs Marsden,' he began formally, 'please take all the time you need. The shop can manage—'

'No,' Victoria cut in, her voice stronger than she felt. 'No, Ted... Ted found peace here, among the books. He never said as much but I believe he found sanctuary here. The books helped his mind escape the memories that hounded him every day. I need to be here; I want to feel close to him.'

She moved to the small table where Ted had spent so many

hours, running her fingers over the scratches in the wood. Ted had confided only to their small circle how some books spoke to him; they said something he couldn't express himself.

'He helped others, you know,' Alice said quietly. 'In his own way. I saw him once, recommending a book to a young veteran who looked as lost as Ted himself did when he first came home. He didn't say much, but the books he chose... they were exactly what that boy needed.'

Victoria nodded, remembering how Ted would carefully note which poems spoke to different kinds of pain, the ones that helped with the nightmares, the ones that eased the anxiety, the ones that gave words to the grief that so many returning soldiers couldn't express.

'Most people here didn't even know he was Victoria's husband,' Molly observed, watching the early morning staff begin to arrive, their curious glances quickly averted from Victoria's grief. 'He preferred it that way. Said it was easier to just be another customer, another reader seeking solace in words.'

Victoria remembered how the first weeks after the armistice had been particularly difficult for Ted. While London celebrated peace, he had retreated further into himself, overwhelmed by the noise of the city's jubilation. Only here in Foyles, among his books and his small circle of understanding friends, had he found any peace at all.

Victoria noticed Ted's notebook on the floor where it fell out of his pocket. She picked it up. She held it tight before opening it and seeing the pages filled with his careful handwriting. He'd been making lists of poems, planning to share them with his doctor who was trying to help other veterans through literature.

'I think,' Victoria said slowly, 'I think I'd like to continue his work. Not obviously, not publicly; he wouldn't have wanted that.

But quietly, the way he did it. Helping other veterans find the right words, the right books...'

Alice squeezed her friend's hand. 'We'll help, just as we always have.'

Mr Leadbetter, who had been hovering uncertainly, finally spoke. 'The poetry section... it could use some reorganising. Perhaps... perhaps a quiet corner, with comfortable chairs? For reading?'

Victoria managed a small smile, recognising the offer of support in his practical suggestion. 'Ted would have liked that. He always said bookshops needed more quiet corners.' She opened her handbag and carefully placed the notebook inside.

The rest of the staff began their morning routines, their hushed movements and respectful distance showing they understood something significant had happened, even if they didn't know the details.

Mr Leadbetter passed Victoria her own notebook, which he had found on her desk.

'Thank you, I'm not sure I'll be needing this now.'

Mr Leadbetter watched her closely. 'Don't make any hasty decisions; now is not the time.'

Victoria nodded before opening it. Her scrawling handwriting filled each page she flicked through. They were filled with plans for future events, ideas for expanding the shop's role in the community. On the last page, she had written, *The war may have changed us, but it hasn't broken us. We can build something new from the pieces.*

The words, penned in her own hand, would haunt them all in the days to come. For while the war had officially ended, its shadows continued to claim victims, turning moments of hope into tragedy, and leaving those who remained to somehow find a way forward in a world where peace brought no guarantee of safety.

The story of Ted's death would be told in whispers around Foyles for years to come, a reminder that the war's true cost couldn't be measured only in battlefield casualties, but in the countless ways it continued to echo through the lives of those who had survived it.

As the winter sun finally broke through the morning mist, Victoria carefully closed her notebook, placing it in her bag. Those final words resonated now more than ever. Tomorrow, she would return to work. She would continue Ted's quiet mission of matching troubled souls with the words they needed. She would honour his memory not with grand gestures or public declarations, but with the same gentle, understated care he had shown to others who carried war's invisible wounds.

Bells from a nearby church began to ring out, marking the hour. London was still looking forward to its first Christmas Day of peace, but here in this quiet corner of Foyles, Victoria and her friends mourned a man who had fought his own private war until the end, finding solace in books and passing that comfort on to others in his own quiet way.

* * *

The December morning brought a bitter wind that whipped at the mourners' black coats as they gathered at the small church near Foyles. Victoria stood at the entrance, her face pale but composed, accepting condolences from the handful of people who had come to pay their respects. The crowd was small, exactly as Ted would have wanted it, she thought, with a sad smile. Daisy stood next to her, holding back the tears for the sake of her sister.

Alice and Freddie arrived first, followed closely by Molly and

Andrew. They formed a protective circle around Victoria, understanding better than anyone the true depth of her loss. These
were the people who had known the real Ted, not just the quiet
customer who haunted Foyles' poetry section, but the man who
fought daily battles with his memories of war.

'The doctor came,' Alice murmured to Victoria, nodding
towards a distinguished-looking man in a dark coat. 'The one
who was helping Ted with his therapy.'

Dr Harrison had become more than just Ted's doctor in
recent months. He'd been a bridge between Ted's inner turmoil
and the outside world, using literature to help him express what
he couldn't say aloud. Now he stood quietly at the back of the
church, respectfully holding his trilby hat in front of him.

Inside, the church was modestly decorated with winter green-
ery. Victoria had refused the traditional lilies, remembering how
their heavy scent had triggered one of Ted's worst episodes last
Easter. Instead, she'd chosen simple holly and ivy, their quiet
resilience seeming more fitting for a man who had fought so hard
to find peace in a post-war world.

'There are more people than I expected,' Molly whispered,
nodding towards a group of unfamiliar faces filing into the pews.

Victoria recognised them with a start. They were the young
veterans she'd seen Ted speaking to in Foyles, men who had
found comfort in his carefully chosen book recommendations
and quiet understanding. They sat together near the back, their
postures reflecting the military bearing they couldn't quite shake.

The service began, traditional hymns echoing off stone walls.
The vicar, who had only met Ted a handful of times, spoke of
duty and sacrifice, of service to king and country. Victoria felt a
flash of anger. Ted had been so much more than his war service,
had fought so hard to be more than just another returning
soldier.

When it came time for the eulogy, Victoria rose shakily to her feet. Alice squeezed her hand as she passed, a gesture of support that nearly broke her composure.

'Ted found his voice in other people's words,' Victoria began, her voice steady despite her trembling hands. 'He believed that poetry could speak what we ourselves cannot. He had hopes and dreams, as everyone does. He was slowly moving forward and managing the torment that haunted him, as I know it does many veterans. He had grown so much and grew to understand his own struggles.' She paused, taking a deep breath to try to calm her own shaking voice and stem the tears that were threatening to overflow. 'He was much more than a war veteran. My sister, Daisy, taught him how to cook breakfast for me. He was kind and caring, he had a love of nature and searched for the kindness around him. He wanted to help others who felt lost in a never-ending cycle as he once did. He was the love of my life and I'm grateful for the time we had together.'

In the pews, Freddie and Andrew sat straighter, recognition flickering in their eyes. These were words they understood too well, the search for beauty in a world that war had made ugly. Alice and Molly drew closer together, remembering how long Victoria had loved Ted. That love had never wavered.

After the service, the small group made their way to the cemetery. The December sun broke briefly through the clouds as they lowered Ted's casket, casting weak shadows across the fresh-turned earth. Victoria placed a book of poetry on top of the coffin – Keats, whose words about beauty and truth had given Ted hope in his darkest moments.

The young veterans from Foyles approached Victoria one by one, each leaving a single book on Ted's grave. Poetry collections, novels, memoirs, books that had helped them find their way back to themselves, recommended by a quiet man who understood their unspoken pain.

'He saved my life,' one young man murmured to Victoria, his voice rough with emotion. 'That copy of *Paradise Lost* he suggested... it gave me something to hold on to when the memories got too dark.'

Victoria hadn't known the full extent of the help Ted gave to others; he had been a very private man, never mentioning any details of his quiet mission of literary salvation. But looking at the growing pile of books, each representing a soul he had helped heal, she felt a fierce pride cutting through her grief.

Later, at the small wake held in the back room of Foyles, Victoria found herself surrounded by her closest friends. Mr Leadbetter had closed the shop for the afternoon, and the familiar smell of books provided a comforting backdrop to their shared memories.

'He was getting better,' she said softly, touching the worn spine of Ted's notebook. 'The groups he was attending were helping. He was starting to talk about the future...'

'He was,' Alice agreed, her hand finding Victoria's. 'And he helped others find their way towards healing too. That's his legacy, not the war that haunted him, but the peace he helped others find.'

As darkness fell outside, the small group remained in the bookshop, sharing quiet stories of Ted, his gentle recommendations, his careful notes in margins, his way of finding exactly the right words to ease another's pain. They were the ones who had known him best, who had understood both his struggles and his strength.

Victoria lingered in Ted's corner long after the others had gone, running her fingers along the spines of the poetry books he had loved so well. Tomorrow, she would begin the task of living without him. Tomorrow, she would start to build something new from the pieces of her shattered world. But for now, she sat in the quiet of the bookshop, surrounded by the words that had given Ted peace, and she let herself remember.

* * *

Alice sat at her bedroom window seat, watching the winter rain trace patterns down the glass, while Lily paced the small room like a caged animal. Their father had left for Norwich that morning, no longer bothering to hide where he was really going, now that the truth was out.

'I thought the pretence was bad enough, but this is even worse,' Lily burst out, running her hands through her dark hair in frustration. 'The way he just announces he's going to see his other family, as if it's the most natural thing in the world. Did you see Mother's face at breakfast?'

Alice nodded, remembering how their mother's hands had trembled slightly as she poured the tea, her smile fixed and brittle. 'She's trying to be strong, to make the best of an impossible situation.'

'But why should she have to?' Lily demanded, stopping her pacing to face her sister. 'Why are we all tiptoeing around Father's feelings when he's the one who created this mess?'

'Because what's the alternative?' Alice asked quietly. 'Mother's chosen to try to salvage something from this and we have to respect that.'

Lily sank onto Alice's bed, slightly deflated. 'And what about Peter? Our brother? We don't even know if he's seen your letter. He may not even know he's our brother. Are we supposed to just... accept that too?'

Alice turned from the window, studying her sister's face. 'I've been thinking about that, about Peter.'

Lily sighed. 'He has no idea, does he? That his whole life is built on lies, just like ours was.'

'He does. I thought I told you but I tied myself up in knots over it. I kept rewriting the letter and in the end I told him I was his sister. I also told him about you, Charles and Robert.' Alice spoke softly. 'But maybe... maybe it's too much for him to deal with. I'm hoping that he will give us the opportunity to build something new. Something true, even if it starts small, just letters about books, shared interests. We could get to know him as a person before... before anything else.'

'And what happens when he discovers the whole truth? You know, when he finds out his father lied about his circumstances. Because he will – secrets like this don't stay buried forever.'

Alice moved to sit beside her sister on the bed. 'Then we'll be there for him. We'll help him understand that none of this is his fault. That he has sisters who want to know him, to be part of his life.'

'Does he though?' Lily asked, her voice small. 'Have sisters, I mean. Can we really claim that relationship when we've never even met him properly?'

'Blood is blood,' Alice said firmly. 'But more than that, we share something unique. Maybe... maybe our situations gives us a connection that's worth building on.'

They sat in silence for a moment, listening to the rain and the distant sound of their mother moving about downstairs. Finally, Lily spoke again, her voice thoughtful. 'Maybe...'

Alice took her sister's hand. 'Would you like to meet him properly? We could both go to Norwich, visit the shop where Peter works...'

'As customers? As Father's daughters? What would we say?'

'As book lovers first,' Alice suggested. 'Just like in my letter, I introduced us but didn't go into any detail. I'm hoping his mother will do that. We should let him get to know us as people before... before anything else.'

Lily was quiet for a moment, considering. 'And Mother? What do we tell her?'

'The truth,' Alice said firmly. 'We don't add to the lies in this family. We tell her we want to know our brother, but we'll respect her feelings about it.'

'She might surprise us,' Lily mused. 'She already said she doesn't blame Peter, and she told me yesterday she doesn't blame Margaret either. Said they're as much victims of Father's choices as we are.'

'Mother's always been wiser than we give her credit for,' Alice agreed. 'Maybe that's something else we've inherited from her: the ability to see beyond hurt to what might be possible.'

A knock at the door made them both start. Their mother's voice came through: 'Girls? I've made some tea, if you'd like to come down.'

The sisters exchanged glances. 'Coming, Mother,' they called in unison, then shared a small smile at the childhood habit.

As they stood to go downstairs, Lily caught Alice's arm. 'It's going to be all right isn't it?'

Alice hugged her sister tightly. 'It will. Whatever else Father's done, he's given us a brother. That's something worth building on, isn't it?'

As they made their way downstairs to join their mother, both sisters felt a slight lightening of the burden they'd been carrying. The future was uncertain, complicated by their father's choices and the weight of family secrets. But together, perhaps eventually with Peter too, they would find a way forward, building something new from the fragments of truth they now possessed.

The rain continued outside, washing away the last leaves of autumn, making way for whatever the new season might bring. Inside, two sisters and their mother gathered around the kitchen table, taking the first small steps toward a future none of them could have imagined just months before.

* * *

The kitchen was warm despite the December chill outside, and steam was rising from three teacups on the worn wooden table. Alice wrapped her hands around her cup, drawing comfort from its warmth as she looked at her mother and sister. They'd been sitting in companionable silence since she and Lily had come downstairs.

Sarah picked up her cup and sipped the hot dark liquid before placing it back on its matching saucer. 'How did Ted's funeral go? I should have gone, you know, offered some support, but I just couldn't face it.'

'It was a beautiful service,' Alice said, her voice soft in the quiet kitchen. 'Simple, dignified, just as Ted would have wanted.'

'How's Victoria holding up?' Lily asked, stirring a second spoon of sugar into her tea, a habit from childhood that surfaced when she was upset.

'She's...' Alice paused, searching for the right words. 'She's stronger than anyone could expect. But it's the little things that catch her off guard. Someone had left a poetry book on her desk at Foyles, and she just... crumbled.'

Sarah reached across the table to squeeze her daughter's hand. 'Loss is like that. It's not the big moments that break us; it's the small ones. The everyday reminders of what has been lost.'

Alice caught the shadow that crossed her mother's face, knowing she was thinking of her own marriage, of the everyday reminders of their father's deception. The parallel wasn't lost on any of them, how secrets and pain could lurk beneath the surface of seemingly perfect lives.

'Did many people attend?' Lily asked, changing the subject slightly.

'Not many, but the people who really knew him were there, who understood his struggles.' Alice took a sip of tea. 'Though there were some faces I wasn't overly familiar with – young men, veterans. Apparently, Ted had been helping them, recommending books that helped him cope with his own shell shock.'

'Had he ever mentioned that?' Lily said softly.

'He wouldn't have. Ted wasn't one for drawing attention to himself, just like Freddie and Andrew. They just want to be there for others, to help them forget their own pain.' Alice smiled sadly. 'While Victoria had seen him talking to soldiers when he was in Foyles she didn't know the full extent of it. One young man told her that Ted's book recommendations had saved his life. It was very moving.'

Their mother nodded thoughtfully. 'Sometimes the quietest people leave the deepest marks on others' lives.'

'Like ripples in a pond,' Lily added. 'You don't see how far they spread until later.'

Alice thought about Ted's corner in Foyles, how empty it would feel now. 'He was getting better, you know. His reading was helping. He and Victoria were making plans for the future...'

'Oh, my dear,' Sarah said softly, seeing the tears in Alice's eyes. 'Sometimes healing isn't a straight line. Some wounds run too deep.'

Alice whispered. 'After surviving the trenches, the flu, the shell shock, and everything else, he ran out in front of a car. I don't think in the end he knew much about it.'

Lily stood abruptly, moving to put the kettle on again. Alice recognised it as her sister's way of handling emotion – staying busy, staying useful. 'Will Victoria keep working at Foyles?' she asked over her shoulder.

'Yes. She says it's what Ted would have wanted. She's going to continue his work with the veterans too, helping them find the right books, the right words to express what they can't say.'

'Good,' their mother said firmly. 'Having a purpose helps. Something to focus on beyond the grief.'

The kettle whistled, and Lily busied herself making fresh tea. When she returned to the table, her eyes were suspiciously bright. 'I keep thinking about Father,' she admitted. 'About how lucky we are that his... his betrayal didn't end like this. That we still have a chance to work things out, to build something new from the truth.'

Alice reached for her sister's hand. 'Ted taught me something about that, actually. About how words, the right words at the right time, can bridge almost any gap. Even when the truth seems impossible to face.'

Their mother smiled sadly. 'Perhaps that's Ted's real legacy then, teaching us that healing can come in unexpected ways. Through books, through quiet conversations, through simply being present for others who are struggling.'

'I was thinking about offering to help Victoria sort through Ted's books, it's going to be painful for her to do it alone, and we've always been there for each other when things are difficult.' Alice said. 'He left notes in the margins of so many of them, little observations about which passages might help other veterans, which words might offer comfort to someone struggling like he was.'

'Would you like us to come with you?' Lily offered. 'When you go to help her?'

Alice nodded gratefully. 'I think... I think Ted would have

liked that. He believed in the power of people coming together, even if he couldn't always manage it himself.'

The kitchen fell quiet again, but it was a different kind of silence now, contemplative rather than heavy. Outside, the winter afternoon was drawing to a close, shadows lengthening across the kitchen floor. The three women sat together, sharing tea and memories, each lost in their own thoughts about loss and healing, about the quiet ways people touch each other's lives.

'To Ted,' Sarah said suddenly, raising her teacup in a small salute. 'Who showed us that sometimes the deepest wounds can lead to the most profound healing.'

'To Ted,' Alice and Lily echoed, their cups clinking gently together.

The sound seemed to linger in the warm kitchen, a reminder that even in loss, even in grief, there was still family, still love, still the possibility of finding new ways to heal old wounds. Ted would have understood that, Alice thought. He would have found just the right poem to express it.

* * *

The morning light filtered through Foyles' windows, casting long shadows between the bookshelves. Victoria had arrived early, before the shop opened, to set up a comfortable corner for Molly near the poetry section. She positioned the old armchair carefully, making sure it was close enough to the counter for Molly to help customers, but far enough from the draught from the door to keep her warm.

'Victoria, you don't have to fuss so much,' Molly said from the doorway, one hand supporting her heavily pregnant belly as she made her way into the shop. 'I'm perfectly capable of—'

'Of following doctor's orders and taking care of yourself and that baby,' Victoria finished firmly, arranging a footstool. 'Andrew told me about your dizzy spell last week. You're to sit as much as possible.'

Molly eased herself into the chair, trying to hide her relief at being off her feet. 'It's not fair that you've got Andrew spying on me now.'

'He's not spying, he's caring – as am I. Now that you no longer work here, he worries about you being indoors by yourself, so here you are where we can all keep an eye on you. Let's face it it's no hardship; you're always here anyway, so stop moaning.' Victoria tucked a warm blanket around Molly's legs. 'Ted would never forgive me if I didn't look after you properly.'

The mention of Ted's name slipped out naturally, and Victoria's hands stilled for a moment on the blanket. Molly reached out to squeeze her friend's arm, but Victoria had already straightened up, brushing off the moment.

'Now, I've put the payment pad here where you can reach it easily, although everyone has been told you no longer work here, I know you won't be able to resist trying to help out when we're busy.' She continued briskly, 'And there's a bell if you need anything. Ellen or Rosie will be near you at all times – they are under strict instructions. Mr Leadbetter said if you must do something you're only to focus on recording sales and reading stories to the children. No climbing ladders or carrying heavy boxes.'

'Victoria,' Molly said softly, 'it's all right to say his name, to miss him.'

Victoria's movements became more precise, more controlled. 'I have work to do. There's so many books that need to be shelved before we open.'

She disappeared downstairs. Molly could hear her methodically unpacking books, her actions almost mechanical in their precision. The sound of pages turning, covers being checked, spines being aligned, all the familiar rhythms of the bookshop that Ted had loved so much.

Then, suddenly, silence.

'Victoria?' Molly called, struggling to push herself up from the chair.

'Don't get up,' Victoria's voice came back, strained and odd. 'I'm fine. I just...'

Molly ignored the instruction, making her way downstairs. She found Victoria standing frozen, holding a volume of Keats's poems. A piece of paper had fallen from between its pages, covered in Ted's neat handwriting.

'Oh, Victoria,' Molly breathed.

Victoria's hands were shaking as she picked up the note. 'He was... he was making a list. Poetry that helped with different kinds of war memories. Listen to this: Brooke's "The Soldier", when homesickness hits hardest. Thomas's "Rain", for the nights when sleep won't come...'

Her voice broke on the last words. Molly reached her just as Victoria's knees gave way, helping her sink to the floor between the shelves. Victoria clutched the note to her chest, her whole body shaking with silent sobs.

'He was getting better,' she whispered. 'He was helping others get better. Why wasn't it enough? Why couldn't he just hold on a little longer?'

Molly eased herself down beside her friend, ignoring the discomfort of her pregnant belly. 'He was making a difference, Victoria. Those notes prove it. He'd found a way to take his pain and turn it into help for others; that's healing of the deepest kind.'

Victoria leaned into Molly's shoulder, tears soaking into her friend's dress. 'I keep finding unexpected pieces of him at home. Little notes in margins, books marked with his thoughts, even his pencil still on the table where he left it. How do I... how do I work with books without him?'

'You don't, you work with him,' Molly said firmly. 'Every note he left, every book he marked – that's his legacy. Not just to you, but to every soldier who comes in here looking for words to explain what they're feeling.'

Victoria wiped her eyes, looking down at the note again. 'He's categorised them, the appropriate poems for the different struggles. He was... he was building a resource for other veterans. I should complete his work.'

'We'll help you,' Molly promised. 'When I'm not too pregnant to move, and Alice has time... we'll help you catalogue everything he noted down. Make sure his work wasn't left undone.'

The sound of Mr Leadbetter unlocking the front door made them both start. Victoria quickly wiped her face but made no move to get up from their spot on the floor.

'I'm not ready,' she whispered. 'To face customers, to be normal.'

'Then we'll sit here a bit longer,' Molly said, adjusting herself more comfortably against the bookshelf. 'Mr Leadbetter can handle things for a few minutes.'

Victoria carefully smoothed Ted's note, her fingers tracing his handwriting. 'He loved it here,' she said softly. 'Among the books. He said poetry made sense of things he couldn't explain himself.'

'Then that's what we'll do,' Molly said, taking her friend's hand. 'We'll help others find the words they need, just like Ted did. One book, one poem, one soldier at a time.'

They sat there in the quiet of the poetry section, surrounded by the books Ted had loved, sharing the grief that came in waves. Outside, they could hear the shop coming to life, Mr Leadbetter greeting early customers, the bell above the door chiming, the familiar sounds of another day beginning at Foyles.

Victoria finally took a deep breath, pulled herself up before squeezing Molly's hand. 'Let's get you up and then you're getting straight back into that chair – no arguments.'

Molly smiled, accepting Victoria's help to her feet. 'Ted would be proud of you, you know, for carrying on and caring so much about everyone else even when your own heart is breaking.'

Victoria tucked Ted's note carefully into her pocket. 'He'd be proud of all of us,' she said quietly. 'Now, let's get you settled before Andrew appears to scold us both.'

As Victoria fussed with the blanket again, Molly noticed how she kept one hand in her pocket, touching Ted's note like a talisman. Some wounds never fully healed, she reflected, but perhaps they could learn to carry them with grace, just as Ted had done.

* * *

The evening candlelight cast a warm glow across Molly and Andrew's sitting room. Molly sat in her favourite armchair, her feet propped up on a footstool, one hand resting on her swollen belly as she darned a sock. Andrew paced before the fireplace, his banker's suit exchanged for more comfortable attire, but his worried expression firmly in place.

'Dr Williams was quite clear, Molly,' he said, running a hand through his hair, a gesture that reminded her of their war days. 'He said you should be resting more, especially after that dizzy spell last week.'

Molly set down her darning with deliberate care. 'I am resting. Mr Leadbetter has given me a comfortable chair behind the counter, and I'm not lifting anything heavier than a novel.'

'But all the walking, the winter weather, the long hours—'

'Victoria needs me,' Molly cut in softly, 'especially now, after Ted.'

Andrew stopped his pacing, his expression softening as he looked at his wife. 'I understand that, love, really, I do, but you're seven months pregnant. Our baby has to come first and Victoria has a lot of people looking out for her.'

'Ted's only been gone three weeks,' Molly said, her hand moving in slow circles over her bump. 'You didn't see her face this morning, Andrew. She was organising the poetry section and found one of Ted's notes tucked in a book. She tries to be strong, but...'

Andrew knelt beside her chair, placing his hand over hers on her belly. 'I know it's hard. Ted was... he was one of us. He understood about the war, about the memories. But Molly, you can't help Victoria if you make yourself ill.'

'I'm not ill,' Molly protested. 'I'm pregnant. There's a difference.'

'Is there?' Andrew's voice was gentle. 'Because I remember how exhausted you looked after you got home yesterday. How you barely touched your dinner, and how you've been having trouble sleeping...'

Molly felt tears prick at her eyes. 'That's not because of work, I just... I keep thinking about Victoria, alone in the house, I know Daisy is there, but Ted isn't. It could have easily been you, or Freddie. Ted fought so hard to get better, to build a future. I think about this little one, who'll never meet their Uncle Ted...'

Andrew gathered her into his arms as best he could, given her condition. 'Oh, love. I know. I miss him too. Those quiet conversations we had, soldier to soldier. He understood things that even Alice and Victoria couldn't, about the dreams, the memories.'

They sat in silence for a moment, the clock ticking softly on the mantel. Finally, Molly spoke again. 'What if we compromise?'

Andrew pulled back slightly to look at her. 'I'm listening.'

'I'll reduce the hours I'm there. Mornings only, three days a week. That way I can still be there for Victoria, but I'll have plenty of time to rest.' She managed a small smile. 'And you can pick me up in your lunch break, so no more walking too far on my own.'

Andrew considered this, his thumb absently stroking her belly where their child had just kicked. 'And you'll remind Mr Leadbetter you need to sit down all the time, and you no longer work there?'

'I promise. Victoria's already set up a comfortable corner for me near the poetry section. She says...' Molly's voice caught slightly. 'She says Ted would have liked that, having someone watching over his favourite part of the shop.'

Andrew was quiet for a moment, and Molly knew he was thinking of his own conversations with Ted, the shared understanding between men who carried war's invisible scars.

'All right,' he said finally. 'Three mornings a week, but if Dr Williams says you need to stop going out completely, or if you have any more dizzy spells...'

'Then I'll listen,' Molly assured him. 'This baby is my priority too, you know. I want to give them the best possible start.'

Andrew smiled, leaning down to speak to her bump. 'Did you hear that, little one? You might as well learn early that your mother's the most stubborn woman in London, so you'll never win an argument, but she loves you more than anything.'

'Not more than anything,' Molly corrected, running her fingers through her husband's hair. 'Equal to how much I love your father.'

Andrew looked up at her, his eyes suddenly bright. 'What did we do to deserve such happiness, Molly? When so many others...'

'Like Ted,' she finished softly. 'I know. That's why we have to help Victoria through this. Why we have to hold on to each other, cherish what we have.'

'Three mornings a week,' Andrew repeated firmly, but his

tone was gentle. 'And I'll see if I can adjust my lunch breaks to match your schedule.'

Molly nodded, relief flooding through her. 'Thank you, for understanding, for everything.'

Andrew pressed a kiss to her belly, then stood, offering her his hand. 'Come on, love. Let's get you and our little one to bed. Tomorrow's one of your Foyles mornings, and Victoria will need you bright and early.'

As they prepared for bed, Molly caught Andrew watching her with a mixture of love and concern. She knew he worried about her and the baby. The war had left its mark on him that way, making him desperately protective of those he loved.

'Andrew?' she said softly as they lay in bed, her head on his shoulder.

'Hmm?'

'Ted would have been proud of us, wouldn't he? All of us? Finding ways to carry on, to take care of each other?'

Andrew's arm tightened around her. 'Yes, love, though he probably would have expressed it through some obscure poetry quote that only Victoria would fully understand.'

They shared a quiet laugh at that, and Molly felt their baby kick in response. In the darkness, she sent up a silent prayer for Victoria's healing, for Andrew's peace of mind, for their child's future, and for Ted's soul, finally free from war's long shadow.

* * *

The sound of the front door shutting echoed through Alice's home like a thunderclap. She was in the kitchen with her mother and Lily, the remains of afternoon tea spread before them, when they heard Luke's voice in the hallway, followed by others.

'Sarah?' Luke called out. 'Alice, Lily, are you home?'

They heard a woman's voice but couldn't catch what was being said.

Alice's mother froze, her teacup halfway to her lips. Lily grabbed Alice's hand under the table, her fingers cold with tension.

'We're in the kitchen,' Sarah called back, her voice remarkably steady despite the whiteness of her knuckles as she set down her cup.

Footsteps approached, too many footsteps. Alice felt her heart thundering against her ribs as her father appeared in the doorway. Behind him stood a woman. Alice recognised her immediately from her visit to Norwich, and beside her...

'Peter,' Alice breathed, barely audible.

The boy hovered uncertainly in the doorway, his father's features unmistakable in his young face. He looked bewildered, his eyes darting between the women at the table and back to his mother, who stood with one hand protectively on his shoulder.

'I thought,' Luke said into the devastating silence, 'it was time we stopped living in shadows. Time everyone met properly.'

'Without warning?' Lily's voice cracked like ice. 'Without asking if we were ready?'

'Lily,' Sarah said quietly, rising from her chair. Her face was pale but composed as she looked at Margaret and Peter. 'Please, come in. Would you like some tea? I can make fresh.'

Margaret stepped forward, her movements hesitant. 'Sarah, I...' She turned to look at Luke. 'I said this wasn't... these things take a bit of...'

'Wasn't what?' Sarah asked, still in that eerily calm voice. 'Wasn't the right time? When is the right time to meet your husband's other family?'

Peter shifted uncomfortably, and Alice saw something familiar in the gesture, the same way she fidgeted when tensions rose at family dinners. Their father's trait, passed down to both her and Charles. Lily and her older brother, Robert, were always more able to speak out when the tensions arose within the family.

'I don't understand,' Peter said suddenly, his voice smaller than his fifteen years. 'Father, you said we were coming to meet...' He paused and glanced at them sitting at the table. 'Sorry, I got the letter you wrote, Alice. This has all come as a bit of a shock and I'm not sure I've taken it all in yet.'

'Don't worry, it has for all of us,' Alice said gently, standing slowly.

Peter's eyes widened with recognition, then confusion, then something like dawning hurt as he looked at his father. 'You told me you were a widower, that your wife died before I was born, how could you lie about such a thing? You said...'

'He told us he was on business trips,' Lily cut in, her voice sharp. 'Every time he went to see you and your mother, he told us it was business.'

'Stop it, all of you,' Sarah said firmly. She moved to the stove, her hands steady as she filled the kettle. 'Peter, dear, please sit down. Margaret... please. We might as well be comfortable while we sort through this mess, yet again, that Luke has created.'

Luke flinched at her words, but no one contradicted them. Slowly, awkwardly, they arranged themselves around the kitchen table, this strange collection of people bound by one man's choices.

'I'm sorry,' Margaret said softly to Sarah. 'I never wanted... when I found out he was married... I can tell you we never shared a bed after that.'

'But you continued seeing him,' Lily couldn't help saying.

'Lily,' Alice warned, seeing Peter's face crumple.

'No, she's right to be angry,' Margaret said. 'You all do, but we had a child together. What Luke and I did... the choices we made... they've hurt so many people.'

'I thought I could keep everyone happy,' Luke said, looking desperately around the table. 'Keep both my families safe, protected...'

'Protected from what?' Peter burst out. 'From knowing I had sisters and two brothers before the war started? From knowing my whole life has been a lie?'

Sarah set cups of tea in front of Margaret and Peter with gentle precision. 'No one in this room is to blame except your father, Peter. Not you, not your mother, not my girls. The fault lies entirely with the man who thought he could live two lives without consequences.'

Alice watched her mother with newfound admiration. This quiet strength, this grace under unimaginable circumstances, it was something she'd never fully appreciated before.

'I've read your letter,' Peter said suddenly, looking at Alice. 'About Foyles, about you driving an ambulance during the war... Was any of it real?'

'All of it,' Alice assured him. 'Every word, I wanted... we wanted to know our brother.'

'You have his smile,' Lily said unexpectedly. 'When you're thinking hard about something, it's just like Father's. You also remind me of our elder brother, Robert.'

Peter touched his mouth unconsciously, then looked at Lily with the first hint of curiosity rather than hurt.

As the siblings began to talk, carefully finding their way toward some kind of connection, Sarah and Margaret exchanged a long look across the table. Something passed between them, an understanding, perhaps, or at least the beginning of one.

Luke sat silent, watching his fractured family begin the

painful process of healing around him rather than because of him.

'Well,' Sarah said finally, pouring more tea. 'This isn't how I expected to spend my afternoon, but perhaps it's better to have everything in the open. Now we can all decide how to move forward, together or apart, but at least with truth between us.'

'I'd like to get to know my sisters, and my brother, Charles,' Peter said quietly. 'If... if that's all right.'

Alice reached across the table, offering her hand. After a moment, Peter took it. Lily added hers on top, and for a moment, the three siblings formed a connection that had nothing to do with their father's choices and everything to do with their own.

The afternoon light slanted through the kitchen windows, illuminating this strange gathering: two mothers, three children, and the man whose choices had brought them all to this moment. Outside, London continued its daily rhythms, unaware that in this ordinary kitchen, two families were becoming one, shaped by truth rather than lies, by choice rather than deception.

It wasn't perfect, wasn't easy, but it was real. And perhaps, Alice thought, watching Peter's tentative smile as Lily told him about Ted's poetry section at Foyles, that was the best place to start.

19

The December morning brought with it a light dusting of snow, the first of the season. Foyles' windows were decorated for Christmas, paper chains and holly sprigs artfully arranged around displays of leather-bound classics and children's picture books. Alice stood with Peter outside, watching his eyes widen as he took in the grandeur of the shop.

'It's so much bigger than the shop I work in,' he breathed, his breath fogging in the cold air.

'Wait until you see inside.' Alice smiled, squeezing his shoulder. 'Molly and Victoria are already here. They're excited to meet you properly.'

Peter shifted nervously. 'You told them about... about everything?'

'They might not be blood, but they are part of my family,' Alice said simply. 'We've been through the war and everything life has thrown at us, including Victoria's own loss recently; her husband, Ted, passed away last month.'

Peter nodded solemnly. At fifteen, he carried himself with a gravity that reminded Alice painfully of their father.

Before Alice could respond, the shop door opened and Molly appeared, her pregnancy now very pronounced beneath her winter coat. 'Are you two planning to stand out here all morning? Mr Leadbetter's got the fire going out the back, and there's hot chocolate.'

Peter's eyes went immediately to Molly's bump. 'Is it true you can feel it kick?' he blurted out, then blushed furiously.

Molly laughed warmly. 'Come inside and I'll let you feel for yourself. This little one's particularly active this morning.'

The shop was warm and inviting, Christmas decorations softening the usual scholarly atmosphere. Victoria stood behind the counter, arranging a display of poetry volumes. She looked up as they entered, and Alice saw her friend straighten her shoulders slightly. Every day brought new challenges.

'You must be Peter,' Victoria said, coming forward with a gentle smile. 'Alice has told us so much about you. I understand you like working in a bookshop too.'

Peter ducked his head. 'I just like helping people find the right book. Sometimes they don't know what they're looking for until they find it.'

'A true bookseller's instinct,' came Mr Leadbetter's voice as he emerged from his office, 'just like the ladies here.'

Alice smiled. 'Mr Leadbetter, this is my brother, Peter. He lives in Norwich with his mother.'

Alice watched Peter's face light up at the casual acknowledgement of their relationship. It was still new to him, having sisters, being part of this larger family.

Mr Leadbetter smiled. 'It's lovely to meet you, Peter.'

'Would you like a tour?' Molly offered, settling into her designated chair near the poetry section. 'Though you'll have to excuse me from walking around too much – doctor's orders.'

'Is the baby due soon?' Peter asked, hovering nearby until Molly took his hand and placed it on her bump. His face broke into a delighted grin as he felt a kick.

'January or February,' Molly confirmed. 'Now you'll have to visit regularly to meet your honorary niece or nephew.'

Victoria had drifted back to the poetry section, her hands running along the spines of books in a way Alice recognised; she was touching the volumes Ted had loved best. Peter noticed too, his expression growing serious.

'Alice told me about your husband,' he said quietly to Victoria. 'That he found comfort in poetry after the war. We... we get soldiers in the shop sometimes, looking for the same thing.'

Victoria's hands stilled on the books. 'Ted believed that poetry could speak what we ourselves cannot find words for,' she said softly. 'He left notes, suggestions for other veterans. I'm trying to continue his work.'

Peter moved closer to the poetry shelves, his eyes scanning the titles. 'Siegfried Sassoon and Rupert Brooke,' he read. 'We have trouble keeping those books in stock. The soldiers say they understood...'

'Would you like to see Ted's notes?' Victoria asked suddenly. 'His suggestions for different kinds of war memories, different kinds of pain? You might find them useful for your customers in Norwich.'

As Victoria showed Peter Ted's careful annotations, Alice joined Molly by her chair. 'He fits, doesn't he?' she murmured. 'Like he was always meant to be part of this.'

'Of course, he fits,' Mr Leadbetter said, appearing with cups of hot chocolate. 'Books have a way of bringing the right people together.'

They watched as Victoria and Peter bent their heads over a

volume of poetry, discussing which verses spoke most strongly to returning soldiers. Despite their age difference, they shared the same serious approach to helping others find solace in words.

'I've been thinking,' Mr Leadbetter said carefully, 'We could perhaps arrange some sort of exchange program with the shop in Norwich. Share inventory lists, special orders... It would give you more excuses to visit your brother.'

Alice felt tears prick at her eyes at the thoughtfulness of the suggestion. 'That would be wonderful, Mr Leadbetter. Thank you.'

The morning passed quickly, Peter absorbing everything with eager interest. He helped Victoria reorganise a display, discussed customer service techniques with Mr Leadbetter, and kept returning to check on Molly, fascinated by the baby's movements.

'Will you come back for the Christmas evening?' Molly asked as the day drew to a close. 'We're having carols and readings next week. Your mother would be welcome too.'

Peter glanced at Alice, who nodded encouragingly. 'I'd like that,' he said. 'Though...' he looked at Victoria '...is it all right? Having Christmas celebrations, when...'

'Ted loved Christmas at Foyles,' Victoria said firmly. 'He'd want the traditions to continue. Want us to find joy where we can.'

As they prepared to leave, Peter paused in the doorway, looking back at the warm interior of Foyles. 'Thank you,' he said simply. 'For sharing this with me, for... for wanting me to be part of it.'

Alice hugged her brother close, still marvelling at the ease with which she could do so now. 'You'll always have a place here,' she promised. 'With all of us.' Alice turned to Molly. 'I've just realised Andrew hasn't come to pick you up and it's nearly the end of the day.'

Molly laughed. 'No, he told me he would be late and I'm to sit still until he gets here.'

With that the shop door swung open, the bell rang out, and a breathless Andrew came rushing in. 'Oh Molly, I'm so sorry, are you alright?'

Molly laughed. 'Of course I am.' She slowly shunted herself forward to the edge of the chair.

Andrew stepped forward and took her arm. 'Come on, let's get you home.'

Molly stood on tiptoes to kiss his cheek. 'Don't worry, I love being here all day, especially this time of year. It's wonderful to hear children laughing and seeing the happiness that fills this shop. I'm sure Mr Leadbetter won't mind if I stay here all day for now.'

Andrew chuckled. 'No, I'm sure he won't, he's always had a soft spot for you.'

Outside, the snow was falling more heavily, but inside Foyles, the silver Christmas decorations twinkled warmly. Victoria returned to Ted's poetry section, her movements more peaceful than they had been earlier. Mr Leadbetter hummed carols as he balanced the day's accounts.

And Alice walked home with her brother, planning future visits, future connections, future chances to blend their two worlds into one. Christmas, she thought, had come early this year, bringing with it the gift of family, not just the one they were born to, but the one they had chosen and built for themselves among the bookshelves of Foyles.

* * *

Molly was looking through the returns that they had collected on the children's section as she sat in her comfortable corner of

Foyles when Mr Leadbetter approached, fidgeting with his bow tie in a way that suggested he had something delicate to discuss. Glancing through the shop window, she could see the Christmas decorations appearing in neighbouring shops, a reminder that the season was fast approaching.

'Mrs Greenwood,' Mr Leadbetter began. He cleared his throat, another sign he was nervous about his request. 'I wonder if I might have a word?'

Molly set down the book she was holding, adjusting her position to ease her aching back. At nearly eight months pregnant, even sitting had become an exercise in finding comfort. 'Of course, Mr Leadbetter. Is everything all right?'

He settled into the chair opposite her – the one Victoria had positioned perfectly for customer consultations. 'Well, you see... it's about our Christmas celebrations, the children, specifically.'

Understanding dawned, and Molly felt her heart squeeze. 'You're wondering about Andrew playing Father Christmas again.'

'The children loved him so much last year,' Mr Leadbetter said quickly. 'He had such a way with them, even the shy ones. And that voice he did, the jolly laugh...' He trailed off, noticing Molly's expression. 'But of course, if he's not feeling up to it this year... especially with the baby due soon, I would understand.'

Molly thought of last Christmas, before the worst of Andrew's shell shock had manifested. He'd been magnificent as Father Christmas, his natural charm shining through the white beard and red suit. The children had been entranced, and for a few precious hours, the shadows of war had lifted from his eyes.

But things were different now. Memories he'd thought buried had come to the forefront of his mind and he sometimes found crowds overwhelming.

'He's been doing better,' Molly said carefully, one hand resting on her bump. 'The doctor says his progress is encouraging. But a room full of excited children...' She hesitated before letting her thoughts be known. 'It's not a problem at the bank where he works, he's in the office doing some kind of bookkeeping, so he doesn't come into contact with a lot of noise, or people.'

'Of course, of course.' Mr Leadbetter nodded quickly. 'I shouldn't have asked. We can find someone else—'

'No, wait,' Molly interrupted. 'Let me talk to him about it. He loved it as much as the children so it might do him good to feel the excitement and happiness he's spreading.' She looked thoughtful. 'If need be, maybe we could make some adjustments? Have the children come in smaller groups to keep the noise levels down?'

Mr Leadbetter's face brightened. 'We could schedule appointments – it might make it more exclusive, special. And Mrs Marsden mentioned setting up in the poetry section, where it's quieter, and Andrew could always take a break there if he needs it, or obviously out the back. I'm sure everyone would understand if he needed extra breaks.'

Molly smiled, touched by his eagerness to accommodate Andrew's needs. 'Thank you. I'll speak to him when I get home.'

Mr Leadbetter nodded. 'I think having Andrew as Father Christmas might help Victoria too. Give her something familiar to hold on to this first Christmas without...'

He didn't finish the sentence, but Molly understood. They were all trying to find ways to support Victoria through her grief, to keep Ted's memory alive while helping her to move forward.

'I'll talk to Andrew tonight,' Molly promised. 'But please don't be disappointed if he can't do it. He wants to help, to be part of things, but sometimes...'

'Sometimes the war comes back,' Mr Leadbetter finished gently. 'We understand, my dear, all of us. This shop has seen enough returning soldiers to know that healing takes its own time.'

Just then, Alice appeared with a fresh pot of tea. 'I couldn't help overhearing,' she said, pouring a cup for Molly. 'What if Freddie and I helped? We could be there as... as a buffer of sorts. Help keep things calm, step in if Andrew needs a break.'

Molly felt tears prick at her eyes. 'You'd do that?'

'Of course we would,' Alice said firmly. 'Andrew helped Freddie through some of his darkest days after the war. We all help each other, don't we?'

Mr Leadbetter stood, straightening his bow tie. 'Well then, Mrs Greenwood, take your time discussing it with Andrew. Whatever he decides, we'll make it work.'

After he left, Alice perched on the arm of Molly's chair. 'Do you think Andrew might want to do it?'

Molly thought about how Andrew's face still lit up when he talked about last Christmas, about the letters some of the children had sent thanking Father Christmas for their books. 'I think... I think he might. If we can make it manageable for him. He misses feeling useful, being part of things.'

'Then we'll make it work,' Alice said simply. 'Between all of us – you, me, Freddie, Victoria, Mr Leadbetter – we'll create a Christmas that works for everyone.'

Molly felt the baby kick, as if in agreement. 'Ted would have loved this,' she said softly. 'Finding ways to help each other heal, to bring joy back into difficult lives.'

'He still is helping.' Alice smiled. 'Through all of us, through what he taught us about caring for each other.'

Later that evening, when Molly broached the subject with Andrew, she was surprised to see a flicker of interest in his eyes.

'We'd understand if it's too much,' she assured him quickly. 'No one would think less of you—'

'I'd like to try,' Andrew interrupted quietly. 'If... if you'll all be there to help. Those children, their faces last year... it was like the war didn't exist for a little while. Like I was just Father Christmas, not a broken soldier.'

Molly reached for his hand across the dinner table. 'You're not a broken soldier, love, you're healing and maybe this is part of that, finding ways to bring joy to others, even when it's difficult. Besides which you are much more than a soldier – you are a caring, wonderful husband and a man who is about to become a father and that's without all the help you give others, so please don't underestimate the good that you do.'

Andrew squeezed her hand, his other moving to rest on her bump. 'Our little one will be here next Christmas,' he said wonderingly. 'Perhaps... perhaps being Father Christmas this year is practice for all the Christmases to come.'

Molly felt hope bloom in her chest. Tomorrow, she would tell Mr Leadbetter that Operation Father Christmas was on, with maybe a few modifications on standby. They would create something magical, not just for the children who visited Foyles, but for their own healing hearts as well.

* * *

The sound of carol singers drifted through Foyles' windows as dusk settled over London. A small crowd had gathered outside the shop, their voices rising clear and sweet in the winter air: 'Silent Night, Holy Night, all is calm, all is bright...'

Victoria paused in her arrangement of the Christmas display, her hands stilling on a copy of *A Christmas Carol*. 'It's different this year, isn't it?' she said softly. 'The singing, no air-raid sirens to interrupt, no blackout curtains to worry about.'

Molly shifted in her chair, both hands resting on her prom-

inent bump. 'First Christmas of peace in four years,' she agreed.
'Though I must admit, I've barely thought about Christmas
preparations. With everything that's happened...'

'Ted's death, Peter coming into our lives, Molly's pregnancy –
it's certainly been an eventful year for us. That's not even
mentioning the flu epidemic or Albert being our hero when he
saved Ellen from the spy and then volunteering to drive the van
so we could deliver the books to our customers.' Alice listed
quietly, moving to stand beside Victoria at the window. 'Sometimes it feels like peace has brought as many challenges as war.'

The carol singers moved on to 'God Rest Ye Merry Gentle-
men', their voices carrying a joy that had been absent in previous
years. Customers in the shop paused to listen, some humming
along, others wiping away sudden tears.

'I haven't bought a single present,' Victoria admitted, turning
away from the window. 'I kept putting it off, thinking I needed to
feel more... festive. More ready for celebration.'

'Oh, thank goodness,' Molly breathed. 'I thought I was the
only one. I've been so busy worrying about everyone, let alone
the baby coming, that Christmas has seemed almost abstract.'

Alice laughed softly. 'Well, that makes three of us then.
Though I did pick up something small for Peter – a book of
poetry he mentioned liking. But otherwise...'

'What do you say we go shopping together?' Victoria
suggested suddenly. 'Tomorrow after work? We could help each
other choose gifts, make it less... overwhelming.'

'Yes, please,' Molly said fervently. 'Though you'll have to be
patient with my waddling. This little one seems to get heavier by
the hour.'

'We'll take care of you,' Alice assured her. 'And perhaps...
perhaps we could look for something special for Andrew? For
being Father Christmas again?'

Victoria nodded. 'That's a good idea.'

Outside, the carol singers had started 'O Little Town of Bethlehem'. A young mother passing by had stopped to listen, her small child's face alight with wonder at the music.

'Look at that child's face,' Molly whispered. 'That's what peace looks like, isn't it? Children who won't grow up knowing air raids and rationing.'

'Your little one will be born into peace,' Victoria said, touching Molly's bump gently. 'A proper peace baby.'

'Though sometimes,' Alice added thoughtfully, 'I think peace is harder than war, in its own way. During the war, everything was about survival, about getting through. Now we have to learn how to live again, how to be happy.'

'Ted would have had a poem for that,' Victoria said, her voice catching slightly. 'Something about hope and renewal...'

Molly reached for her friend's hand. 'We'll find our own words,' she said firmly. 'Our own way to celebrate this first Christmas of peace.'

'Starting with shopping tomorrow,' Alice added, trying to lighten the mood. 'Though God knows what we'll find in the shops. Everything's still so scarce.'

'It's not about the gifts though, is it?' Victoria mused, watching the young mother outside point out the Christmas star to her child. 'It's about... about being together, about surviving and spreading happiness.'

'About building something new,' Molly agreed. 'Speaking of which, I had an idea for Peter's Christmas gift from all of us. What if we created a special shelf in the poetry section? "Recommended by Norwich's Finest" or something similar? Let him contribute his own suggestions alongside yours, Victoria?'

Victoria's eyes lit up at the idea. 'Yes, and we could do the same in the shop he works in, if they are happy to do it. They could have a "Foyles Recommends" section. It could help build bridges between our two worlds.'

'See?' Alice smiled. 'We're getting into the Christmas spirit already. And tomorrow we'll brave the shops together, take care of each other like we always do.'

The carol singers had moved further down the street, their voices fading into the gathering darkness, but the shop seemed to hold on to the echoes of their songs. The Christmas display glowed warmly in the lamplight.

'I miss Ted,' Victoria said suddenly, her voice small. 'But being here, with you both, with the carols and the preparations... it helps. He would have loved this Christmas, I think. The first one without fear of bombs or telegrams.'

'He's still part of it,' Molly said gently. 'In the poetry section, in the ways we care for each other, in how we're helping Andrew and Freddie face their demons to bring joy to others.'

Alice wrapped an arm around Victoria's shoulders. 'And tomorrow we'll find presents that would make him smile. Books for soldiers still struggling to find their peace, poetry for those who need words to heal, toys for children who will grow up knowing only peace.'

The last rays of sun caught the gilt lettering on the Christmas books, making them shine like promises. Outside, London prepared for its first peaceful Christmas in years. Inside Foyles, three friends stood together, supporting each other as they had through war and loss and change, ready to face whatever challenges peace might bring.

'Right then,' Molly said briskly, struggling to her feet. 'Help me up, and let's make a list of what we need to buy tomorrow. Starting with something for Mr Leadbetter. Did you see him shed a tear during "Silent Night"?'

As they gathered around Molly's table, planning their shopping expedition and sharing ideas for gifts, the spirit of Christmas seemed to settle over them properly for the first time. It wouldn't be a perfect Christmas – too much had been lost, too much had changed – but it would be their Christmas, built on friendship and understanding and the precious gift of peace.

20

Oxford Street glittered with Christmas decorations, shops making an extra effort this year to celebrate the first peaceful Christmas since 1913. The windows of Selfridges drew crowds of admirers, their displays more elaborate than had been possible during the war years. Among the shoppers, Alice, Victoria, and Molly made their way slowly down the street, mindful of Molly's condition.

'Let's stop for a moment,' Alice suggested, noticing Molly's slight breathlessness. 'These crowds are worse than I expected.'

'Everyone's making up for lost time,' Victoria observed, guiding Molly to a quiet doorway. 'Four years of restricted cele-brations... it's like the whole city is determined to make this Christmas count.'

They watched as a group of children pressed their faces against a toy shop window, their excitement palpable. No more tin soldiers or war games on display, instead there were dolls houses, train sets, and teddy bears.

'It's strange,' Molly said, one hand resting on her bump.

'Seeing toys that aren't about war. Makes you realise how much it affected everything, even children's play.'

'Speaking of children's gifts,' Alice said, pulling out her list, 'what should we get for Peter? I know we're doing the poetry section idea, but I'd like to give him something personal too, other than the book of poems I've already got for him. Something that says "sister".'

Victoria squeezed her friend's arm. 'I saw some lovely leather-bound notebooks in Selfridges. For him to write his own book recommendations, perhaps, continuing the family tradition of bookselling.'

'Perfect.' Alice smiled. 'Though I still can't quite believe I'm shopping for another brother this Christmas. This time last year, we had no idea...'

'So much has changed,' Victoria murmured, her eyes catching on a display of men's gifts. Ted would have loved the fountain pen in the window, she thought, then pushed the pain aside.

Molly noticed her friend's expression. 'Let's go to Liberty's next,' she suggested. 'I need to find something for Andrew to thank him for being Father Christmas. And Victoria, you can help me choose – you always know what will appeal to soldiers who've... who've seen too much.'

They made their way through the crowds, Alice and Victoria forming a protective barrier around Molly. The decorations seemed brighter this year, the shop windows more enticing without the fear of air raids to dim their sparkle.

'Oh!' Molly stopped suddenly, pressing a hand to her side.

'The baby?' Alice asked anxiously.

'Just kicking,' Molly assured them. 'I think all the excitement is catching. Though I wouldn't mind sitting down soon.'

'There's that tea shop around the corner,' Victoria remembered. 'We could rest and make proper plans and work out what else we need to buy.'

The tea shop was busy but warm, festive garlands draped across its windows. They found a quiet corner table, and Victoria went to order while Alice helped Molly settle into her chair.

'I want to find something special for my mother,' Alice said once they were settled. 'She's been so strong through everything with my father and Peter.'

'She'd love that.' Molly smiled. 'She's a strong woman, probably stronger than any of you realised, and full of compassion too.'

Victoria returned with tea and fresh scones, setting them out carefully. 'Speaking of survival... You know I've been thinking about Ted's poetry collection. I'd like to share it – perhaps give some volumes to the veterans who found comfort in his recommendations. I could also give some to his doctor as he was encouraging Ted to read. I'll keep some special ones for... for when I need help to feel close to him.'

Her friends reached for her hands across the table, understanding the magnitude of this decision.

'That's a wonderful idea,' Molly said softly. 'A way to keep his work going, helping others find healing through words.' She looked thoughtful for a moment. 'Maybe we could ask Ellen if John could get some poetry lists, along with Ted's thoughts on them, printed at the newspaper office; after all, he's practically in charge now.'

Victoria's face tightened a little. 'That would depend on how much it would cost. I don't think printing is cheap.'

Molly nodded. 'Maybe not, but it's worth an ask. He might give us a good price because it's for a good cause, and don't forget he's a veteran himself.'

Victoria smiled. 'We'll ask for a price.'

'We could add it to our shopping list,' Alice suggested gently. 'Maybe we could find some nice boxes or bookplates, make it a special gift for each recipient.'

Outside, carol singers had started up, their voices carrying through the tea shop windows. 'We wish you a merry Christmas, we wish you a merry Christmas' floated in, and Victoria smiled through sudden tears.

'Ted loved carols,' she said. 'Said they were poetry set to music. Last Christmas, he...'

'Tell us,' Molly encouraged, squeezing her hand.

As Victoria shared memories of her last Christmas with Ted, their tea grew cold, but none of them minded. This too was part of Christmas shopping: taking time to remember, to share, to support each other through moments of joy and grief.

Finally, refreshed and rested, they gathered their bags and lists and ventured back into the Oxford Street crowds.

'Right then,' Alice said briskly, linking arms with her friends. 'Liberty's for Andrew's gift, then the stationer's for Peter's notebook, and perhaps the bookshop on the corner for Mother?' She giggled. 'I almost forgot my own family and the children; something tells me it's not all going to get done tonight.'

'And we need decorations for Foyles,' Victoria added. 'Something special for the children's Christmas party. Maybe some new stockings for Father Christmas to fill...'

'And don't forget Mr Leadbetter,' Molly reminded them. 'Though what do you get for the bookseller who has everything?'

Alice laughed. 'Maybe a new bow tie.'

Molly chuckled. 'Joking aside, that's not a bad idea.'

They made their way through the gathering dusk, the streetlamps casting a warm glow over the Christmas crowds. Every so often they would stop for Molly to rest, and for Victoria to gather herself when memories hit too hard, as well as Alice to jot down new gift ideas in her notebook.

It wasn't the carefree Christmas shopping they might have imagined in peacetime, but it was their reality, three friends supporting each other through grief and joy, through endings and new beginnings, through the complex process of learning to live in peace again.

As they finally turned towards home, their arms full of carefully chosen gifts, snowflakes began to fall. They paused to watch, remembering other winters, other Christmases, other snows.

'Next year,' Molly said suddenly, 'we'll have a baby to shop for too.'

'And Peter will be with us properly,' Alice added. 'Part of everything.'

'And Ted...' Victoria took a deep breath. 'Ted will be with us in our hearts, in the gifts we give, in the way we care for each other.'

The snow fell faster as they made their way home, transforming London's streets into something magical. Behind them, Oxford Street's Christmas decorations twinkled like stars, promising hope and renewal in this first peaceful winter since the war began.

* * *

Molly's arms were aching from carrying her shopping bags as she approached her front door, but she forgot all the weariness she felt when she heard something unexpected through the window: Andrew's voice, softly humming 'O Christmas Tree'. She paused, listening, hardly daring to believe what she was hearing.

Opening the door carefully, she was enveloped by the fresh scent of pine. There, in their small sitting room, stood Andrew, carefully hanging ornaments on a modest but perfectly shaped

Christmas tree. He turned at her entrance, a slightly sheepish smile on his face.

'I thought...' He hesitated. 'I thought if I'm to be Father Christmas at Foyles, we should have a proper tree at home, only for practice you understand.'

Molly felt tears spring to her eyes. 'Oh, Andrew,' she breathed, taking in the scene. He'd pushed the armchair aside to make room for the tree, and several boxes of decorations sat open on the floor.

'Here, let me take those,' he said, moving to relieve her of the shopping bags. 'You shouldn't be carrying so much. Doctor's orders, remember?'

As he took the bags, Molly noticed his hands were steady today, no visible tremors from the shell shock. This was one of his good days, a gift in itself. 'Shall we have tea?'

'Tea sounds perfect,' Andrew agreed, carefully setting down the shopping bags. 'Though you stay right there, and I'll bring it to you. Father Christmas's orders.'

'Where did you find the tree?' she asked, easing herself into the armchair he'd positioned perfectly for her to watch his decorating efforts.

Andrew returned with two cups of tea and placed them on a side table next to Molly's chair. He beamed.

Molly smiled at his happiness. 'You can tell me about the tree, then I'll tell you about our shopping adventures.'

Andrew glanced at the partially decorated tree. 'Do you remember a while back I mentioned Mr Jenkins, from my unit, and how ill he looked?'

Frowning, Molly nodded. 'Oh, please don't tell me he's died.'

Andrew smiled at her worried expression. 'No, he runs a small Christmas tree lot now, and it's only down the street. Another returning soldier, trying to make his way.' Andrew returned to his decorating, moving a bauble to another position. He glanced at Molly; his smile faded. 'We got talking about... about our last Christmas in the trenches, how we'd tried to make it festive with whatever we could find and somehow I then found myself buying a tree.'

Molly watched as he hung another ornament, one of her mother's old glass baubles that had survived four years of war when so much hadn't. 'It's beautiful,' she said softly. 'Perfect for our first peaceful Christmas. And the baby's first Christmas, even if it doesn't arrive until the end of January.'

Andrew's hand moved to touch a small silver rattle hanging among the other decorations. 'I got this today too,' he admitted. 'Our first decoration for the little one, I thought... I thought they should be part of Christmas from the start. Does that sound daft?'

'No, that's a beautiful thought.' Molly felt the baby kick, as if in appreciation. 'I think the baby feels the same, come and have a feel,' she said, holding out her hand to Andrew. 'Someone's excited about their first Christmas tree.'

Andrew knelt beside her chair, his hand gentle on her bump. When the baby kicked again, his face lit up with that look of wonder that never failed to melt Molly's heart.

'I've been thinking,' he said, still keeping his hand on her belly. 'I've been thinking about Christmas, and about being Father Christmas at Foyles. I suppose I've been thinking about everything. The war took so much from us all, but this peace, this baby, this chance to bring joy to children, it's like getting pieces of myself back that I thought were lost forever.'

Molly ran her fingers through his hair, feeling the slight tremble that ran through him at the admission. 'You never lost those pieces, love. They were just waiting for the right moment to shine again.'

Andrew leaned into her touch. 'There are still bad days,' he admitted. 'Days when the memories are too loud, when I can barely face leaving the house. But then I think about this little one coming, about those children at Foyles who'll be looking for Father Christmas, it somehow helps.'

'That's because you have the biggest heart of anyone I know,' Molly said firmly. 'Even when it's hurting, it still finds ways to love, to give.'

Andrew stood, returning to the tree but staying close to her chair. 'I found something else today too,' he said, reaching into one of the decoration boxes. 'Look.'

He held up a small, worn card. Molly recognised it immediately; it was their first Christmas card as a married couple. Inside was a picture of them, smiling at each other, with a sprig of holly drawn around the edges.

'I thought we could hang it on the tree,' Andrew said. 'To remind us how far we've come. And next year, we'll add a picture with the baby.'

Molly felt fresh tears spill over. 'It's perfect,' she managed. 'Everything is perfect.'

Andrew carefully tied a ribbon to the card and hung it on the tree. Then he stepped back, studying his work. 'It needs something on top,' he mused. 'A star, perhaps?'

'There's one in that box by your feet,' Molly said. 'It was my grandmother's. I've been saving it for when the time felt right.'

Andrew opened the box reverently, lifting out the delicate glass star. It caught the late afternoon light, sending prisms dancing across the walls. With gentle hands, he placed it on top of the tree.

'There,' he said softly. 'Now it's ready for Christmas.'

Molly struggled to her feet, wanting to stand beside him to admire their tree. Andrew's arm slipped around her waist, supporting her, and the baby kicked again as if adding its approval.

'Happy Christmas, little one,' Andrew whispered, his free hand cradling Molly's bump. 'Your first of many, I promise. And they'll all be peaceful ones.'

As the winter light faded outside their window, the tree seemed to glow with its own inner light. Molly leaned against her husband, feeling his strength, his love, his gradual healing. This Christmas was about more than peace in the world. She realised it was about finding peace within themselves, about building new traditions from the ashes of war, about looking forward instead of back.

Molly laughed, the sound merging with the baby's kicks and Andrew's returning hum of Christmas carols. Outside, London prepared for its first peaceful Christmas in years. Inside, in their sitting room with its perfect tree, Molly and Andrew created their own peace, one moment, one decoration, one shared smile at a time.

* * *

The evening lamp cast a warm glow in Alice's family sitting room, but there was an undercurrent of tension as Sarah folded and refolded her handkerchief, a habit her daughters had come to recognise as a sign of her internal struggle. Alice and Lily sat on either side of her on the settee, waiting for their mother to voice what was clearly weighing on her mind.

'I've been thinking about Christmas,' Sarah finally said, her voice careful and measured. 'About, about family.'

Alice and Lily exchanged glances over their mother's head. They knew what was coming, the question they'd all been avoiding.

'Peter is your brother,' Sarah continued, smoothing the handkerchief for the hundredth time. 'And whatever your father's choices, whatever pain they've caused... that boy is innocent in all this.'

'Mother,' Lily started, her voice tight with protective anger, 'you don't have to—'

'Yes, I do,' Sarah cut in with unexpected firmness. 'I do have to think about this, to make decisions about it. Because if we don't, if we just let the situation fester...' She took a deep breath. 'I'm considering inviting Margaret and Peter for Christmas dinner.'

The silence that followed was profound. Alice found herself holding her breath, while Lily practically vibrated with suppressed emotion.

'What about Father?' Alice asked carefully. 'Would he be here too?'

Sarah's hands stilled on the handkerchief. 'I've told your father he can have Christmas lunch with them in Norwich, and dinner here with us. Or the other way around, if they prefer. But I won't have him pretending any more. No more trying to keep his two worlds separate.'

'But Mother,' Lily burst out, 'why should you have to arrange anything? Why should you have to be the one making accommodations for his... his—'

'His other family?' Sarah finished quietly. 'Because they are family now, Lily. Whether we like it or not, Peter is your brother, and he's just a boy who's had his whole world turned upside down.'

Alice reached for her mother's hand. 'Are you sure about this? It won't be easy.'

Sarah gave a small, sad laugh. 'Nothing about this situation is easy, my dear. But I keep thinking about that boy, about how much he looks like your father, about how none of this is his fault. And I think about you girls, about having a brother you're just getting to know, and should my pain prevent that relationship from growing?'

'Your pain matters,' Lily insisted fiercely. 'You're allowed to be hurt, to be angry.'

'Yes, I am,' Sarah agreed. 'And I am hurt, and angry, but I'm also... I'm also tired of letting your father's choices control all our lives. Perhaps this is a way to take that control back. To decide for ourselves what kind of family we want to be.'

Alice thought about Peter, about his enthusiasm for books about the way his face lit up when she called him 'brother'. 'He asked me, when I took him to Foyles, if we had any family Christmas traditions. He tried to make it sound casual, but—'

'But he was really asking if he had a place in them,' Sarah finished softly.

'And what about Margaret?' Lily asked, her voice smaller now 'How are we meant to act around her?'

Sarah was quiet for a moment, considering. 'She's a mother who loves her son,' she said finally. 'Whatever else she is, whatever choices she and your father made, that much I understand Perhaps that's where we start.'

'We could...' Alice hesitated, then pressed on. 'We could make it Christmas tea instead of dinner. Less formal, easier to end if it becomes too difficult. And Victoria and Molly could be here too, as a buffer. They've been such a support through everything.'

Sarah squeezed her daughter's hand. 'That's a good idea, and perhaps we could ask Margaret to bring one of their family traditions. Show Peter that we're trying to blend our families, not erase his.'

'I still think it's too much to ask of you,' Lily said, but her voice had lost some of its anger. 'You're being so... so...'

'So much like a mother,' Alice finished. 'Putting the children first, even when it hurts.'

Sarah pulled both her daughters close, breathing in the familiar scent of their hair. 'You're all my children now,' she said softly. 'You, Lily, Charles, and now Peter as well. Whatever your father did, however he went about it... he gave me another child to love, I am very blessed, and that's not including my wonderful grandchildren, Arthur and David as well. I can't ignore that, not at Christmas.'

'Then we'll help,' Alice decided. 'We'll make it work somehow, for Peter, for you, for all of us.'

'But if it becomes too much,' Lily added, 'if you need to stop, or step away, or... or anything. You just say the word.'

Sarah nodded, her eyes bright with tears. 'I know, my dears. And having you both with me, supporting me like this... it makes me even more certain that we need to try. Because you've shown me that love can grow, can expand, can heal even the deepest wounds.'

Lily frowned. 'What about grandpa? Are you going to tell him the truth?'

Sarah raised her eyebrows. 'I will at some point but not at Christmas. He's never liked your father very much and I don't want the day being ruined. I'll just tell him they are family friends, which isn't a total lie, for now.'

The lamp flickered slightly, casting shifting shadows on the walls. Outside, carol singers could be heard in the distance, their voices carrying messages of peace and goodwill. Inside, three women held each other, planning a Christmas that would be different from any they'd known before – a Christmas of new beginnings, of brave attempts at healing, of family redefined by choice rather than just blood.

'I'll write to Margaret tomorrow,' Sarah said finally. 'Invite them for Christmas tea. Of course they won't be able to travel on Christmas Day so your father will have to find them somewhere to stay and I'll tell him so. And whatever happens... we'll all know the truth and that's what matters.'

Alice and Lily tightened their embrace, their mother strong between them. Whatever happened at Christmas, they would be there, ready to support, to protect, to help build something new from the pieces of their broken family.

The carol singers drew closer, and Sarah raised her head to listen. 'Silent Night,' she murmured. 'How appropriate – because whatever else this Christmas brings, we've found our way to honesty at last. No more secrets, no more silence, just truth, and the hope of healing.'

21

The early morning quiet of Foyles provided the perfect moment. Alice had arrived early specifically for this conversation, knowing her friends would be there before the shop opened. Victoria was arranging the poetry section, as she did every morning, keeping Ted's careful organisation system intact. Molly sat in her usual chair, one hand resting on her prominent bump as she sorted through invoices, while Andrew helped Mr Leadbetter unpack a new delivery of books before he went to work.

Alice cleared her throat. 'Could I... could I have everyone's attention for a moment?'

They gathered around Molly's chair, their usual meeting spot now, and Alice couldn't help but feel grateful for these people who had become such an important part of her life.

'Mother's decided to invite Margaret and Peter for Christmas tea,' she said quietly, watching their reactions carefully. 'And I... we... would very much like all of you to be there, as you are all family too.'

Victoria was the first to respond, reaching for Alice's hand. 'Of course, we'll come, won't we?' She looked at Molly.

Molly shifted in her chair, trying to find a comfortable position. 'Are you sure your mother's ready for this? It's such a big step.'

'That's exactly why we need you there,' Alice explained 'You've all been such a support through everything with Father's... situation. Having you there would make it easier, especially for Mother. Oh, and Victoria, your invitation also includes Daisy and Stephen, if he's home by then.'

Victoria nodded. 'I've had a letter from him and he's staying with a friend who's on his own and suffering a little, so as much as I want him home, I know he's doing the right thing, helping someone else.'

Andrew, who had been standing quietly behind Molly's chair spoke up. 'What time, and are you talking about Christmas Day because I'll need to work around the Father Christmas duties here at the shop.'

'Yes, maybe late afternoon, say, four o'clock,' Alice said. 'The children's party is on Christmas Eve so Father Christmas duties will be safe.' She laughed. 'Mr Leadbetter,' she turned to the bookseller, who had been trying to fade discreetly into the background. 'We'd very much like you to come too, because you've also been a big part of everything.'

Mr Leadbetter adjusted his bow tie, clearly touched. 'My dear I wouldn't want to intrude on a family—'

'You are family,' Victoria interrupted firmly. 'All of you are That's what Foyles has given us: a family we chose for ourselves.'

'Besides,' Molly added with a gentle smile, 'who better to help break the ice than a bookseller? You, Peter and Margaret can talk books if nothing else.'

Alice saw Mr Leadbetter's expression soften at that. He'd been curious about the small bookshop in Norwich, though he'd never said so directly.

'It won't be easy,' Alice admitted. 'Mother's trying so hard to be brave about it all, but having you there... knowing she has support...'

'Will Lily be all right with us all being there?' Andrew asked perceptively, remembering the conversation he and Molly had about Alice's trips to Norwich. 'She's been... protective of your mother.'

Alice nodded. 'It was partly her idea, actually. She thought having you all there might make it feel more like a gathering of friends than a... a forced family union.'

'Which is exactly what it should be,' Victoria said decisively. 'A gathering of people who care about each other, no matter how they came to be family.'

'We could bring things,' Molly suggested, her practical nature emerging. 'I'll make those mince pies Andrew loves, enough to share. Victoria, you could bring some of Ted's favourite poetry books to show Peter...'

'And I might have some first editions that might interest Peter. I'll also see what food I can muster up, although I'm sure my cooking isn't as wonderful as your mother's,' Mr Leadbetter mused, clearly warming to the idea.

Alice felt tears threatening. 'Thank you,' she managed. 'All of you, for understanding, for helping—'

'That's what family does,' Victoria said simply. 'And we've all learned this year that family is about more than blood. It's about who stands by you through the hard times.'

'Speaking of hard times,' Andrew said quietly, 'would it help if I came in my Father Christmas outfit? Might break the tension a bit.'

The suggestion startled a laugh out of Alice, exactly as Andrew had intended. Even Mr Leadbetter chuckled.

'Perhaps not.' Alice smiled. 'Though knowing you'll have had a busy Christmas Eve bringing joy to children here at Foyles... it feels right somehow. Like everything's connected.'

'Because it is,' Molly said softly. 'Foyles, family, friends, Christmas... it's all part of healing, isn't it? Of finding our way forward together.'

Victoria nodded, her hand straying to the poetry section where Ted's presence still lingered. 'And some of us will be there in spirit too, watching over us all.'

The shop bell tinkled as the first customer of the day entered, breaking the moment. They dispersed to their various tasks, but Alice noticed the gentle way they moved around each other, the supportive glances, the silent understanding.

Mr Leadbetter spoke quietly as he passed Alice. 'I should like to bring a proper Christmas pudding, if that would be appropriate?'

'That would be perfect.' Alice smiled. 'Mother always says Christmas isn't Christmas without a pudding, and she's been so focused on everything else...'

'Then it's settled,' he said firmly. 'We'll all come, we'll all bring something to share, and we'll all help make this Christmas tea something positive, a beginning rather than an ending.'

As Alice watched her friends go about their morning duties, Victoria straightening books with extra care, Molly making notes about mince pies, Andrew and Mr Leadbetter discussing the logistics of the children's party – she felt a wave of gratitude so strong it nearly overwhelmed her as she walked towards her counter, ready to serve customers.

These people, this place... they had helped her family survive its darkest revelations. Now they would help build something new, something honest, something filled with the possibility of healing. It wouldn't be a perfect Christmas tea, but with these friends beside them, it would be real and maybe that was the greatest gift of all.

* * *

The children's section of Foyles had been transformed into a Christmas grotto. Twinkling lights and paper chains created a magical atmosphere, while stacks of carefully wrapped books waited beside Father Christmas's chair. Andrew sat regally in his red suit and white beard, with Freddie and Alice managing the excited queue of children that stretched between the book-shelves.

'Remember,' Alice was saying softly to a small girl with pigtails, 'Father Christmas has very sensitive ears, so we must approach quietly and calmly.'

Freddie stood at the head of the queue, his policeman's experience proving invaluable in maintaining order. He'd developed a system of letting small groups approach at a time, preventing Andrew from becoming overwhelmed by noise and sudden movements.

'Next three, please,' he called quietly, ushering forward a boy of about seven and two smaller children who were clearly siblings.

The children approached with wide eyes, the older boy holding his younger siblings' hands. Andrew's voice, when he spoke, was warm and gentle, nothing like the haunted tones he sometimes used when the memories became too much.

'Well, well,' he said, his eyes twinkling behind the spectacles that completed his costume, 'what have we here? Three young readers, I believe?'

The smallest child, a girl no more than four, gasped in delight. 'How did you know we can read?'

'Father Christmas knows everything about books,' Alice said, stepping forward with wrapped presents. 'That's why he's visiting Foyles today.'

Andrew leaned forward conspiratorially. 'And what kind of books do you enjoy?'

The older boy spoke up shyly. 'I... I like adventure stories. And my sister Ruth likes fairy tales, and little Emma likes anything with animals.'

'Ah,' Andrew said, his voice full of warmth as he reached for three specific packages. 'Then I believe I have just the right books here.'

Alice watched as he handed the children their gifts, noting how his hands remained steady, how he managed to make each child feel special without becoming overwhelmed himself. Freddie stood ready nearby, prepared to step in if needed, but so far, Andrew was handling everything beautifully.

'Is it true,' the boy asked suddenly, 'that you visited soldiers during the war? My father said Father Christmas never forgot the soldiers, even in the trenches.'

A shadow passed briefly over Andrew's face, but he recovered quickly. 'Indeed I did,' he said softly. 'Every soldier, no matter where they were, got a little reminder of home at Christmas.'

Alice felt Freddie tense beside her, but Andrew continued smoothly, 'And now that peace has come, I can spend more time with wonderful young readers like yourselves.'

The children beamed, clutching their books. As they turned to leave, the oldest boy paused. 'My father didn't come back from France,' he said quietly. 'But he wrote to us about the Christmas presents you brought them there.'

Andrew's eyes met Alice's for a moment, and she saw the depth of emotion in them. 'Your father,' he said gently, 'was very brave. And I'm sure he'd be proud to see what good care you're taking of your sisters.'

The boy straightened his shoulders, nodding solemnly before leading his siblings away. Alice quickly moved forward, squeezing Andrew's shoulder as Freddie called the next group.

'Would anyone like to hear a Christmas story while they wait?' Alice called to the queue, noticing that Andrew needed a moment to compose himself. She opened a nearby copy of 'The Night Before Christmas' and began to read, giving Andrew time to steady his breathing.

The day continued in this way, small groups approaching the grotto, each child receiving a carefully chosen book, Freddie maintaining calm order, and Alice providing distraction when needed. They had developed an unspoken rhythm, the three of them working together to create magic while protecting Andrew from becoming overwhelmed.

Mr Leadbetter appeared occasionally, bringing cups of tea and beaming at the success of the event. 'You're doing wonderfully,' he whispered to Andrew during one such visit. 'The group reading in the poetry section seems popular and appears to be going well. Ted would have loved seeing it being used in that way.'

The readers were surrounded by the poetry books Ted had so carefully organised. There was a sense of his presence watching over them. Victoria had helped decorate the space the night before, incorporating small touches that would have made Ted smile, a volume of Christmas poems displayed prominently, a sprig of holly marking his favourite reading spot.

As the morning wore on, Molly appeared, easing herself into her usual chair to watch. The children were fascinated by her obvious pregnancy, and several asked Father Christmas if he would bring the baby a book when it arrived.

'The baby's first book is already wrapped and waiting,' Andrew assured them, catching Molly's eye with a smile.

One little girl, approaching the grotto alone, stopped suddenly, her face anxious. 'Are you... are you really magic?' she whispered to Andrew. 'Only, my brother has bad dreams about the war, and I wondered if...'

Alice stepped forward quickly, but Andrew handled it with remarkable grace. 'The best magic,' he said gently, 'is the magic of stories. Perhaps you and your brother could read this book together?' He handed her two wrapped packages instead of one. 'Stories have a way of helping with bad dreams, you see.'

The girl's face lit up as she clutched the books. 'Thank you, Father Christmas.'

After she left, Freddie moved closer to Andrew. 'Do you need a break?'

But Andrew shook his head. 'No,' he said softly. 'No, I think I need to keep going. To keep reminding myself that there's still magic in the world. Still hope.'

Alice arranged more wrapped books within easy reach, each one carefully chosen to bring joy to a child in this first peaceful Christmas since the war. She watched as Andrew continued to greet each child with warmth and attention, saw how Freddie maintained the calm atmosphere that made it possible, felt the spirit of Ted watching over them all from his beloved poetry section.

This, she thought, was what healing looked like, not the absence of pain, but the courage to create joy despite it. The courage to put on a red suit and white beard, to face crowds of excited children, to transform war memories into Christmas magic.

As another group of children approached the grotto, their faces shining with excitement, Alice caught Andrew's eye and saw in it a reflection of the same magic he was creating for others: the magic of books, of Christmas, of peace, of hope renewed.

* * *

The Taylor family dining room had been arranged for a careful balance of formality and comfort. Sarah had set out her best china, while Alice and Lily had decorated with holly and candles. The Christmas tree in the corner sparkled with ornaments, each one holding memories of happier, simpler times.

Freddie's footsteps could be heard upstairs, with Mrs Headley, getting the children ready for bed. Arthur had been up half the night waiting for Father Christmas to come, consequently waking David in his excitement. Freddie and Charles had enjoyed playing on the floor with the boy's gifts of train sets and cars, but now he was reading one of the many books they had also been given.

Downstairs, Margaret and Peter had arrived first – Peter clutching a wrapped package that he kept glancing at nervously. Victoria came next with Daisy, followed by Mr Leadbetter with his promised Christmas pudding, and finally Andrew and Molly, the latter moving more slowly than usual, one hand supporting her very prominent bump.

'The children's party was a great success,' Andrew was saying, helping Molly into a comfortable chair. 'Though I'm glad to be out of that Father Christmas beard; it was rather itchy.'

'You were wonderful with them,' Victoria added, skilfully shifting the conversation away from the awkward silence that had fallen when Margaret entered. 'Especially that little boy who'd lost his father in France.'

Charles yawned as he walked in. 'Oh my goodness, I'm shattered, playing with the boys' toys was wonderful but very tiring. He smiled as he flopped into an armchair.

Alice laughed. 'You did very well today, I think you are now their favourite uncle.'

Lily chuckled. 'That'll teach you.'

Sarah emerged from the kitchen carrying a tea tray, her face composed despite the strain around her eyes. 'Shall I pour?' she offered, her voice steady. 'Peter, would you like to sit here, next to Alice?'

Peter moved to the indicated chair, still holding his package. 'I... I brought something,' he said suddenly. 'For the tree, if that's... if that's allowed.'

'Of course it is,' Alice said warmly, as Lily leaned forward with interest. 'What is it?'

Peter carefully unwrapped a hand-painted glass ornament. 'It's from our own Christmas tree. I painted it myself,' he explained.

Freddie walked in catching Peter's words. 'It looks like you have a real talent there.'

Alice smiled at Freddie, thankful for his encouragement.

Peter beamed. 'Thank you, it's something I quite enjoyed doing.' He paused. 'Mother said... she said maybe we could start sharing traditions.'

Sarah's hands trembled slightly as she poured the tea, but her voice remained calm. 'That's a lovely thought, Peter. Perhaps you could hang it yourself? Choose a special spot?'

As Peter moved to the tree, Margaret spoke softly to Sarah. 'Thank you for inviting us. I know it can't be easy...'

'No,' Sarah agreed quietly. 'But it's right, if only for the children's sake.'

Mr Leadbetter cleared his throat. 'Margaret, I understand

from Peter, your local bookshop has a remarkable collection of first editions?'

The conversation gradually began to flow more naturally, helped along by shared interests in books and bookselling. Peter, returning from the tree, found himself drawn into a discussion with his sisters about their favourite childhood stories.

Molly shifted uncomfortably in her chair, and Andrew immediately leaned toward her. 'Are you all right, love?'

'Just the usual aches,' she assured him. 'This little one's very active today. I'll be glad when it's arrived. I feel permanently uncomfortable.'

Victoria was watching Peter as he talked animatedly with Alice about a customer he had served. 'He has your expressions, Alice. The way you both use your hands when you're excited about a book.'

The observation hung in the air for a moment, a reminder of shared blood, of family connections that existed despite the complicated circumstances.

Sarah's father glanced from Alice to Peter to Luke. He frowned. He was always suspicious about Luke's trips to Norfolk and now it was clear.

'More tea?' Sarah offered, her voice only slightly strained. 'And maybe a slice of Mr Leadbetter's Christmas pudding – it looks wonderful.' She caught her father's look but now wasn't the time. Whatever happened between them was her decision and she knew that her father would accept it eventually.

As they passed plates and cups, the atmosphere slowly relaxed. Peter shared stories about his childhood, while Alice and Lily told him about growing up around books. Margaret and Mr Leadbetter discovered a shared passion for rare editions, and Victoria added occasional quiet observations that made everyone smile.

'Oh!' Molly exclaimed suddenly, her hand going to her bump. Everyone turned to look at her.

'Just a strong kick,' she said, but her face looked uncertain. 'Though...'

A moment later, her eyes widened. 'Oh dear,' she said very calmly. 'I think... I think my water just broke.'

The room erupted into controlled chaos. Andrew jumped up, knocking over his teacup. Alice and Victoria moved to Molly's side, while Mr Leadbetter began talking about calling for a doctor.

'But it's too early,' Molly protested, even as another contraction hit. 'The baby's not due until January at the earliest.'

'Babies come when they choose,' Margaret said unexpectedly, moving forward with practical efficiency. 'Sarah, do you have clean towels?'

Alice grabbed Peter's arm. 'Peter, dear, run and fetch Dr Williams. His surgery is just around the corner.'

Margaret frowned. 'Do you know where he lives?'

Peter looked startled at being given a task but nodded quickly. 'I... I know where it is. Alice showed me on our walk yesterday.'

Freddie stepped forward and touched Peter's arm. 'I'll go with you; it'll make it easier because he knows who I am.'

Molly moaned. 'Alice, why can't Mrs Headley deliver the baby? She delivered Arthur when your waters broke.'

Alice smiled. 'That was a few years ago and Mrs Headley isn't getting any younger.'

Sarah was already heading for the linen cupboard, her hostess instincts taking over despite the unusual circumstances. 'We'll set up in the spare room,' she said decisively. 'Alice, Victoria, help Molly up the stairs. Lily, fetch some hot water. Margaret... would you help me prepare the room?'

The two women's eyes met for a moment, two mothers,

despite everything else between them. Margaret nodded, and they moved efficiently together, their differences temporarily set aside in the face of more urgent matters.

'Well,' Mr Leadbetter said, watching Andrew pace anxiously. 'It seems this Christmas tea will be more memorable than we anticipated.'

'A Christmas baby,' Victoria smiled, supporting Molly as they helped her up. 'How perfect.'

'Perfect timing,' Alice said, trying to keep her voice light to keep Molly calm, aware the baby was coming at least a month early. She prayed her dates are wrong and the baby will be born safely. 'Just when we have everyone here to help.'

As they guided Molly upstairs, Sarah and Margaret working together to prepare the room, Peter running for the doctor, and Andrew alternating between excitement and panic, Alice couldn't help but think how life had its own way of bringing people together. Here they all were, their complicated family dynamics temporarily forgotten in the face of new life making its unexpected arrival.

The Christmas tree sparkled in the corner, Peter's ornament catching the light among the old familiar ones. Below it, the abandoned tea things sat in disarray, cups half-empty, Christmas pudding barely touched, all plans for a formal family gathering disrupted by the imminent arrival of the newest member of their extended family.

'Someone better save me a piece of that Christmas pudding,' Molly called out as they helped her up the stairs. 'After all this excitement, I think I'll have earned it.'

The laughter that followed seemed to break the last of the tension, as everyone found their roles in this unexpected drama.

* * *

The spare bedroom at the Taylor house had been transformed into a makeshift birthing room. Towels and bowls of hot water took up every available space. Hours had passed since Molly's water broke during their Christmas tea, and now the winter evening was drawing in. Dr Williams moved efficiently around the bed where Molly lay groaning, while Sarah and Margaret worked together with the unspoken understanding of experienced mothers.

Andrew paced the hallway outside, alternating between quiet panic and determined calm. Freddie sat patiently supporting his friend, while Alice, Victoria, and Lily took turns bringing up fresh hot water and clean linens, along with cups of tea for those who could drink it.

'Almost there, Mrs Greenwood,' Dr Williams encouraged. 'The baby is nearly here.'

Molly gripped Sarah's hand tightly. 'I can't... I don't think I can...'

'Yes, you can,' Sarah said firmly. 'You're the strongest person I know. Just one more push.'

Margaret dabbed Molly's forehead with a cool cloth. 'Think of all the books you'll read to this little one,' she said softly. 'All the stories waiting to be shared.'

Suddenly, the room filled with a new sound, the loud, healthy cry of a newborn baby. Molly fell back against the pillows as Dr Williams announced triumphantly, 'It's a girl!'

The news travelled quickly through the house. Downstairs, Andrew stopped his pacing at the sound of his daughter's first cry. Freddie clapped him on the back while Peter, who had stayed to help run messages, broke into a broad grin.

'A girl,' Mr Leadbetter said softly, dabbing at his eyes with his handkerchief. 'How wonderful.'

Upstairs, Dr Williams had checked the baby and declared her

perfectly healthy despite her early arrival. 'She's eager to meet the world, this one.' He smiled, placing the wrapped bundle in Molly's arms.

'She's beautiful,' Molly whispered, tears streaming down her face. 'Andrew, Andrew should see her.'

Alice went to fetch him, finding her friend pale but composed. 'Would you like to meet your daughter?' she asked softly.

Andrew entered the room as if in a dream, his eyes fixed on the small bundle in Molly's arms. 'A daughter,' he breathed. 'We have a daughter.'

'What will you call her?' Victoria asked, having slipped in behind him.

Molly and Andrew exchanged a look. 'Elizabeth,' Molly said. 'After my grandmother and Andrew's sister, Elizabeth Victoria Alice.' She looked at her friends with shining eyes. 'After the women who've been our strength through everything.'

Victoria gasped softly, while Alice felt tears spring to her eyes. Sarah and Margaret exchanged glances, their shared experience as mothers transcending their complicated situation.

'Elizabeth,' Andrew repeated, gently touching his daughter's tiny hand. 'Our peace baby. Born in the first peaceful Christmas since the war began.'

'And surrounded by so much love,' Sarah added, looking around the room at this unlikely gathering of people.

Peter hovered in the doorway, uncertain of his place in this intimate moment until Alice beckoned him forward. 'Come meet your honorary niece.' She smiled.

'I've never seen such a tiny baby,' he said in wonder, peering at Elizabeth's face.

'She'll grow,' Margaret assured him. 'And she'll have quite the extended family to watch over her.'

Mr Leadbetter appeared at the door with a tray of crockery with Freddie holding a large teapot. 'We took the liberty o making tea,' he said. 'And I saved some Christmas pudding fo the new mother, as promised.'

Molly laughed weakly. 'My first meal as a mother, Christmas pudding in borrowed blankets, surrounded by booksellers and family. Perfect.'

The room filled with gentle laughter as Elizabeth was passed carefully from person to person. Andrew hadn't stopped smiling his war memories temporarily banished by the miracle of his daughter. Victoria held the baby with tears in her eyes, thinking of Ted and the future they'd planned.

Daisy reached out and gently touched Elizabeth's little fingers. 'She's beautiful.'

Alice and Lily cooed over their honorary niece while Peter watched in fascination.

'She's a lucky girl,' Sarah said softly to Margaret as they watched the scene. 'To have so many people to love her.'

'And to have women like you to guide her mother,' Margaret replied. 'Your strength today... thank you.'

Outside, carol singers could be heard in the distance, their voices carrying traditional messages of peace and joy. Inside, Eliz abeth slept contentedly, unaware that her arrival had brough together an unlikely group of people, healing old wounds and creating new bonds.

'Welcome to the world, Elizabeth,' Andrew whispered to his daughter as Molly drifted into exhausted sleep. 'Welcome to peace, to family, to love.'

Mr Leadbetter raised his teacup in a quiet toast. 'To Elizabeth Victoria Alice Greenwood,' he said solemnly. 'Born during a Christmas tea, surrounded by books and family. May she inheri all our love of stories, and none of our complications.'

The room filled with soft laughter and murmured agreement. Elizabeth slept on, her tiny face peaceful, while around her, the adults who would shape her world came together in celebration of new life and new beginnings.

Freddie placed his arm around Alice, pulling her close.

Alice peered up at him, her face full of love for her husband.

'Next Christmas will be very different,' Victoria observed, watching the baby sleep. 'A one-year-old opening presents, learning about Father Christmas...'

'Learning to love books,' Alice added with a smile.

'And having the most unusual, wonderful extended family any child could wish for,' Molly murmured sleepily from the bed.

As night fell properly over London, the Taylor house remained lit and warm, filled with the quiet joy of Elizabeth's arrival. The abandoned Christmas tea things downstairs were eventually cleared away, but nobody really noticed or cared. Upstairs, a new family story had begun – one that would be told and retold in years to come, of how a baby girl arrived during Christmas tea, bringing with her the gift of healing and hope.

* * *

MORE FROM ELAINE ROBERTS

In case you missed it, the previous book from Elaine Roberts, *The Foyles Bookshop Girls' Promise*, is available to order now here:
    https://mybook.to/FoylesBGPromiseBackAd

ACKNOWLEDGEMENTS

This is the sixth book in the Foyles Bookshop Girls series, the third with my current publishers, Boldwood. A huge thank you must go to my Editor and all the team at Boldwood Publishing, they are a wonderful supportive company. I was certainly blessed when they wanted to have me in their family of writers.

I would also like to thank everyone who has encouraged and supported me throughout my writing career. My family have been brilliant, friends have listened to me when I've felt over-whelmed with the task. I also have friends that I have met through trying to rebuild my life after my husband passed away, and their straight talking has got me through some difficult times. I have been very blessed to have all these people around me, I don't know what I would have done without them.

A big thank you must go to the most important people, you the readers. I have felt honoured that you have continued to enjoy my books, as I hope you enjoy this one.

ABOUT THE AUTHOR

Elaine Roberts is the bestselling author of historical sagas se[ ] London during the First World War. She joined a creative writ[ ] class in 2012 and shortly afterwards had her first short st[ ] published. She was thrilled when many more followed. H[ ] home is in Dartford, Kent and she is always busy with childr[ ] grandchildren, grand dogs and cats.

Sign up to Elaine Roberts' mailing list for news, competitions a[ ] updates on future books.

Visit Elaine's website: www.elaineroberts.co.uk

Follow Elaine on social media here:

facebook.com/ElaineRobertsAuthor
x.com/RobertsElaine11

ALSO BY ELAINE ROBERTS

A Wartime Welcome from the Foyles Bookshop Girls

The Foyles Bookshop Girls' Promise

Victory for the Foyles Bookshop Girls

Sixpence Stories

Introducing Sixpence Stories!

Discover page-turning historical novels from your favourite authors, meet new friends and be transported back in time.

Join our book club Facebook group

https://bit.ly/SixpenceGroup

Sign up to our newsletter

https://bit.ly/SixpenceNews

Boldwood

Printed in Dunstable, United Kingdom